THE PELICAN SHAKESPEARE

GENERAL EDITORS

STEPHEN ORGEL

A. R. BRAUNMULLER

The Tragical History of
Hamlet Prince of Denmark

David Garrick as Hamlet encountering his father's ghost, from a mezzotint after a painting by Benjamin Wilson. Garrick first played the role in 1742, at the age of twenty-five, and it became his most celebrated tragic part, performed more frequently than any other.
(Courtesy of the Stanford University Library)

William Shakespeare

The Tragical History of
Hamlet Prince of Denmark

EDITED BY A. R. BRAUNMULLER

PENGUIN BOOKS

PENGUIN BOOKS

Published by the Penguin Group
Penguin Putnam Inc., 375 Hudson Street,
New York, New York 10014, U.S.A.
Penguin Books Ltd, 80 Strand, London WC2R 0RL, England
Penguin Books Australia Ltd, 250 Camberwell Road,
Camberwell, Victoria 3124, Australia
Penguin Books Canada Ltd, 10 Alcorn Avenue,
Toronto, Ontario, Canada M4V 3B2
Penguin Books India (P) Ltd, 11 Community Centre,
Panchsheel Park, New Delhi-110 017, India
Penguin Books (N.Z.) Ltd, Cnr Rosedale and Airborne Roads,
Albany, Auckland, New Zealand
Penguin Books (South Africa) (Pty) Ltd, 24 Sturdee Avenue,
Rosebank, Johannesburg 2196, South Africa

Penguin Books Ltd, Registered Offices:
Harmondsworth, Middlesex, England

The Tragical History of
Hamlet Prince of Denmark
edited by Willard Farnham published in the United States of America
in Penguin Books 1957
Revised edition published 1970
This new edition edited by A. R. Braunmuller published 2001

3   5   7   9   10   8   6   4   2

Copyright © Penguin Books Inc., 1957, 1970
Copyright © Penguin Putnam Inc., 2001
All rights reserved

ISBN 0-14-07.1454-5
(CIP data available)

Printed in the United States of America
Set in Adobe Garamond
Designed by Virginia Norey

Contents

Publisher's Note

IT IS ALMOST half a century since the first volumes of the Pelican Shakespeare appeared under the general editorship of Alfred Harbage. The fact that a new edition, rather than simply a revision, has been undertaken reflects the profound changes textual and critical studies of Shakespeare have undergone in the past twenty years. For the new Pelican series, the texts of the plays and poems have been thoroughly revised in accordance with recent scholarship, and in some cases have been entirely reedited. New introductions and notes have been provided in all the volumes. But the new Shakespeare is also designed as a successor to the original series; the previous editions have been taken into account, and the advice of the previous editors has been solicited where it was feasible to do so.

Certain textual features of the new Pelican Shakespeare should be particularly noted. All lines are numbered that contain a word, phrase, or allusion explained in the glossarial notes. In addition, for convenience, every tenth line is also numbered, in italics when no annotation is indicated. The intrusive and often inaccurate place headings inserted by early editors are omitted (as is becoming standard practice), but for the convenience of those who miss them, an indication of locale now appears as the first item in the annotation of each scene.

In the interest of both elegance and utility, each speech prefix is set in a separate line when the speaker's lines are in verse, except when those words form the second half of a verse line. Thus the verse form of the speech is kept visually intact. What is printed as verse and what is printed as prose has, in general, the authority of the original texts. Departures from the original texts in this regard have only the authority of editorial tradition and the judgment of the Pelican editors; and, in a few instances, are admittedly arbitrary.

The Theatrical World

ECONOMIC REALITIES determined the theatrical world in which Shakespeare's plays were written, performed, and received. For centuries in England, the primary theatrical tradition was nonprofessional. Craft guilds (or "mysteries") provided religious drama – mystery plays – as part of the celebration of religious and civic festivals, and schools and universities staged classical and neoclassical drama in both Latin and English as part of their curricula. In these forms, drama was established and socially acceptable. Professional theater, in contrast, existed on the margins of society. The acting companies were itinerant; playhouses could be any available space – the great halls of the aristocracy, town squares, civic halls, inn yards, fair booths, or open fields – and income was sporadic, dependent on the passing of the hat or on the bounty of local patrons. The actors, moreover, were considered little better than vagabonds, constantly in danger of arrest or expulsion.

In the late 1560s and 1570s, however, English professional theater began to gain respectability. Wealthy aristocrats fond of drama – the Lord Admiral, for example, or the Lord Chamberlain – took acting companies under their protection so that the players technically became members of their households and were no longer subject to arrest as homeless or masterless men. Permanent theaters were first built at this time as well, allowing the companies to control and charge for entry to their performances.

Shakespeare's livelihood, and the stunning artistic explosion in which he participated, depended on pragmatic and architectural effort. Professional theater requires ways to restrict access to its offerings; if it does not, and admission fees cannot be charged, the actors do not get paid, the costumes go to a pawnbroker, and there is no such thing as a professional, ongoing theatrical tradition. The answer to that economic need arrived in the late 1560s and 1570s with the creation of the so-called public or amphitheater playhouse. Recent discoveries indicate that the precursor of the Globe playhouse in London (where Shakespeare's mature plays were presented) and the Rose theater (which presented Christopher Marlowe's plays and some of Shakespeare's earliest ones) was the Red Lion theater of 1567. Archaeological studies of the foundations of the Rose and Globe theaters have revealed that the open-air theater of the 1590s and later was probably a polygonal building with fourteen to twenty or twenty-four sides, multistoried, from 75 to 100 feet in diameter, with a raised, partly covered "thrust" stage that projected into a group of standing patrons, or "groundlings," and a covered gallery, seating up to 2,500 or more (very crowded) spectators.

These theaters might have been about half full on any given day, though the audiences were larger on holidays or when a play was advertised, as old and new were, through printed playbills posted around London. The metropolitan area's late-Tudor, early-Stuart population (circa 1590–1620) has been estimated at about 150,000 to 250,000. It has been supposed that in the mid-1590s there were about 15,000 spectators per week at the public theaters; thus, as many as 10 percent of the local population went to the theater regularly. Consequently, the theaters' repertories – the plays available for this experienced and frequent audience – had to change often: in the month between September 15 and October 15, 1595, for instance, the Lord Admiral's Men performed twenty-eight times in eighteen different plays.

Since natural light illuminated the amphitheaters' stages, performances began between noon and two o'clock and ran without a break for two or three hours. They often concluded with a jig, a fencing display, or some other nondramatic exhibition. Weather conditions determined the season for the amphitheaters: plays were performed every day (including Sundays, sometimes, to clerical dismay) except during Lent – the forty days before Easter – or periods of plague, or sometimes during the summer months when law courts were not in session and the most affluent members of the audience were not in London.

To a modern theatergoer, an amphitheater stage like that of the Rose or Globe would appear an unfamiliar mixture of plainness and elaborate decoration. Much of the structure was carved or painted, sometimes to imitate marble; elsewhere, as under the canopy projecting over the stage, to represent the stars and the zodiac. Appropriate painted canvas pictures (of Jerusalem, for example, if the play was set in that city) were apparently hung on the wall behind the acting area, and tragedies were accompanied by black hangings, presumably something like crepe festoons or bunting. Although these theaters did not employ what we would call scenery, early modern spectators saw numerous large props, such as the "bar" at which a prisoner stood during a trial, the "mossy bank" where lovers reclined, an arbor for amorous conversation, a chariot, gallows, tables, trees, beds, thrones, writing desks, and so forth. Audiences might learn a scene's location from a sign (reading "Athens," for example) carried across the stage (as in Bertolt Brecht's twentieth-century productions). Equally captivating (and equally irritating to the theater's enemies) were the rich costumes and personal props the actors used: the most valuable items in the surviving theatrical inventories are the swords, gowns, robes, crowns, and other items worn or carried by the performers.

Magic appealed to Shakespeare's audiences as much as it does to us today, and the theater exploited many deceptive and spectacular devices. A winch in the loft above the stage, called "the heavens," could lower and raise actors playing gods, goddesses, and other supernatural figures to and from the main acting area, just as one or more trapdoors permitted entrances and exits to and from the area, called "hell," beneath the stage. Actors wore elementary makeup such as wigs, false beards, and face paint, and they employed pig's bladders filled with animal blood to make wounds seem more real. They had rudimentary but effective ways of pretending to behead or hang a person. Supernumeraries (stagehands or actors not needed in a particular scene) could make thunder sounds (by shaking a metal sheet or rolling an iron ball down a chute) and show lightning (by blowing inflammable resin through tubes into a flame). Elaborate fireworks enhanced the effects of dragons flying through the air or imitated such celestial phenomena as comets, shooting stars, and multiple suns. Horses' hoofbeats, bells (located perhaps in the tower above the stage), trumpets and drums, clocks, cannon shots and gunshots, and the like were common sound effects. And the music of viols, cornets, oboes, and recorders was a regular feature of theatrical performances.

For two relatively brief spans, from the late 1570s to 1590 and from 1599 to 1614, the amphitheaters competed with the so-called private, or indoor, theaters, which originated as, or later represented themselves as, educational institutions training boys as singers for church services and court performances. These indoor theaters had two features that were distinct from the amphitheaters': their personnel and their playing spaces. The amphitheaters' adult companies included both adult men, who played the male roles, and boys, who played the female roles; the private, or indoor, theater companies, on the other hand, were entirely composed of boys aged about 8 to 16, who were, or could pretend to be, candidates for singers in a church or a royal boys' choir. (Until 1660, professional theatrical companies included no women.) The playing space would appear much more familiar to modern audiences than the long-vanished amphitheaters; the later indoor theaters were, in fact, the ancestors of the typical modern theater. They were enclosed spaces, usually rectangular, with the stage filling one end of the rectangle and the audience arrayed in seats or benches across (and sometimes lining) the building's longer axis. These spaces staged plays less frequently than the public theaters (perhaps only once a week) and held far fewer spectators than the amphitheaters: about 200 to 600, as opposed to 2,500 or more. Fewer patrons mean a smaller gross income, unless each pays more. Not surprisingly, then, private theaters charged higher prices than the amphitheaters, probably sixpence, as opposed to a penny for the cheapest entry.

Protected from the weather, the indoor theaters presented plays later in the day than the amphitheaters, and used artificial illumination – candles in sconces or candelabra. But candles melt, and need replacing, snuffing, and trimming, and these practical requirements may have been part of the reason the indoor theaters introduced breaks in the performance, the intermission so dear to the heart of theatergoers and to the pocketbooks of theater concessionaires ever since. Whether motivated by the need to tend to the candles or by the entrepreneurs' wishing to sell oranges and liquor, or both, the indoor theaters eventually established the modern convention of the non-continuous performance. In the early modern "private" theater, musical performances apparently filled the intermissions, which in Stuart theater jargon seem to have been called "acts."

At the end of the first decade of the seventeenth century, the distinction between public amphitheaters and private indoor companies ceased. For various cultural, political, and economic reasons, individual companies gained control of both the public, open-air theaters and the indoor ones, and companies mixing adult men and boys took over the formerly "private" theaters. Despite the death of the boys' companies and of their highly innovative theaters (for which such luminous playwrights as Ben Jonson, George Chapman, and John Marston wrote), their playing spaces and conventions had an immense impact on subsequent plays: not merely for the intervals (which stressed the artistic and architectonic importance of "acts"), but also because they introduced political and social satire as a popular dramatic ingredient, even in tragedy, and a wider range of actorly effects, encouraged by their more intimate playing spaces.

Even the briefest sketch of the Shakespearean theatrical world would be incomplete without some comment on the social and cultural dimensions of theaters and playing in the period. In an intensely hierarchical and status-conscious society, professional actors and their ventures had hardly any respectability; as we have indicated, to protect themselves against laws designed to curb vagabondage and the increase of masterless men, actors resorted to the near-fiction that they were the servants of noble masters, and wore their distinctive livery. Hence the company for which Shakespeare wrote in the 1590s called itself the Lord Chamberlain's Men and pretended that the public, money-getting performances were in fact rehearsals for private performances before that high court official. From 1598, the Privy Council had licensed theatrical companies, and after 1603, with the accession of King James I, the companies gained explicit royal protection, just as the Queen's Men had for a time under Queen Elizabeth. The Chamberlain's Men became the King's Men, and the other companies were patronized by the other members of the royal family.

These designations were legal fictions that half-concealed an important economic and social development, the evolution away from the theater's organization on the model of the guild, a self-regulating confraternity of individual artisans, into a proto-capitalist organization. Shakespeare's company became a joint-stock company, where persons who supplied capital and, in some cases, such as Shakespeare's, capital and talent, employed themselves and others in earning a return on that capital. This development meant that actors and theater companies were outside both the traditional guild structures, which required some form of civic or royal charter, and the feudal household organization of master-and-servant. This anomalous, maverick social and economic condition made theater companies practically unruly and potentially even dangerous; consequently, numerous official bodies – including the London metropolitan and ecclesiastical authorities as well as, occasionally, the royal court itself – tried, without much success, to control and even to disband them.

Public officials had good reason to want to close the theaters: they were attractive nuisances – they drew often riotous crowds, they were always noisy, and they could be politically offensive and socially insubordinate. Until the Civil War, however, anti-theatrical forces failed to shut down professional theater, for many reasons – limited surveillance and few police powers, tensions or outright hostilities among the agencies that sought to check or channel theatrical activity, and lack of clear policies for control. Another reason must have been the theaters' undeniable popularity. Curtailing any activity enjoyed by such a substantial percentage of the population was difficult, as various Roman emperors attempting to limit circuses had learned, and the Tudor-Stuart audience was not merely large, it was socially diverse and included women. The prevalence of public entertainment in this period has been underestimated. In fact, fairs, holidays, games, sporting events, the equivalent of modern parades, freak shows, and street exhibitions all abounded, but the theater was the most widely and frequently available entertainment to which people of every class had access. That fact helps account both for its quantity and for the fear and anger it aroused.

WILLIAM SHAKESPEARE OF STRATFORD-UPON-AVON, GENTLEMAN

Many people have said that we know very little about William Shakespeare's life – pinheads and postcards are often mentioned as appropriately tiny surfaces on which to record the available information. More imaginatively and perhaps more correctly, Ralph Waldo Emerson wrote, "Shakespeare is the only biographer of Shakespeare. . . . So far from Shakespeare's being the least known, he is the one person in all modern history fully known to us."

In fact, we know more about Shakespeare's life than we do about almost any other English writer's of his era. His last will and testament (dated March 25, 1616) survives, as do numerous legal contracts and court documents involving Shakespeare as principal or witness, and parish records in Stratford and London. Shakespeare appears quite often in official records of King James's royal court, and of course Shakespeare's name appears on numerous title pages and in the written and recorded words of his literary contemporaries Robert Greene, Henry Chettle, Francis Meres, John Davies of Hereford, Ben Jonson, and many others. Indeed, if we make due allowance for the bloating of modern, run-of-the-mill bureaucratic records, more information has survived over the past four hundred years about William Shakespeare of Stratford-upon-Avon, Warwickshire, than is likely to survive in the next four hundred years about any reader of these words.

What we do not have are entire categories of information – Shakespeare's private letters or diaries, drafts and revisions of poems and plays, critical prefaces or essays, commendatory verse for other writers' works, or instructions guiding his fellow actors in their performances, for instance – that we imagine would help us understand and appreciate his surviving writings. For all we know, many such data never existed as written records. Many literary and theatrical critics, not knowing what might once have existed, more or less cheerfully accept the situation; some even make a theoretical virtue of it by claiming that such data are irrelevant to understanding and interpreting the plays and poems.

So, what do we know about William Shakespeare, the man responsible for thirty-seven or perhaps more plays, more than 150 sonnets, two lengthy narrative poems, and some shorter poems?

While many families by the name of Shakespeare (or some variant spelling) can be identified in the English Midlands as far back as the twelfth century, it seems likely that the dramatist's grandfather, Richard, moved to Snitterfield, a town not far from Stratford-upon-Avon, sometime before 1529. In Snitterfield, Richard Shakespeare leased farmland from the very wealthy Robert Arden. By 1552, Richard's son John had moved to a large house on Henley Street in Stratford-upon-Avon, the house that stands today as "The Birthplace." In Stratford, John Shakespeare traded as a glover, dealt in wool, and lent money at interest; he also served in a variety of civic posts, including "High Bailiff," the municipality's equivalent of mayor. In 1557, he married Robert Arden's youngest daughter, Mary. Mary and John had four sons – William was the oldest – and four daughters, of whom only Joan outlived her most celebrated sibling. William was baptized (an event entered in the Stratford parish church records) on April 26, 1564, and it has become customary, without any good factual support, to suppose he was born on April 23, which happens to be the feast day of Saint George, patron saint of England, and is also the date on which he died, in 1616. Shakespeare married Anne Hathaway in 1582, when he was eighteen and she was twenty-six; their first child was born five months later. It has been generally assumed that the marriage was enforced and subsequently unhappy, but these are only assumptions; it has been estimated, for instance, that up to one third of Elizabethan brides were pregnant when they married. Anne and William Shakespeare had three children: Susanna, who married a prominent local physician, John Hall; and the twins Hamnet, who died young in 1596, and Judith, who married Thomas Quiney – apparently a rather shady individual. The name Hamnet was unusual but not unique: he and his twin sister were named for their godparents, Shakespeare's neighbors Hamnet and Judith Sadler. Shakespeare's father died in 1601 (the year of *Hamlet*), and Mary Arden Shakespeare died in 1608 (the year of *Coriolanus*). William Shakespeare's last surviving direct descendant was his granddaughter Elizabeth Hall, who died in 1670.

Between the birth of the twins in 1585 and a clear reference to Shakespeare as a practicing London dramatist in Robert Greene's sensationalizing, satiric pamphlet, *Greene's Groatsworth of Wit* (1592), there is no record of where William Shakespeare was or what he was doing. These seven so-called lost years have been imaginatively filled by scholars and other students of Shakespeare: some think he traveled to Italy, or fought in the Low Countries, or studied law or medicine, or worked as an apprentice actor/writer, and so on to even more fanciful possibilities. Whatever the biographical facts for those "lost" years, Greene's nasty remarks in 1592 testify to professional envy and to the fact that Shakespeare already had a successful career in London. Speaking to his fellow playwrights, Greene warns both generally and specifically:

> . . . trust them [actors] not: for there is an upstart crow, beautified with our feathers, that with his tiger's heart wrapped in a player's hide supposes he is as well able to bombast out a blank verse as the best of you; and being an absolute Johannes Factotum, is in his own conceit the only Shake-scene in a country.

The passage mimics a line from *3 Henry VI* (hence the play must have been performed before Greene wrote) and seems to say that "Shake-scene" is both actor and playwright, a jack-of-all-trades. That same year, Henry Chettle protested Greene's remarks in *Kind-Heart's Dream,* and each of the next two years saw the publication of poems – *Venus and Adonis* and *The Rape of Lucrece,* respectively – publicly ascribed to (and dedicated by) Shakespeare. Early in 1595 he was named as one of the senior members of a prominent acting company, the Lord Chamberlain's Men, when they received payment for court performances during the 1594 Christmas season.

Clearly, Shakespeare had achieved both success and reputation in London. In 1596, upon Shakespeare's application, the College of Arms granted his father the now-familiar coat of arms he had taken the first steps to obtain almost twenty years before, and in 1598, John's son – now permitted to call himself "gentleman" – took a 10 percent share in the new Globe playhouse. In 1597, he bought a substantial bourgeois house, called New Place, in Stratford – the garden remains, but Shakespeare's house, several times rebuilt, was torn down in 1759 – and over the next few years Shakespeare spent large sums buying land and making other investments in the town and its environs. Though he worked in London, his family remained in Stratford, and he seems always to have considered Stratford the home he would eventually return to. Something approaching a disinterested appreciation of Shakespeare's popular and professional status appears in Francis Meres's *Palladis Tamia* (1598), a not especially imaginative and perhaps therefore persuasive record of literary reputations. Reviewing contemporary English writers, Meres lists the titles of many of Shakespeare's plays, including one not now known, *Love's Labor's Won,* and praises his "mellifluous & hony-tongued" "sugred Sonnets," which were then circulating in manuscript (they were first collected in 1609). Meres describes Shakespeare as "one of the best" English playwrights of both comedy and tragedy. In *Remains . . . Concerning Britain* (1605), William Camden – a more authoritative source than the imitative Meres – calls Shakespeare one of the "most pregnant witts of these our times" and joins him with such writers as Chapman, Daniel, Jonson, Marston, and Spenser. During the first decades of the seventeenth century, publishers began to attribute numerous play quartos, including some non-Shakespearean ones, to Shakespeare, either by name or initials, and we may assume that they deemed Shakespeare's name and supposed authorship, true or false, commercially attractive.

For the next ten years or so, various records show

Shakespeare's dual career as playwright and man of the theater in London, and as an important local figure in Stratford. In 1608-9 his acting company – designated the "King's Men" soon after King James had succeeded Queen Elizabeth in 1603 – rented, refurbished, and opened a small interior playing space, the Blackfriars theater, in London, and Shakespeare was once again listed as a substantial sharer in the group of proprietors of the playhouse. By May 11, 1612, however, he describes himself as a Stratford resident in a London lawsuit – an indication that he had withdrawn from day-to-day professional activity and returned to the town where he had always had his main financial interests. When Shakespeare bought a substantial residential building in London, the Blackfriars Gatehouse, close to the theater of the same name, on March 10, 1613, he is recorded as William Shakespeare "of Stratford upon Avon in the county of Warwick, gentleman," and he named several London residents as the building's trustees. Still, he continued to participate in theatrical activity: when the new Earl of Rutland needed an allegorical design to bear as a shield, or *impresa,* at the celebration of King James's Accession Day, March 24, 1613, the earl's accountant recorded a payment of 44 shillings to Shakespeare for the device with its motto.

For the last few years of his life, Shakespeare evidently concentrated his activities in the town of his birth. Most of the final records concern business transactions in Stratford, ending with the notation of his death on April 23, 1616, and burial in Holy Trinity Church, Stratford-upon-Avon.

The Question of Authorship

The history of ascribing Shakespeare's plays (the poems do not come up so often) to someone else began, as it continues, peculiarly. The earliest published claim that someone else wrote Shakespeare's plays appeared in an 1856 article by Delia Bacon in the American journal *Putnam's Monthly* – although an Englishman, Thomas Wilmot, had shared his doubts in private (even secretive) conversations with friends near the end of the eighteenth century. Bacon's was a sad personal history that ended in madness and poverty, but the year after her article, she published, with great difficulty and the bemused assistance of Nathaniel Hawthorne (then United States Consul in Liverpool, England), her *Philosophy of the Plays of Shakspere Unfolded*. This huge, ornately written, confusing farrago is almost unreadable; sometimes its intents, to say nothing of its arguments, disappear entirely beneath near-raving, ecstatic writing. Tumbled in with much supposed "philosophy" appear the claims that Francis Bacon (from whom Delia Bacon eventually claimed descent), Walter Ralegh, and several other contemporaries of Shakespeare's had written the plays. The book had little impact except as a ridiculed curiosity.

Once proposed, however, the issue gained momentum among people whose conviction was the greater in proportion to their ignorance of sixteenth- and seventeenth-century English literature, history, and society. Another American amateur, Catherine P. Ashmead Windle, made the next influential contribution to the cause when she published *Report to the British Museum* (1882), wherein she promised to open "the Cipher of Francis Bacon," though what she mostly offers, in the words of S. Schoenbaum, is "demented allegorizing." An entire new cottage industry grew from Windle's suggestion that the texts contain hidden, cryptographically discoverable ciphers – "clues" – to their authorship; and today there are not only books devoted to the putative ciphers, but also pamphlets, journals, and newsletters.

Although Baconians have led the pack of those seeking a substitute Shakespeare, in *"Shakespeare" Identified* (1920), J. Thomas Looney became the first published

"Oxfordian" when he proposed Edward de Vere, seventeenth earl of Oxford, as the secret author of Shakespeare's plays. Also for Oxford and his "authorship" there are today dedicated societies, articles, journals, and books. Less popular candidates – Queen Elizabeth and Christopher Marlowe among them – have had adherents, but the movement seems to have divided into two main contending factions, Baconian and Oxfordian. (For further details on all the candidates for "Shakespeare," see S. Schoenbaum, *Shakespeare's Lives,* 2nd ed., 1991.)

The Baconians, the Oxfordians, and supporters of other candidates have one trait in common – they are snobs. Every pro-Bacon or pro-Oxford tract sooner or later claims that the historical William Shakespeare of Stratford-upon-Avon could not have written the plays because he could not have had the training, the university education, the experience, and indeed the imagination or background their author supposedly possessed. Only a learned genius like Bacon or an aristocrat like Oxford could have written such fine plays. (As it happens, lucky male children of the middle class had access to better education than most aristocrats in Elizabethan England – and Oxford was not particularly well educated.) Shakespeare received in the Stratford grammar school a formal education that would daunt many college graduates today; and popular rival playwrights such as the very learned Ben Jonson and George Chapman, both of whom also lacked university training, achieved great artistic success, without being taken as Bacon or Oxford.

Besides snobbery, one other quality characterizes the authorship controversy: lack of evidence. A great deal of testimony from Shakespeare's time shows that Shakespeare wrote Shakespeare's plays and that his contemporaries recognized them as distinctive and distinctly superior. (Some of that contemporary evidence is collected in E. K. Chambers, *William Shakespeare: A Study of Facts and Problems,* 2 vols., 1930.) Since that testimony comes from Shakespeare's enemies and theatrical competitors as well as from his co-workers and from the Elizabethan equivalent of literary journalists, it seems unlikely that, if any of these sources had known he was a fraud, they would have failed to record that fact.

Books About Shakespeare's Theater

Useful scholarly studies of theatrical life in Shakespeare's day include: G. E. Bentley, *The Jacobean and Caroline Stage,* 7 vols. (1941-68), and the same author's *The Professions of Dramatist and Player in Shakespeare's Time, 1590-1642* (1986); E. K. Chambers, *The Elizabethan Stage,* 4 vols. (1923); R. A. Foakes, *Illustrations of the English Stage, 1580-1642* (1985); Andrew Gurr, *The Shakespearean Stage,* 3rd ed. (1992), and the same author's *Play-going in Shakespeare's London,* 2nd ed. (1996); Edwin Nungezer, *A Dictionary of Actors* (1929); Carol Chillington Rutter, ed., *Documents of the Rose Playhouse* (1984).

Books About Shakespeare's Life

The following books provide scholarly, documented accounts of Shakespeare's life: G. E. Bentley, *Shakespeare: A Biographical Handbook* (1961); E. K. Chambers, *William Shakespeare: A Study of Facts and Problems,* 2 vols. (1930); S. Schoenbaum, *William Shakespeare: A Compact Documentary Life* (1977); and *Shakespeare's Lives,* 2nd ed. (1991), by the same author. Many scholarly editions of Shakespeare's complete works print brief compilations of essential dates and events. References to Shakespeare's works up to 1700 are collected in C. M. Ingleby et al., *The Shakespeare Allusion-Book,* rev. ed., 2 vols. (1932).

The Texts of Shakespeare

AS FAR AS WE KNOW, only one manuscript conceivably in Shakespeare's own hand may (and even this is much disputed) exist: a few pages of a play called *Sir Thomas More,* which apparently was never performed. What we do have, as later readers, performers, scholars, students, are printed texts. The earliest of these survive in two forms: quartos and folios. Quartos (from the Latin for "four") are small books, printed on sheets of paper that were then folded in fours, to make eight double-sided pages. When these were bound together, the result was a squarish, eminently portable volume that sold for the relatively small sum of sixpence (translating in modern terms to about $5.00). In folios, on the other hand, the sheets are folded only once, in half, producing large, impressive volumes taller than they are wide. This was the format for important works of philosophy, science, theology, and literature (the major precedent for a folio Shakespeare was Ben Jonson's *Works,* 1616). The decision to print the works of a popular playwright in folio is an indication of how far up on the social scale the theatrical profession had come during Shakespeare's lifetime. The Shakespeare folio was an expensive book, selling for between fifteen and eighteen shillings, depending on the binding (in modern terms, from about $150 to $180). Twenty Shakespeare plays of the thirty-seven that survive first appeared in quarto, seventeen of which appeared during Shakespeare's lifetime; the rest of the plays are found only in folio.

The First Folio was published in 1623, seven years after Shakespeare's death, and was authorized by his fellow actors, the co-owners of the King's Men. This publication was certainly a mark of the company's enormous respect for Shakespeare; but it was also a way of turning the old plays, most of which were no longer current in the play-house, into ready money (the folio includes only Shakespeare's plays, not his sonnets or other nondramatic verse). Whatever the motives behind the publication of the folio, the texts it preserves constitute the basis for almost all later editions of the playwright's works. The texts, however, differ from those of the earlier quartos, sometimes in minor respects but often significantly – most strikingly in the two texts of *King Lear,* but also in important ways in *Hamlet, Othello,* and *Troilus and Cressida.* (The variants are recorded in the textual notes to each play in the new Pelican series.) The differences in these texts represent, in a sense, the essence of theater: the texts of plays were initially not intended for publication. They were scripts, designed for the actors to perform – the principal life of the play at this period was in performance. And it follows that in Shakespeare's theater the playwright typically had no say either in how his play was performed or in the disposition of his text – he was an employee of the company. The authoritative figures in the theatrical enterprise were the shareholders in the company, who were for the most part the major actors. They decided what plays were to be done; they hired the playwright and often gave him an outline of the play they wanted him to write. Often, too, the play was a collaboration: the company would retain a group of writers, and parcel out the scenes among them. The resulting script was then the property of the company, and the actors would revise it as they saw fit during the course of putting it on stage. The resulting text belonged to the company. The playwright had no rights in it once he had been paid. (This system survives largely intact in the movie industry, and most of the playwrights of Shakespeare's time were as anonymous as most screenwriters are today.) The script could also, of course, continue to change as the tastes of audiences and the requirements of the actors changed. Many – perhaps most – plays were revised when they were reintroduced after any substantial absence from the repertory, or when they were performed

by a company different from the one that originally com-
missioned the play.

Shakespeare was an exceptional figure in this world
because he was not only a shareholder and actor in his
company, but also its leading playwright – he was literally
his own boss. He had, moreover, little interest in the
publication of his plays, and even those that appeared
during his lifetime with the authorization of the company
show no signs of any editorial concern on the part of
the author. Theater was, for Shakespeare, a fluid and
supremely responsive medium – the very opposite of the
great classic canonical text that has embodied his works
since 1623.

The very fluidity of the original texts, however, has
meant that Shakespeare has always had to be edited. Here
is an example of how problematic the editorial project in-
evitably is, a passage from the most famous speech in
Romeo and Juliet, Juliet's balcony soliloquy beginning "O
Romeo, Romeo, wherefore art thou Romeo?" Since the
eighteenth century, the standard modern text has read,

> What's Montague? It is nor hand, nor foot,
> Nor arm, nor face, nor any other part
> Belonging to a man. O be some other name!
> What's in a name? That which we call a rose
> By any other name would smell as sweet.
>
> (II.2.40-44)

Editors have three early texts of this play to work from,
two quarto texts and the folio. Here is how the First
Quarto (1597) reads:

> Whats *Mountague?* It is nor band nor foote,
> Nor arme, nor face, nor any other part.
> Whats in a name? That which we call a Rofe,
> By any other name would fmell as fweet:

Here is the Second Quarto (1599):

> Whats *Mountague*? it is nor hand nor foote,
> Nor arme nor face, ô be some other name
> Belonging to a man.
> Whats in a name that which we call a rose,
> By any other word would smell as sweete,

And here is the First Folio (1623):

> What's *Mountague*? it is nor hand nor foote,
> Nor arme, nor face, O be some other name
> Belonging to a man.
> What? in a names that which we call a Rose,
> By any other word would smell as sweete,

There is in fact no early text that reads as our modern text does – and this is the most famous speech in the play. Instead, we have three quite different texts, all of which are clearly some version of the same speech, but none of which seems to us a final or satisfactory version. The transcendently beautiful passage in modern editions is an editorial invention: editors have succeeded in conflating and revising the three versions into something we recognize as great poetry. Is this what Shakespeare "really" wrote? Who can say? What we can say is that Shakespeare always had performance, not a book, in mind.

Books About the Shakespeare Texts

The standard study of the printing history of the First Folio is W. W. Greg, *The Shakespeare First Folio* (1955). J. K. Walton, *The Quarto Copy for the First Folio of Shakespeare* (1971), is a useful survey of the relation of the quartos to the folio. The second edition of Charlton Hinman's *Norton Facsimile* of the First Folio (1996), with a new introduction by Peter Blayney, is indispensable. Stanley Wells, Gary Taylor, John Jowett, and William Montgomery, *William Shakespeare: A Textual Companion,* keyed to the Oxford text, gives a comprehensive survey of the editorial situation for all the plays and poems.

THE GENERAL EDITORS

Introduction

ABOUT 1600, WHEN Shakespeare turned, or perhaps he returned, to write *The Tragicall Historie of Hamlet, Prince of
Denmarke* (as an early printing calls it), that "Tragicall Historie" had already had a long life in northern European
writing, for the tale was thought to be, and might truly
have been, "Historie" – that is, a relatively accurate account
of deeds done. Some of its elements have been traced
to Norse sagas, the half-historical, half-legendary stories
recording the earliest history of northern European peoples;
the story achieved historical legitimacy when Saxo Gram-
maticus included it in his twelfth-century *Historiae Danicae*
("Danish History" or "History of the Danes"). François de
Belleforêt ("Belleforest" to English readers) included a version in his popular *Histoires tragiques* ("Tragic Stories"), a
sixteenth-century French prose work where Shakespeare
and his contemporaries found many plot suggestions.

Shakespeare might be said to have returned to the
Hamlet story about 1600 because it seems likely that an
English-language Hamlet play was being performed in the
late 1580s or 1590s, and it is possible that Shakespeare revised this early Hamlet play at some point. Numerous references and seeming echoes of actual language from that
hypothetical play come down to us, though the play itself,
often called the *Ur-Hamlet*, has not. Many scholars have
thought the *Ur-Hamlet* might have been written by
Thomas Kyd, who wrote *The Spanish Tragedy* (circa 1587),
popular and often imitated, often parodied, throughout
the Elizabethan-Jacobean-Caroline period. It is the finest
English revenge tragedy before Shakespeare's *Hamlet*.

Beginning with Thomas Nashe's remarks in his preface
to *Menaphon* (1589), fragmentary references to a now-
lost Hamlet play suggest that the ghost of Hamlet's father

and especially his complicated demand that the son revenge the father's death struck early audiences forcibly. Thomas Lodge's *Wit's Misery* (1596) apparently alludes to the *Ur-Hamlet* when Lodge describes a devil born of Beelzebub and Jealousy: "he walks for the most part in black under colour of gravity, & looks as pale as the Visard of ye ghost which cried so miserally [*sic*] at ye Theator [i.e., The Theatre, an early playhouse dating from 1576] like an oisterwife, *Hamlet, revenge*." Like "Hieronimo is mad again" from *The Spanish Tragedy,* "Hamlet, revenge" became a catchphrase and appears in print as late as Samuel Rowland's *The Night-Raven* (1620), although it does not occur in any of the three early texts of Shakespeare's version we now possess. An unusual sign of *Hamlet*'s early popularity is the record of its having been performed aboard Captain William Keeling's ship *Dragon* off the coast of Sierra Leone in September 1607.*

In 1710, the third earl of Shaftesbury alluded to the play's extreme popularity in a way that assumes his readers know the play, the central character, and the author without having to be told title or names:

> That Piece of his ["Our old dramatick Poet"] which seems to have most affected *English* Hearts, and has perhaps been oftenest acted of any that have come upon our Stage, is . . . a series of deep Reflections, drawn from *one* Mouth, upon the Subject of *one* single Accident and Calamity, naturally fitted to move Horrour and Compassion. It may be said, of this Play . . . that it has properly but ONE *Character* or *principal Part*.†

---

* For the shipboard performance and many of the allusions to the *Ur-Hamlet*, see E. K. Chambers, *William Shakespeare: A Study of Facts and Problems,* 2 vols. (Oxford: Clarendon Press, 1930), 2: 334–35 and 1: 411–12, respectively.

† [Anthony Ashley Cooper,] *Soliloquy, or Advice to an Author* (London, 1710), pp. 117–18, reprinted under Cooper's name in *Characteristicks of Men, Manners, Opinions, Times* (London, 1711), where both Shakespeare and *Hamlet* are identified.

Shaftesbury accurately assessed *Hamlet*'s early-eighteenth-century popularity on stage. And the play has never lost the status of Shakespeare's most performed drama; over the centuries that prominence has extended into many other forms and media – burlesque and satire, novels for young adults, comic books, opera, film, video, among others.

Why is and was *Hamlet* so popular? Centuries ago, Shaftesbury identified accident and calamity, horror, compassion, and the centrality of Hamlet the prince. At the play's very end, Hamlet asks Horatio, "report me and my cause aright . . . To tell my story" (V.2.322, 332), and the first draft of that story comes quickly:

> So shall you hear
> Of carnal, bloody, and unnatural acts,
> Of accidental judgments, casual slaughters,
> Of deaths put on by cunning and forced cause,
> And, in this upshot, purposes mistook
> Fall'n on th' inventors' heads.
>
> (V.2.363–68)

Horatio stresses, as Shaftesbury did a century later, the play's violent actions – misdirected, unknowingly self-directed – and the labyrinthine ironies of human purpose and human error.

Aware of Thomas Kyd's lead in *The Spanish Tragedy*, Shakespeare saw how the apparently simple and very human demand for revenge could be a way into questions both common and insoluble. Greeted by the anxious terror of first Barnardo and Marcellus and then Horatio ("If thou hast any sound or use of voice, / Speak to me," I.1.128–29), a ghost appears – the observers think it looks like Hamlet's dead father – and says nothing, but "before them and with solemn march / Goes slow and stately by" (I.2.201–2). Its inexplicable appearance requires (but exactly why?) that they tell Prince Hamlet what they have seen. And when Hamlet does indeed see the Ghost walking, he instantly identifies its ambiguity:

> Be thou a spirit of health or goblin damned,
> Bring with thee airs from heaven or blasts from hell,
> Be thy intents wicked or charitable,
> Thou com'st in such a questionable shape
> That I will speak to thee. I'll call thee Hamlet,
> King, father, royal Dane. O, answer me!
>
> (I.4.40–45)

This "questionable shape" is at least doubly questionable. It is an uncertain, a "questionable," shape – is it the ghost of Hamlet's father? is it some demonic "goblin" with "wicked" intents? is it a "spirit of health" come to offer some charity to the living? It is also a "questionable shape" because somehow it demands questions: "O, answer me!" One paradoxical reason for the play's undying popularity is its ceaseless interrogation. Famously, it begins with questions:

> BARNARDO Who's there?
> FRANCISCO
>   Nay, answer me. Stand and unfold yourself.
> BARNARDO Long live the king!
> FRANCISCO Barnardo?
> BARNARDO He.
>
> (I.1.1–5)

As the play goes on, questions and hypotheses proliferate ("I'll call thee Hamlet, / King, father, royal Dane"), but there are few answers ("O, answer me!").

Though the Ghost soon responds to Hamlet's triple naming of him – replies "I am thy father's spirit" (I.5.9), gives a detailed, circumstantial account of "his foul and most unnatural murder" (I.5.25), and requires Hamlet to revenge that murder – all of Hamlet's questions about the questionable shape remain. Those puzzles are not merely Shakespeare's inspired inventions; they would also have been especially troubling for the original audiences, caught as they were among conflicting religious teachings about the afterlife of souls and the possibility of those souls' temporary return as goblin or spirit of health or as some yet more inscrutable being. The Ghost himself testifies, "I am forbid / To tell the secrets of my prison house . . . this eternal blazon must not be / To ears of flesh and blood" (I.5.13-14, 21-22): no living person can possibly know what it is to be dead, "Doomed for a certain term to walk the night, / And for the day confined to fast in fires" (10-11). Yet only knowledge of "The undiscovered country, from whose bourn / No traveler returns" (III.1.79-80) could fully "answer me!" To the ambiguities of the Ghost's condition and intent, his demands add two further excruciatingly difficult provisos: "howsomever thou pursues this act [killing Claudius], / Taint not thy mind, nor let thy soul contrive / Against thy mother aught. Leave her to heaven" (I.5.84-86).

Arising within these imponderable matters, there is the plot's propulsive engine: revenge. Here lies another part of the play's popularity. One loss, the murder of Hamlet's father, should be revenged by another, his murderer's death. In the essay "Of Revenge," Francis Bacon famously called it "a kind of wild justice," and he meant the phrase to be an oxymoron because justice is a quality of civilization, not savagery; savagery is by definition "wild," not civil, and hence without justice. Bacon's pithy remark is more celebrated than the way he finishes his sentence, but his final words neatly catch Hamlet's problem: "Revenge is a kind of wild justice, which the more man's nature runs to, the more ought law to weed it out." Yet there is an appalling, an appealing, symmetry (a justice?) when we see vengeance achieved. Just as Shakespeare's first audiences would have been uncertain about how to understand a ghost, so too Elizabethan views of revenge were deeply ambiguous. Condemned by church and state (Bacon: "the more ought law to weed it out"), personal revenge was nonetheless an entirely possible, even frequent, choice for every social group and class. Moreover, the right to defend and sustain personal honor, the duty to maintain the integrity of name and family by refusing insult and redressing wrong were widely held though controversial components of aristocratic belief and behavior.

If an Elizabethan nobleman could feel compelled to answer a wrong with personal rather than legal or institutional action – a duel, for example – and many did, then how much more likely would it be that a prince, presumptive heir to the throne of Denmark, should feel compelled to revenge his royal father's death? And how much more ambiguously admirable would the first Elizabethan audiences find that revenge? Might the audiences not feel that Hamlet's personal nobility and his promise as future monarch, proclaimed by Ophelia (III.1.150-54) and Fortinbras (V.2.378-81), required him to avenge his father and defend his family's dignity? And are not Laertes' dilemma (a father wrongly killed, a sister driven mad) and his response to his dilemma (threatened regicide and usurpation, attempted murder) almost precisely the same as Hamlet's?

The Ghost's central demand has a frank simplicity, almost an ordinariness, so convincing that the play must shock us into feeling knowledge of how terrifying the demand is. Hardly has that demand been made than Hamlet tersely sums its wide difficulty: "The time is out of joint. O cursèd spite / That ever I was born to set it right!" (I.5.191-92). Regicide and usurpation – these are Claudius's crimes according to the Ghost, and they are so grave they dislocate the social body, the world, "the time." Hamlet portrays himself as a bonesetter, an orthopod restoring straightness to the disjointed, bent nation. He echoes, disturbingly, his uncle:

> Now follows, that you know, young Fortinbras,
> Holding a weak supposal of our worth,
> Or thinking by our late dear brother's death
> Our state to be *disjoint* and out of frame.
> (I.2.17-20; my italics)

Earlier, Hamlet regards himself as a potential gardener when he uses Francis Bacon's metaphor from "Of Re-

venge" and describes Denmark as "an unweeded garden /
That grows to seed" (I.2.135-36).

It is a romantic commonplace that Hamlet is a character who cannot make up his mind, and so Laurence
Olivier's admired film (1948) opens with the text of
Hamlet's sardonic speech on Danish drunkenness and
revelry, spoken aloud by Olivier:

> So oft it chances in particular men
> That (for some vicious mole of nature in them,
> As in their birth, wherein they are not guilty,
> Since nature cannot choose his origin)
> By the o'ergrowth of some complexion,
> Oft breaking down the pales and forts of reason,
> Or by some habit that too much o'erleavens
> The form of plausive manners – that (these men
> Carrying, I say, the stamp of one defect,
> Being nature's livery, or fortune's star)
> His virtues else, be they as pure as grace,
> As infinite as man may undergo,
> Shall in the general censure take corruption
> From that particular fault.
>
> (I.4.23-36)

Then, while the text lingers in sight and memory, Olivier
tells us in voice-over Hamlet's "particular fault": "This is
the tragedy of a man who could not make up his mind."
Commonplace and film are simplistic. Hamlet understands
his duty of revenge very well and says so almost at once:
"Haste me to know't, that I, with wings as swift / As meditation or the thoughts of love, / May sweep to my revenge"
(I.5.29-31). What he does not know and must seek to learn
is the truth of the Ghost's claims. And always as he learns
the truth or when he chooses to believe he has learned the
truth, he endures the agony of thinking and feeling the ex-
travagance of revenge itself. It is not ordinary at all.

Hamlet's validating of the Ghost's claims determines
the skeleton of the play's action. Sometimes horribly,

sometimes comically, sometimes satirically, he tests the Ghost by testing the truthfulness of those around him – Ophelia, Rosencrantz and Guildenstern, Polonius (especially in II.2) and Gertrude (especially in III.4) and Laertes (see, for instance, V.2.204 ff.). In each case, Hamlet finds or suspects the enmity of his mighty opposite, King Claudius (see V.2.62). Distrusting most others, Hamlet repeatedly affirms his trust in Horatio – "thou art e'en as just a man / As e'er my conversation coped withal" (III.2.53 ff.), and Horatio justifies that trust. As we saw, Hamlet relies on Horatio to explain and defend the prince's actions after his death. In the middle of the play, Hamlet makes Horatio a trusted witness to the elaborate deception called "The Mousetrap," the celebrated play-within-the-play wherein Hamlet hopes to "catch the conscience of the king" (II.2.544).

This playlet (III.2.131 ff.) reproduces in pantomime and spoken action a version of Claudius murdering old Hamlet. Like Hamlet's elaborate cuing of the lead actor's speeches as "The rugged Pyrrhus" at the fall of Troy (II.2.392 ff.), and Hamlet's later condescending, schoolmasterish advice to professional actors on how to perform their parts (III.2.1 ff.), the play-within-the-play is part of Shakespeare's examination of roles and role-playing. What is art for the actor is hypocrisy and deceit in real life, and the strongly praised art of acting may, so Hamlet hopes, reveal the true hypocrisy of the Danish court. Yet Hamlet has warned his friends not to be surprised if he "perchance hereafter shall think meet / To put an antic disposition on" (I.5.174-75). The Hamlet who instructs the actors is himself portrayed by a consummate professional actor (probably Richard Burbage in the earliest performances) and is, moreover, an actor who plays the role of a man playing many roles in order to discover the roles other characters (themselves also other *actors*) have assumed.

Examples abound of the play's self-reflexivity through its treatment of actors and acting, of deceit as artistry and deceit as conspiracy and threat. Polonius's fatuous commentary on the "rugged Pyrrhus" speech, for instance, finds him criticizing in others the faults he so flagrantly commits himself ("This is too long"!). When Claudius concocts a plan with Laertes to kill Hamlet (IV.7.125 ff.), the two characters, who we know are also actors, in fact create an elaborate charade, one that Claudius desperately seeks to prolong – "O, yet defend me, friends. I am but hurt" (V.2.307) – beyond that charade's final, grotesque failure to convince its onstage audience.

A third example of the play's reflexivity occurs in the soliloquy (II.2.488-544) beginning "O, what a rogue and peasant slave am I!" and ending with Hamlet's assertion that "The Mousetrap" will reveal Claudius's guilt once and for all. The speech begins with Hamlet's typical sense of his superior social rank, as his speeches so often remark; he lacerates himself with déclassé terms ("rogue" = vagabond, vagrant; "peasant" = agricultural worker bound to the land), categories most unsuited to a prince. Without the character (Hamlet) quite seeming to realize it, the soliloquy demonstrates the process Hamlet intends to apply to Claudius. The principle has folkloric support:

I have heard that guilty creatures sitting at a play
Have by the very cunning of the scene
Been struck so to the soul that presently
They have proclaimed their malefactions.
(II.2.528-31)

Yet "guilty" or not, Hamlet himself has also been "sitting at a play." He has been brought to this moment by watching and hearing an actor who "But in a fiction, in a dream of passion" has forced "his soul so to his own conceit" that tears come to his eyes, he appears distracted, and his voice breaks with emotion. Hamlet here and Claudius in prospect are victims of the actor's deceit; each man reveals (Hamlet) or is expected to reveal (Claudius) true feelings through responding to dramatic fictions. Hamlet's language becomes increasingly exaggerated, stuffed with rhetorical excess and nearly parodic sound devices: "*Bloody, b*awdy villain! / Re-m*orseless,* trea*cherous,* le*cherous,* kind*less* villain!" (II.2.519-20; my italics stress the exaggerated sonic echoes).

Stimulated to this self-contempt by an actor's artifice, Hamlet finally compares himself to that other profession skilled in artificial passion and financially rewarding deceit:

> . . . I, the son of a dear father murdered,
> Prompted to my revenge by heaven and hell,
> Must like a *whore* unpack my heart with words
> And fall a-cursing like a very *drab,*
> A *stallion!*
>
> (II.2.522–26; my italics)

Actor, whore, hero. The shifting analogies among them may disconcert us, but they reveal the possibilities of deception and revelation, truth found through falsehood or pretense, truth found to *be* falsehood and apparent falsehood found to be true that make Hamlet's and the play's understanding of revenge and its ambiguities so powerful and imponderable.

Parallel to this overt, plot-motivating exploration is the mental and emotional exploration of what revenge means and what it means to revenge. This exploration generates many of what Shaftesbury calls the play's "deep Reflections, drawn from *one* Mouth" and helps explain why he found "that it has properly but ONE *Character* or *principal Part.*" Those reflections appear in Hamlet's soliloquies, the speeches that have made the play so popular with actors and so memorable for audiences: "To be, or not to be . . ." (III.1.56 ff.); "O, what a rogue and peasant slave am I! . . ." (II.2.488 ff.); "How all occasions do inform against me . . ." (IV.4.32 ff.), for instance.

Grandiloquent and sublime, sometimes both and more simultaneously, these soliloquies purport to be meditative and reflective, the words of a speaker pondering ideas, possibilities, choices. And so the speeches are, but they are also a dramatic convention, and that convention died long ago.

Producers of the play have found it a difficult convention because it strongly resists being naturalized and made to seem "realistic." Hamlet complains that Rosencrantz and Guildenstern treat him as a musical instrument upon which they may play, and he taunts them: "you would pluck out the heart of my mystery" (III.2.359-60). The complaint is a neat piece of Shakespearean sleight of hand because it tempts us to think we have privileged entry into Hamlet's "mystery" through his soliloquies. We do not. It is vital to understand that the soliloquies, like everything else in the script, are part of Shakespeare's design upon our hearts and minds. We draw inferences from the soliloquies, and we are meant to. Shakespeare's art makes us believe we have unmediated access to the character's thoughts and feelings, but Hamlet the character has no thoughts and feelings because the character is a dramatic creation, not a thinking, feeling human being.

Thus, the soliloquies often prompt feelings and thoughts in us that the character cannot self-consciously know or feel in any realistic sense, as we saw in "O, what a rogue and peasant slave am I!" In that soliloquy, the triple parallel of actor, hero, and whore was created within Hamlet's imagined consciousness and unconsciousness so that Shakespeare could develop revenge's ambiguous nature. If we turn our attention from these matters and back to the overt actions of the play, we find that parallelism also organizes a great deal of the action and hence organizes our response to it.

In a scene Derek Jacobi performs brilliantly in Kenneth Branagh's film of the play (1996), Claudius (Jacobi) inveigles the help of the dead Polonius's son, Laertes, in a plot against Hamlet. Claudius first recalls (for the audience) the transitoriness of love when he uses the language of the Player King in "The Mousetrap":

> Not that I think you did not love your father,
> But that I know love is begun by time,
> And that I see, in passages of proof,
> Time qualifies the spark and fire of it.

There lives within the very flame of love
A kind of wick or snuff that will abate it,
And nothing is at a like goodness still,
For goodness, growing to a plurisy,
Dies in his own too-much.

(IV.7.108–16)

Or as the Player King says in "The Mousetrap,"

I do believe you think what now you speak,
But what we do determine oft we break.
Purpose is but the slave to memory,
Of violent birth, but poor validity,
Which now, the fruit unripe, sticks on the tree,
But fall unshaken when they mellow be.

(III.2.182–87)

Claudius (in IV.7) and the Player King (in III.2) speak to audiences that have, or wish to have, an unbreakable conviction that human love, desire, trust, fidelity will survive time and time's passing.

Humans and their wants can and will triumph over time's jaws. So we wish and so we may hope, but the analogy between the Player King and the player who plays Claudius toying with Laertes (also an actor-player) warns the audience and underlines one of the play's many parallelisms: Laertes lost a father, Polonius, mistakenly killed by Hamlet; Hamlet lost a father, old Hamlet, killed deliberately by Claudius. Beyond the Danish royal family, there is another lost father. Old Norway, we learn, lost a competition with old Hamlet:

Such was the very armor he [old Hamlet, now a
    ghost] had on
When he the ambitious Norway combated.
So frowned he once when, in an angry parle,
He smote the sledded Polacks on the ice.

(I.1.60–63)

"Ambitious Norway" lost the battle (the duel?), and the victor, old Hamlet, fostered a legacy of competition and hatred. His son, Hamlet, and old Hamlet's successor, Claudius, oppose and echo old Norway and his nephew, Fortinbras.

Horatio continues with a confusing account of the past conflict between Denmark and Norway, old Hamlet and a Norwegian king who has the same name, "Fortinbras," as the character first mentioned at I.1.95 ("young Fortinbras") and the character who arrives at the play's end to claim, with young Hamlet's "voice," or vote, the throne of Denmark:

> Our last king [old Hamlet],
> Whose image [i.e., the Ghost] even but now appeared
>   to us,
> Was as you know by Fortinbras of Norway,
> Thereto pricked on by a most emulate pride,
> Dared to the combat; in which our valiant [old]
>   Hamlet
> (For so this side of our known world esteemed him)
> Did slay this Fortinbras; who, by a sealed compact
> Well ratified by law and heraldry,
> Did forfeit, with his life, all those his lands
> Which he stood seized of to the conqueror;
> Against the which a moiety competent
> Was gagèd by our king, which had returned
> To the inheritance of Fortinbras
> Had he been vanquisher, as, by the same comart
> And carriage of the article designed,
> His fell to Hamlet.
>
>   (I.1.80-95)

There's no denying that this account is confusing, and it's probably not an instance of Shakespeare's archaic language confusing a modern spectator. The speech is manifestly contorted, and we may guess that it stumped many of its original hearers. How did such a state of affairs come about, and why?

One possibility is that Shakespeare is trying to convey

more narrative and expository detail than he can organize and we can comfortably absorb. That might be the case. If we suppose, however, that the playwright who had navigated the always shifting shoals of the English history plays he wrote in the 1590s is by now (around 1600) masterfully in control of historical sources and their dramatic representation, then we must wonder if this confusing farrago of "he" and "his," of a Fortinbras killed by one Hamlet and another Fortinbras who turns up at the play's conclusion to solemnize the death of another Hamlet, of an old Norway now alive in the play's present who is (it seems) uncle to the young Fortinbras we first encounter in V.2, has a deliberated aesthetic purpose. Rather than imagine that we have detected Shakespeare compounding error upon error, we had better suppose that Shakespeare knows his craft – he is, probably, playing a sophisticated dramatic and narrative game. If so, again, why?

This cloud of Hamlets young and old, of Fortinbrasses young and old, not to mention "Norway, uncle of young Fortinbras – / . . . impotent and bedrid" (I.2.28-29), surrounds a personal and political world defined by and grounded in families, most obviously fathers and sons, kings and their princely heirs, Danes and Norwegians. Closer to Danish Elsinore than Norway, there's a third family, not royal but presumably noble: a father, Polonius, a daughter, Ophelia, and a son, Laertes. And this family is joined with the Danish and Norwegian royal families through dutiful service and romantic love. Councillor Polonius seeks to resolve Dano-Norwegian political problems and the more intimate familial problem of a daughter who loves, he and his son fear, above her social status. As Laertes tells his sister, Hamlet may love her now

> And now no soil nor cautel doth besmirch
> The virtue of his will, but you must fear,
> His greatness weighed, his will is not his own.
> He may not, as unvalued persons do,

Carve for himself, for on his choice depends
The safety and health of this whole state,
And therefore must his choice be circumscribed
Unto the voice and yielding of that body
Whereof he is the head.

(I.3.15–23)

Laertes advises his sister to distrust Hamlet's proffered love because Hamlet is not his own man, not just the son of old Hamlet, but prospectively the father, the "head," of the national family and social body and therefore responsible for "The safety and health of this whole state." King Claudius himself has just said as much when he names Hamlet "the most immediate to our throne" (I.2.109). Valued beyond any particular, personal worth, Hamlet has a public worth he may neither deny nor escape: "He may not . . . / Carve for himself." Nor of course in a very different way may Ophelia choose freely; just as political demands trap Hamlet, so political and patriarchal constraints control Ophelia's choices and set her on the path to frustration, madness, and suicide.

Families and family values, it seems, are everywhere, and now Shakespeare's apparently confusing exposition of Hamlets and Norways, Fortinbrasses and Denmarks begins to make sense. As so often in his major tragedies, Shakespeare here focuses public, political issues through the family and its difficulties, its conflicts and dynamic relations. Longing for his dead father and subdued to his ghost's will, Hamlet still has a living mother, Gertrude, now married to his father's murderer. The parallel Danish family, Polonius's, has a father and brother, but no mother; here, Laertes takes the mother's traditional advisory role. Hamlet's absent father and present mother have been fertile sources for scholars and critics. At least as long ago as Sigmund Freud's *The Interpretation of Dreams* (1900), readers and spectators have wondered if Hamlet's enmity toward Claudius arises not only from filial loyalty and justified anger but from a less expressible sexual envy: son desires mother sexually, and that desire is made the more acknowledgeable because the mother's seducer-lover-husband is uncle and stepfather, not father. True or not, these possibilities intensify and complicate our sense of Hamlet's problems as he seeks to know the truth of the Ghost's assertions and then seeks to act upon his own conclusions.

Whatever Shakespeare may have designed, or allowed us to find, in the Gertrude-Hamlet relation, it is clear that Hamlet finds sexuality troubling (I.2.146: "frailty, thy name is woman"), most evidently in his relation with Ophelia and then his brutal rupture of it (III.1.103 ff.), followed by his obscene and cruel banter before "The Mousetrap" (III.2.110 ff.). Generations of audiences have speculated about Ophelia and Hamlet's relation "before the play begins," and the question concerns actors very deeply. We cannot know the answer, and presumably Shakespeare did not see a dramatic purpose to offering one. What we can fairly infer, however, is that Ophelia and Hamlet's relation is politicized first by her brother and father, and soon after by Claudius and then by Hamlet himself when he begins to believe – "Are you honest?" (III.1.103) – that she has become a pawn or cat's-paw in his conflict with King Claudius. Polonius explicitly frames his anxieties about his daughter's relation with the prince as political: "What majesty should be, what duty is . . ." (II.2.87).

This speech and others like it are his versions of Laertes' attempts to warn Ophelia against Hamlet, and by joining sexuality with politics father and brother point us to one of the play's most important though sometimes overlooked concerns: succession to the throne. Royal succession, especially primogeniture (father succeeded by eldest surviving son), the system familiar to Shakespeare's audiences, is a legal, political, and personal nexus where family, sexuality, and politics meet. (One slightly confusing feature of *Hamlet* is the references to an elective monarchy, which Denmark historically had been, but Shakespeare writes other lines invoking his audience's native system of succession.) Whatever system of royal succession we imagine in the play's world, we do see Hamlet's family line end in the play's final bloodbath. A new line must start from this instant, and it is Norway, a foreign, albeit neighboring, nation that provides Denmark's next ruler.

With only a little changing, this imagined Danish political situation might have seemed rather familiar to Shakespeare's early-seventeenth-century audiences. A queen who had ruled for as long as most of her subjects could remember, Elizabeth I, was now visibly aging and certain to remain childless; the English succession had become so controversial and potentially divisive that public discussion of it had been banned. The leading candidate was King James VI of Scotland, and when the Tudor family line died with Elizabeth in March 1603, he was the man and his the family who replaced the Tudors on the throne. James, of course, was king of a foreign, albeit neighboring, nation. As Laertes had said long ago of Hamlet, a royal figure cannot freely choose to follow personal desires without risking public calamity. What we might call the reciprocal is true too: a royal figure's every personal desire and act are made inescapably political. So, Hamlet.

From high political issues refracted through the family, we have here returned to what Shaftesbury "said, of this Play . . . that it has properly but ONE *Character* or *principal Part.*" *Hamlet,* that is, is Hamlet. Shaftesbury may be correct, especially for the theater's *Hamlet,* and it is even more likely that we will agree with him when watching productions that omit Fortinbras and the international political matters entirely, as performances from the eighteenth century onward have often done.* Yet even in such

* See Robert Hapgood, ed., *Hamlet,* Shakespeare in Production (Cambridge, England: Cambridge University Press, 1999), p. 275, n. to V.2.340 s.d.; Hapgood's volume is an excellent guide to *Hamlet's* history of performance.

truncated performances, we will – or we may – also attend to the play's complicated representation of roles and role-playing, actors on stage and actors in life, and its profound investigations of the nature of knowledge and knowing. Responding to the play's epistemological intricacies, many people have argued that the play portrays Hamlet's quest for self-knowledge. That claim lessens the play by plucking out the heart of its mysteries. Even if we do not presume to say what knowledge Hamlet achieves, to suppose that that knowledge is the play's goal or its artistic purpose diminishes its power. Doing so, we tame into knowledge something better enjoyed as wild and unconfinable.

A. R. BRAUNMULLER
University of California, Los Angeles

Note on the Text

THIS IS A MODERNIZED text of the Second Quarto (Q2, published 1604-5) of *Hamlet*. "Modernized" means that earlier forms of words English speakers still use appear in the forms they now speak or read. Thus, where the text here edited mentions a creature English speakers call "porcupine," that is the way the creature's name appears, although the 1604–5 text here edited spells the creature's name "porpentine," an archaic word. Words that are no longer current – e.g., "eisel," which means "vinegar" – appear in their early forms because English speakers no longer have those words. The meaning of "the Second Quarto of *Hamlet*" and the text chosen for this edition of *Hamlet* are the subjects of the next paragraphs.

"*The Tragicall Historie of Hamlet, Prince of Denmarke. By William Shakespeare.*" appeared in three early texts: a quarto in 1603 (Q1), a second quarto in 1604-5 (Q2, with the title just cited), and in Shakespeare's collected dramatic works, a folio, in 1623 (F, or "First Folio").

Hamlet Q1 is a mysterious text and very rare (only two copies, both imperfect, are known). It is quite short (about 2,154 lines), has characters named Gertred, Rossencraft, and Gilderstone as well as Corambis (analogous to the character the later texts call Polonius), and has a plot order different from Q2 and F – Hamlet's "To be, or not to be" soliloquy and his "nunnery" scene (III.1 in editions of Q2 and F) with Ophelia ("Ofelia" in Q1) appear before his instructions to the actors (II.2 in editions of Q2 and F) rather than after, making a direct link between Hamlet's decision to use a play to "catch the conscience of the king" and the performance of "The Mousetrap." Q1 lacks almost all the international and political elements in Q2 and F, and, finally, it often has less vivid and wrought language than the other two texts.* Q1 shows signs of deriving from or being a text prepared for performance, almost certainly not by Shakespeare. Nevertheless, because of Q1's clear connection with the stage, modern acting and reading texts often include stage directions derived from or influenced by it, and some modern productions have gone so far as to use Q1's plot order and language drawn from Q2 and F.

Q2 is much the longest of the three surviving early texts, about 3,674 lines, it shows fewer signs (some scholars say none) of having been readied for performance, and it includes many passages not in Q1 or F, most notably Hamlet's soliloquy beginning "How all occasions do inform against me" and the associated discussion of Fortinbras's army (IV.4 in editions of Q2) and other speeches, such as the one including Horatio's memorable "A mote it is to trouble the mind's eye" (I.1.112), a phrase Hamlet seems to echo in both Q2 and F when he startles Horatio by saying he has recently seen old Hamlet, "In my mind's eye" (I.2.185). Q2 is generally thought to derive from Shakespeare's draft for the play and was published with a blurb claiming, "Newly imprinted and enlarged to almost as much againe as it was [i.e., as published in Q1], according to the true and perfect Coppie."

The folio of 1623 (F), about 3,535 lines long, includes, roughly, 70 lines not in Q2 and lacks 230 that Q2 prints; it seems that F derives from a script prepared for performance and includes many lines that scholars regard as "actors' additions" – that is, additional words recording what actors said and by implication what they *did* on stage. The most notorious of these supposed "additions" are the letters or sounds that follow Hamlet's final words in Q2, ". . . the rest is silence." F adds, "O, o, o, o." And presumably some comic actor thought it worth his while to elaborate Polonius's catalogue of dramatic genres in II.2 with

* For a text and discussion of Q1, see Kathleen O. Irace, ed., *The First Quarto of Hamlet*, The New Cambridge Shakespeare: The Early Quartos (Cambridge, England: Cambridge University Press, 1998).

"tragical-historical, tragical-comical-historical-pastoral," an over-the-top addition to Q2's already laden joke.

Which early text should be the basis for a modernized reading edition? Q1 is unsatisfactory because it prints relatively little of what Q2 and F agree is Shakespearean as, indeed, Q2's title page testifies. One solution, formerly very popular, is to combine Q2 and F and retain in a conflated text as many of the lines unique to Q2 and to F as possible. In doing so, however, one creates of two long plays a still longer play: uncut performances of Q2 or F run about four hours plus; either text is almost certainly too long for uncut Elizabethan-Jacobean performance. Further, the conflated text never existed, so far as we know, as an option for Shakespeare's actors or readers. Better, then, to choose one early text, Q2 or F, and change it as little as can be reconciled with intelligibility.

But which early text? On the relatively strong probability that Q2 has passed through fewer amending agencies than F (with its probable theatrical provenance, at least in places), the Q2 text has a higher percentage of Shakespeare's writing than F. I therefore chose Q2 as the version of the play to represent here. Undoubtedly, there are lines in F and not in Q2 that seem important to the plot and unlikely to be evidence of actors eager to display their talents or extend their roles – that is, lines by Shakespeare and perhaps the result of his revision; there are also a few occasions where lines seem to have been omitted from Q2 through printing accident (see, for example, the note on II.2.211–12). In these few cases, words from F are included in this edition within brackets if they constitute three contiguous words or more; shorter additions or substitutions are cited in the Emendations (pp. lv–lviii). All changes and additions to the stage directions have been bracketed; the speech prefixes and characters' names have been silently normalized and modernized. Q2 has no act or scene divisions and F very few; most here are editorial and traditional; they are included only to make reference to specific lines easier.

Finally, it must also be noted that F includes lines that

have entered English speech and literary allusion – for instance, Hamlet's dismissive remark on the deaths of Rosencrantz and Guildenstern: "Why, man, they did make love to this employment" (V.2 in F). The line does not appear in this edition because it does not appear in Q2. For the same reason, Hamlet's superb remark that he understands Laertes' unhappy situation as similar to his own – "by the image of my cause I see / The portraiture of his" (V.2 in F) – is not included here. Both appear in the Folio-only Passages that follow.*

The list of emendations (pp. lv–lviii) seeks to record all places where this edition diverges from Q2 and also offers readings from Q1 and F that appear to be possible or arguable alternatives to the Q2 reading printed here.

The original Pelican edition of *Hamlet* was prepared by Willard Farnham; text and introduction here are entirely new, the notes and emendations thoroughly revised and expanded.

---

* For more elaborate treatments of the extremely complex and always heavily hypothetical editorial problem in *Hamlet,* see Stanley Wells, Gary Taylor, John Jowett, and William Montgomery, *William Shakespeare: A Textual Companion* (Oxford: Clarendon Press, 1987), pp. 396–402, and Harold Jenkins, ed., *Hamlet,* Arden Shakespeare (London: Methuen, 1982), pp. 18–82.

FOLIO-ONLY PASSAGES

The principal passages in the First Folio (F) *Hamlet* not in this edition of *Hamlet* Q2 follow in modernized spelling and with notes where necessary.

1. After "His greatness weighed, his will is not his own" (1.3.17), F reads:

> For he himself is subject to his birth.

2. After "But your news is not true" (II.2.238-39), F reads:

> HAMLET   Let me question more in particular. What have   240
> you, my good friends, deserved at the hands of For-
> tune that she sends you to prison hither?
> GUILDENSTERN   Prison, my lord?
> HAMLET   Denmark's a prison.
> ROSENCRANTZ   Then is the world one.
> HAMLET   A goodly one; in which there are many confines,   246
> wards, and dungeons, Denmark being one o' th' worst.   247
> ROSENCRANTZ   We think not so, my lord.
> HAMLET   Why, then 'tis none to you, for there is nothing
> either good or bad but thinking makes it so. To me it is   250
> a prison.
> ROSENCRANTZ   Why, then your ambition makes it one.
> 'Tis too narrow for your mind.
> HAMLET   O God, I could be bounded in a nutshell and
> count myself a king of infinite space, were it not that I
> have bad dreams.
> GUILDENSTERN   Which dreams indeed are ambition, for
> the very substance of the ambitious is merely the
> shadow of a dream.
> HAMLET   A dream itself is but a shadow.   260
> ROSENCRANTZ   Truly, and I hold ambition of so airy and
> light a quality that it is but a shadow's shadow.
> HAMLET   Then are our beggars bodies, and our mon-   263

264   archs and outstretched heroes the beggars' shadows.
265   Shall we to th' court? for, by my fay, I cannot reason.
266   BOTH   We'll wait upon you.

    HAMLET   No such matter. I will not sort you with the
    rest of my servants, for, to speak to you like an honest
    man, I am most dreadfully attended.

---

246 *confines* places of imprisonment   247 *wards* cells   263 *bodies* solid substances, not shadows (because *beggars* lack ambition)   264 *outstretched* elongated as shadows (with a corollary implication of far-reaching with respect to the ambitions that make both *heroes* and *monarchs* into *shadows*)   265 *fay* faith   266 *wait upon* attend

3. After "No indeed, are they not" (II.2.305), F reads:

    HAMLET   How comes it? Do they grow rusty?

    ROSENCRANTZ   Nay, their endeavor keeps in the wonted
309   pace, but there is, sir, an eyrie of children, little eyases,
310   that cry out on the top of question and are most tyran-
    nically clapped for't. These are now the fashion, and so
312   berattle the common stages (so they call them) that
313   many wearing rapiers are afraid of goosequills and dare
    scarce come thither.

    HAMLET   What, are they children? Who maintains 'em?
316   How are they escoted? Will they pursue the quality no
317   longer than they can sing? Will they not say afterwards,
    if they should grow themselves to common players (as it
    is most like, if their means are no better), their writers
320   do them wrong to make them exclaim against their own
    succession?

    ROSENCRANTZ   Faith, there has been much to do on
323   both sides, and the nation holds it no sin to tarre them
    to controversy. There was, for a while, no money bid
325   for argument unless the poet and the player went to
    cuffs in the question.

    HAMLET   Is't possible?

    GUILDENSTERN O, there has been much throwing about
    of brains.

330   HAMLET   Do the boys carry it away?

ROSENCRANTZ   Ay, that they do, my lord – Hercules
and his load too.

332

309 *eyrie* nest; *eyases* nestling hawks   310 *on the top of question* above
others on matter of dispute   312 *berattle* berate; *common stages* "public" theaters of the "common" players, who were organized in companies mainly composed of adult actors (allusion being made to the
"War of the Theaters" in Shakespeare's London)   313 *goosequills*
pens (of satirists who made out that the London public stage showed
low taste)   316 *escoted* supported; *quality* profession of acting   317
sing i.e., with unchanged voices   323 *tarre* incite   325 *argument*
matter of a play   332 *load* i.e., the whole world (with a topical reference to the sign of the Globe theater, a representation of Hercules
bearing the world on his shoulders)

4. After ". . . historical-pastoral" (II.2.341), F reads:

   tragical-historical, tragical-comical-historical-pastoral

5. After "That's good" (II.2.444), F reads:

   "Mobled queen" is good.

6. After "No, my lord" (III.2.111), F reads:

   HAMLET   I mean, my head upon your lap?
   OPHELIA   Ay, my lord.

7. After "The king rises" (III.2.261), F reads:

   HAMLET   What, frighted with false fire?

   false fire a blank, a gun fired with noisy powder but no bullet

8. After "Pray you be round" (III.4.5), F reads:

   HAMLET   *(Within)* Mother, mother, mother.

9. After "Safely stowed" (IV.2.1), F reads:

   GENTLEMEN   *(Within)* Hamlet, Lord Hamlet.

10. After "Bring me to him" (IV.2.27), F reads:

    Hide fox, and all after.

11. After "... an old man's life" (IV.5.160), F reads:

161 Nature is fine in love, and where 'tis fine,
162 It sends some precious instance of itself
  After the thing it loves.

---

161 *fine* refined, purified 162 *instance* specimen, sample

12. After "... ever bore arms" (V.1.33), F reads:

OTHER Why, he had none.
CLOWN What, art a heathen? How dost thou understand the Scripture? The Scripture says Adam digged. Could he dig without arms?

---

arms (a joke on "limbs" and "coat of arms")

13. After "So Guildenstern and Rosencrantz go to't" (V.2.56), F reads:

HAMLET
Why, man, they did make love to this employment.

14. After "... is't not perfect conscience?" (V.2.66), F reads:

 To quit him with this arm? And is't not to be damned
68 To let this canker of our nature come
 In further evil?
HORATIO
70 It must be shortly known to him from England
 What is the issue of the business there.
HAMLET
 It will be short; the interim is mine,
 And a man's life's no more than to say "one."
 But I am very sorry, good Horatio,
 That to Laertes I forgot myself,
 For by the image of my cause I see
 The portraiture of his. I'll court his favors.

But sure the bravery of his grief did put me   78
   Into a tow'ring passion.

HORATIO   Peace, who comes here?

------

68 *canker* cancer, ulcer   **78** *bravery* ostentatious display

EMENDATIONS

Except for noncontroversial modernizations and for a few corrections of obvious typographical errors, all departures from the text of *Hamlet* Q2 (1604-5) are listed below, with the adopted reading in italics followed by the Q2 reading in roman. (Q2 appeared with some pages in two states, uncorrected and corrected, and those two versions are noted where relevant, even if the "corrected" state is not adopted.) Most of the adopted non-Q2 readings are from F, the First Folio (1623) of Shakespeare's dramatic works; where relevant, readings that also appear in *Hamlet* Q1 (1603) are noted. Readings adopted from other editions are attributed to those who first printed them. Occasionally, quartos later than Q2 are cited, and they are identified by publication date (Q 1611, Q 1637, Q 1676). Changes and additions to the stage directions of Q2 are bracketed in the text but not listed here unless controversial; most derive from Q1 and/or F.

I.1 **16** *soldier* (Q1, F) souldiers   **44** *harrows* (F) horrowes   **63** *Polacks* (Malone) pollax   **68** *my* (Q1, F) mine   **73** *why* (Q1, F) with; *cast* (F) cost   **87** *heraldry* (Q1, F) heraldy   **88** *those* (Q1, F) these   **91** *returned* (F) returne   **94** *designed* (Pope) desseigne   **121** *feared* (Collier) feare   **127 s.d.** *He* (Q 1676) It
I.2 **s.d.** *Councillors* (Wilson) Counsaile: as   **16** *all,* (Johnson) all   **58** *He hath* (Q1, Q 1611) Hath   **67** *so* (F) so much   **77** *good* (F) coold   **82** *shapes* (Q 1611) chapes (Q2) shewes (F)   **129** *sullied* (Q2: sallied) solid

(F) 132 *self-* (F) seale 133 *weary* (F) wary 137 *to this* (F) thus 143 *would* (Q1, F) should 178 *see* (Q1, F) not in Q2 209 *Where, as* (Q1) Whereas 213 *watched* (F) watch 257 *Foul* (Q1, F) fonde

I.3 3 *convoy is* (F) conuay, in 12 *bulk* (F) bulkes 48 *like* (F) not in Q2 73 *Are* (F) Or 74 *be* (F) boy 75 *loan* (F) loue 82 *invites* (F) inuests 108 *Running* (Collier) Wrong 128 *implorators* (F) imploratotors 129 *bawds* (Theobald) bonds 130 *beguile* (F) beguide

I.4 2 *a* (F) not in Q2 9 *swaggering* (Q1, F) swaggring 17 *revel* (Q 1611) reueale 27 *the* (Pope) their 36 *evil* (Keightley) eale 37 *often dout* (Steevens) of a doubt 82 *artire* (F) arture 87 *imagination* (Q1, F) imagion

I.5 43 *wit* (Pope) wits 47 *a* (F) not in Q2 55 *lust* (Q1, F) but 56 *sate* (Q1, F) sort 68 *posset* (F) possesse 95 *stiffly* (F) swiftly 96 *while* (F) whiles

II.1 s.d. *man* (Parrott-Craig) man or two 3 *marvelous* (Q 1611) meruiles (Q2) maruels (F) 57 *gaming,* (F) gaming 62 *takes* (F) take 104 *passion* (F) passions

II.2 57 *o'erhasty* (F) hastie 90 *since* (F) not in Q2 108 s.d. *letter* (placed as in F; at line 116 in Q2) 112 *Thus:* (Malone) thus 126 *above* (F) about 137 *winking* (F) working 143 *his* (F) her 148 *watch* (F) wath 149 *a* (F) not in Q2 167 s.d. *reading on a book* (F) not in Q2 209 *sanity* (F) sanctity 211–12 *and . . . him* (F) not in Q2 223 *excellent* (F) extent 227 *overhappy* (F) euer happy 228 *cap* (F) lap 274 *moving how* (F) moouing, how 275 *admirable,* (F) admirable; *action* (F) action,; *angel,* (F) Angell 276 *apprehension* (Q 1637) apprehension, 279 *woman* (Q1, F) women 290 *of* (F) on 293–94 *the clown . . . sere,* (Q1, F) not in Q2 295 *blank* (Q1, F) black 316 *lest my* (F) let me 367 *By'r* (F) by 371 *e'en to't* (Rowe) ento't (Q2) e'ne to't (F); *French falconers* (Q1, F) friendly Fankners 387 *tale* (Q1, F) talke 394 *the* (Q1, F) th' 414 *Then . . . Ilium* (F) not in Q2 421 *And* (F) not in Q2 435 *fellies* (F4) follies 454 *husband's* (Q1, F) husband 479 *a* (F) not in Q2 480 *dozen* (Q1, F) dosen lines 492 *his* (F) the 499 *the cue* (F) that 518 *ha'* (Wilson) a 522 *father* (Q1, Q 1611) not in Q2, F 526 *About,* (Theobald) About 538 *devil . . . devil* (F) deale . . . deale

III.1 28 *too* (F) two 32 *lawful espials* (F) not in Q2 46 *loneliness* (F) lowlines 55 *Let's* (F) not in Q2 83 *of us all* (Q1, F) not in Q2 85 *sicklied* (F) sickled 99 *the* (F) these 107 *your honesty* (F) you 129 *all* (Q1, F) not in Q2 144 *lisp* (F) list 145–46 *your ignorance* (F) ignorance 152 *expectancy* (F) expectation 156 *music* (F) musickt 157 *that* (F) what 159 *feature* (F) stature 188 *unwatched* (F) vnmatcht

III.2 27 *the which* (F) which 29 *praise* (F) praysd 44 s.d. *Enter . . . Rosencrantz* (placed as in F; placed after *work* in Q2) 88 *detecting* (F) detected 96 *now.* (Johnson) now 132 *is* (Q1, F) not in Q2; *miching* (Q1, F) munching 137 *counsel* (Q1, F) not in Q2 151 *orbèd* (F) orb'd the 159 *your* (F) our 164 *In neither* (F) Eyther none, in neither 165 *love* (F) Lord 195 *joys* (F) joy 215 *An* (Theobald) And 219 *once a* (Q1, F) once I be a; *be* (Q1, F) be a 224 s.d. *Exit* (Q1, F) Exeunt 248 *mis-take* (Jenkins) mistake 252 *Confederate* (Q1, F) Considerat 254 *infected* (Q1, Q 1611) inuected 303 *start* (F) stare

312 *my* (F) not in Q2   **352** *thumb* (F) the vmber   **361** *the top of* (F) not in Q2   **365** *can fret me* (Q1, F) fret me not   **379–80** *POLONIUS I . . . friends* (F) Leaue me friends. / I will, say so. By and by is easily said,   **382** *breathes* (F) breakes   **384** *bitter business as the day* (F) busines as the bitter day   **389** *daggers* (Q1, F) dagger

III.3 22 *ruin* (F) raine   **23** *with* (F) not in Q2   **50** *pardoned* (F) pardon   **58** *shove* (F) showe   **73** *pat* (F) but   **75** *revenged* (F) reuendge   **79** *hire and salary* (F) base and silly   **89** *drunk* (F) drunke,

III.4 6 *warrant* (F) wait   **20** *inmost* (F) most   **53** HAMLET (placed as in F; placed one line earlier in Q2)   **59** *heaven-kissing* (F) heaue, a kissing   **88** *panders* (F) pardons   **89** *eyes into my very soul* (F) very eyes into my soul   **90** *grainèd* (F) greeued   **97** *tithe* (F) kyth   **143** *I* (F) not in Q2   **158** *live* (F) leaue   **162** *evil* (Theobald-Thirlby) deuill   **165** *Refrain tonight* (F) to refraine night   **169** *lodge* (Jenkins, conjectured in Clarendon edition) not in Q2   **186** *ravel* (F) rouell   **215** *foolish* (F) most foolish

IV.2 4 *Compounded* (F) Compound   **16** *ape* (F) apple

IV.3 28 KING (F) King. King.   **42** *With fiery quickness* (F) not in Q2

IV.5 9 *aim* (F) yawne   **16** QUEEN (placed as in Hanmer; placed before l. 17 in Q2)   **82** *their* (F) not in Q2   **98 s.d.** *Enter a Messenger* (placed as in Kittredge; after *A noise within* in Q2)   **106** *They* (F) The   **152 s.d.** *Let her come in* (as F; represented as Laertes' speech at l. 153 in Q2)   **160** *an old* (Q1, F) a poore   **177** *must* (Q1, F) may   **194** *Christian* (F) Christians   **195** *see* (F) not in Q2

IV.6 9 *and't* (F) and   **26** *bore* (F) bord   **30** *He* (F) So   **31** *give* (F) not in Q2

IV.7 6 *proceeded* (F) proceede   **8** *safety,* (F) safetie, greatnes,   **14** *conjunctive* (F) concliue   **22** *loud a wind* (F) loued Arm'd   **24** *had* (F) haue   **44** *your pardon* (F) you pardon   **54** *shall* (F) not in Q2   **55** *didest* (F) didst   **60** *checking* (F) the King   **86** *my* (F) me   **120** *spendthrift* (Q 1637) spend thirsts   **136** *pass* (F) pace   **138** *that* (F) not in Q2   **157** *prepared* (F) prefard   **169** *cold* (F) cull-cold

V.1 9 *se offendendo* (F) so offended   **12** *Argal* (F) or all   **39** *frame* (F) not in Q2   **56** *stoup* (Q1, F) soope   **66** *daintier* (F) dintier   **80** *meant* (F) went   **84** *mazard* (F) massene   **99–100** *Is . . . recoveries,* (F) not in Q2   **101** *his vouchers* (F) vouchers   **102–3** *double ones too* (F) doubles   **114** *O* (F) or   **135** *all* (F) not in Q2   **156** *nowadays* (F) not in Q2   **163** *three and twenty* (F) 23.   **206** *winter's* (F) waters   **219** *have* (F) been   **251** *and* (F) not in Q2   **275** *thus* (F) this   **288** *shortly* (F) thirtie (Q2 uncorrected) thereby (Q2 corrected)

V.2 5 *Methought* (F) my thought   **6** *bilboes* (F) bilbo   **17** *unseal* (F) vnfold   **29** *villainies* (Capell) villaines   **43** *as's* (Rowe) as sir   **52** *Subscribed* (F) Subscribe   **68** *humbly* (Q3, F) humble   **84** *sultry* (F) sully; *for* (F) or   **95** *feelingly* (Q 1611) sellingly (Q2 uncorrected) fellingly (Q2 corrected)   **100** *dozy* (Q2 uncorrected: dosie) dazzie (Q2 corrected)   **126** *his* (Q 1611) this   **143** *might be* (F) be (Q2 uncorrected) be might (Q2 corrected)   **146** *impawned, as* (Malone) all (Q2) impon'd as (F)   **164** *He* (F) not in Q2   **168** *comply* (F) sir (Q2 uncorrected) so sir (Q2 corrected)   **171** *yeasty* (F) histy   **173** *fanned* (Hanmer) prophane; *win-*

nowed (F) trennowed   **193–94** *gaingiving* (F) gamgiuing   **198** *now* (F) not in Q2   **200** *will* (F) well   **218** *Sir . . . audience* (F) not in Q2   **228** *keep* (F) not in Q2; *till* (F) all   **241** *bettered* (F) better   **250** *union* (F) Vnice (Q2 uncorrected) Onixe (Q2 corrected)   **296** *Hamlet, thou* (F) thou   **299** *thy* (Q1, F) my   **308** *murd'rous* (F) not in Q2   **309** *thy union* (Q1, F) the Onixe   **334** *the* (Pope) th'   **341 s.d.** *Dies* (Q1, F) not in Q2   **362** *th' yet* (F) yet   **366** *forced* (F) for no   **375** *on* (F) no

The Tragical History of
Hamlet Prince of Denmark

[Names of the Actors

KING CLAUDIUS, *of Denmark*
HAMLET, *son of the late, and nephew of the present,*
   King
POLONIUS, *Danish councillor*
HORATIO, *Hamlet's friend*
LAERTES, *Polonius's son*
VOLTEMAND ⎫
CORNELIUS ⎪
ROSENCRANTZ ⎬ *courtiers*
GUILDENSTERN ⎪
OSRIC ⎪
A GENTLEMAN ⎭
A PRIEST
MARCELLUS ⎫
BARNARDO ⎬ *soldiers*
FRANCISCO ⎭
REYNALDO, *servant in Polonius's household*
PLAYERS, *including Player King, Player Queen,*
   Player Lucianus
TWO CLOWNS, *one a gravedigger*
FORTINBRAS, *Prince of Norway*
A NORWEGIAN CAPTAIN, *in Fortinbras's army*
ENGLISH AMBASSADORS
QUEEN GERTRUDE, *of Denmark, Hamlet's mother*
OPHELIA, *Polonius's daughter*
GHOST OF HAMLET'S FATHER
LORDS, LADIES, OFFICERS, SOLDIERS, SAILORS,
   MESSENGERS, ATTENDANTS

SCENE: *Denmark*]
*

The Tragical History of Hamlet Prince of Denmark

∾ I.1 *Enter Barnardo and Francisco, two sentinels.*

BARNARDO   Who's there?

FRANCISCO
Nay, answer me. Stand and unfold yourself.

BARNARDO   Long live the king!

FRANCISCO   Barnardo?

BARNARDO   He.

FRANCISCO
You come most carefully upon your hour.   6

BARNARDO
'Tis now struck twelve. Get thee to bed, Francisco.

FRANCISCO
For this relief much thanks. 'Tis bitter cold,
And I am sick at heart.

BARNARDO
Have you had quiet guard?   10

FRANCISCO   Not a mouse stirring.

BARNARDO
Well, good night.
If you do meet Horatio and Marcellus,
The rivals of my watch, bid them make haste.   13

I.1 Elsinore Castle, Denmark: the battlements   **6** *upon your hour* right on
time   **13** *rivals* sharers

Enter Horatio and Marcellus.

FRANCISCO
I think I hear them. Stand, ho! Who is there?

HORATIO
15   Friends to this ground.   And liegemen to the Dane.

MARCELLUS

FRANCISCO
Give you good night.

MARCELLUS   O, farewell, honest soldier.
Who hath relieved you?

FRANCISCO   Barnardo hath my place.
Give you good night.   *Exit Francisco.*

MARCELLUS   Holla, Barnardo!

BARNARDO   Say –
What, is Horatio there?

HORATIO   A piece of him.

BARNARDO
20   Welcome, Horatio. Welcome, good Marcellus.

HORATIO
What, has this thing appeared again tonight?

BARNARDO
I have seen nothing.

MARCELLUS
23   Horatio says 'tis but our fantasy,
And will not let belief take hold of him
Touching this dreaded sight twice seen of us.
Therefore I have entreated him along
With us to watch the minutes of this night,
That, if again this apparition come,
29   He may approve our eyes and speak to it.

HORATIO
30   Tush, tush, 'twill not appear.

BARNARDO   Sit down awhile,
And let us once again assail your ears,

---

15 *liegemen* sworn followers; *Dane* King of Denmark   23 *fantasy* imagination   29 *approve* confirm

That are so fortified against our story,
What we have two nights seen.
HORATIO   Well, sit we down,
And let us hear Barnardo speak of this.
BARNARDO
Last night of all,
When yond same star that's westward from the pole   36
Had made his course t' illume that part of heaven
Where now it burns, Marcellus and myself,
The bell then beating one –
    Enter Ghost.
MARCELLUS
Peace, break thee off. Look where it comes again.   40
BARNARDO
In the same figure like the king that's dead.
MARCELLUS
Thou art a scholar; speak to it, Horatio.
BARNARDO
Looks a not like the king? Mark it, Horatio.   43
HORATIO
Most like. It harrows me with fear and wonder.
BARNARDO
It would be spoke to.
MARCELLUS   Speak to it, Horatio.
HORATIO
What art thou that usurp'st this time of night
Together with that fair and warlike form
In which the majesty of buried Denmark   48
Did sometimes march? By heaven I charge thee, speak.   49
MARCELLUS
It is offended.   50
BARNARDO   See, it stalks away.
HORATIO
Stay. Speak, speak. I charge thee, speak.   *Exit Ghost.*

---

36 *pole* polestar   **43** *a* he   **48** *buried Denmark* the buried King of Denmark (old Hamlet)   **49** *sometimes* formerly

MARCELLUS
'Tis gone and will not answer.

BARNARDO
How now, Horatio? You tremble and look pale.
Is not this something more than fantasy?
What think you on't?

HORATIO
Before my God, I might not this believe
57   Without the sensible and true avouch
Of mine own eyes.

MARCELLUS   Is it not like the king?

HORATIO
As thou art to thyself.
60   Such was the very armor he had on
61   When he the ambitious Norway combated.
62   So frowned he once when, in an angry parle,
He smote the sledded Polacks on the ice.
'Tis strange.

MARCELLUS
65   Thus twice before, and jump at this dead hour,
With martial stalk hath he gone by our watch.

HORATIO
In what particular thought to work I know not;
68   But, in the gross and scope of my opinion,
69   This bodes some strange eruption to our state.

MARCELLUS
70   Good now, sit down, and tell me he that knows,
Why this same strict and most observant watch
72   So nightly toils the subject of the land,
And why such daily cast of brazen cannon
74   And foreign mart for implements of war,
75   Why such impress of shipwrights, whose sore task

---

57 *avouch* assurance   61 *Norway* King of Norway   62 *parle* parley, negotiation under truce (said ironically)   65 *jump* just, exactly   68 *gross and scope* gross scope, general view   69 *strange eruption* unexpected, destructive change   72 *toils* makes toil; *subject* subjects   74 *mart* trading   75 *impress* conscription

Does not divide the Sunday from the week.
What might be toward that this sweaty haste   77
Doth make the night joint laborer with the day?
Who is't that can inform me?
HORATIO   That can I.
At least the whisper goes so. Our last king,   80
Whose image even but now appeared to us,
Was as you know by Fortinbras of Norway,   82
Thereto pricked on by a most emulate pride,   83
Dared to the combat; in which our valiant Hamlet
(For so this side of our known world esteemed him)
Did slay this Fortinbras; who, by a sealed compact
Well ratified by law and heraldry,   87
Did forfeit, with his life, all those his lands
Which he stood seized of to the conqueror;   89
Against the which a moiety competent   90
Was gagèd by our king, which had returned   91
To the inheritance of Fortinbras
Had he been vanquisher, as, by the same comart   93
And carriage of the article designed,   94
His fell to Hamlet. Now, sir, young Fortinbras,   95
Of unimprovèd mettle hot and full,   96
Hath in the skirts of Norway here and there
Sharked up a list of lawless resolutes   98
For food and diet to some enterprise
That hath a stomach in't; which is no other,   100
As it doth well appear unto our state,
But to recover of us by strong hand
And terms compulsatory those foresaid lands
So by his father lost; and this, I take it,

---

77 *toward* in preparation, coming on   82 *Fortinbras of Norway* i.e., father of
young Fortinbras (l. 95)   83 *emulate* jealously rivaling   87 *law and heraldry*
law of heralds regulating combat   89 *seized* possessed   90 *moiety competent*
sufficient portion   91 *gagèd* engaged, staked   93 *comart* joint bargain   94
carriage purport   95 *His* i.e., old Fortinbras's share, had he won   96 *unimprovèd* unused   98 *Sharked* snatched indiscriminately; *list* roll call; *resolutes*
determined people   100 *stomach* promise of danger

Is the main motive of our preparations,
106 The source of this our watch, and the chief head
107 Of this posthaste and rummage in the land.

BARNARDO
I think it be no other but e'en so.
109 Well may it sort that this portentous figure
110 Comes armèd through our watch so like the king
That was and is the question of these wars.

HORATIO
112 A mote it is to trouble the mind's eye.
113 In the most high and palmy state of Rome,
A little ere the mightiest Julius fell,
115 The graves stood tenantless and the sheeted dead
Did squeak and gibber in the Roman streets;
117 As stars with trains of fire and dews of blood,
118 Disasters in the sun; and the moist star
119 Upon whose influence Neptune's empire stands
120 Was sick almost to doomsday with eclipse.
121 And even the like precurse of feared events,
122 As harbingers preceding still the fates
123 And prologue to the omen coming on,
Have heaven and earth together demonstrated
125 Unto our climatures and countrymen.
    Enter Ghost.
But soft, behold, lo where it comes again!
127 I'll cross it, though it blast me. – Stay, illusion.
    [He] spreads his arms.
If thou hast any sound or use of voice,
Speak to me.

---

106 *head* fountainhead, source   **107** *posthaste* bustle, urgency; *rummage* disorder, ransacking   **109** *sort* be fitting; *portentous* ominous   **112** *mote* speck
of dust   **113** *palmy* successful, victorious   **115** *sheeted* in burial shrouds
117 *As* (this line does not follow grammatically from the preceding one, although it continues to list dangerous portents; some words have probably
been omitted accidentally)   **118** *Disasters* omens; *moist star* moon   **119**
stands depends   **120** *sick almost to doomsday* almost as terrible as the Christian Apocalypse   **121** *precurse* foreshadowing   **122** *harbingers* forerunners;
still constantly   **123** *omen* calamity   **125** *climatures* regions   **127** *cross it*
cross its path, confront it

If there be any good thing to be done   *130*
That may to thee do ease and grace to me,
Speak to me.
If thou art privy to thy country's fate,
Which happily foreknowing may avoid,   *134*
O, speak!
Or if thou hast uphoarded in thy life
Extorted treasure in the womb of earth,
For which, they say, your spirits oft walk in death,   *138*
  The cock crows.
Speak of it. Stay and speak. Stop it, Marcellus.

MARCELLUS
Shall I strike it with my partisan?   *140*

HORATIO
Do, if it will not stand.   *141*

BARNARDO   'Tis here.

HORATIO   'Tis here.

MARCELLUS
'Tis gone.   *[Exit Ghost.]*
We do it wrong, being so majestical,
To offer it the show of violence,
For it is as the air invulnerable,
And our vain blows malicious mockery.

BARNARDO
It was about to speak when the cock crew.

HORATIO
And then it started, like a guilty thing
Upon a fearful summons. I have heard
The cock, that is the trumpet to the morn,   *150*
Doth with his lofty and shrill-sounding throat
Awake the god of day, and at his warning,   *152*
Whether in sea or fire, in earth or air,
Th' extravagant and erring spirit hies   *154*

---

134 *happily* haply, perchance   138 *your* (an indefinite usage referring to
hearers in general, not a specific interlocutor; F reads "you")   140 *partisan*
pike (a spearlike weapon)   141 *stand* stop, stand still   152 *god of day* i.e.,
sun   154 *extravagant* wandering beyond bounds; *erring* wandering

To his confine; and of the truth herein
156 This present object made probation.

MARCELLUS
It faded on the crowing of the cock.
158 Some say that ever 'gainst that season comes
Wherein our Savior's birth is celebrated,
160 This bird of dawning singeth all night long,
And then, they say, no spirit dare stir abroad,
162 The nights are wholesome, then no planets strike,
163 No fairy takes, nor witch hath power to charm,
164 So hallowed and so gracious is that time.

HORATIO
So have I heard and do in part believe it.
166 But look, the morn in russet mantle clad
Walks o'er the dew of yon high eastward hill.
Break we our watch up, and by my advice
Let us impart what we have seen tonight
170 Unto young Hamlet, for upon my life
171 This spirit, dumb to us, will speak to him.
Do you consent we shall acquaint him with it,
As needful in our loves, fitting our duty?

MARCELLUS
Let's do't, I pray, and I this morning know
175 Where we shall find him most convenient.   *Exeunt.*

*

156 *probation* test   158 *'gainst* just before   158–59 *season . . . celebrated* i.e.,
Christmastime   162 *strike* work evil by influence   163 *takes* bewitches
164 *gracious* full of (divine) grace   166 *russet* reddish brown rough cloth
171 *dumb* silent   175 *convenient* i.e., conveniently (Shakespeare often uses
adjectives for adverbs)

∾ **I.2** *Flourish. Enter Claudius, King of Denmark,
Gertrude the Queen, Councillors, Polonius and his son
Laertes, Hamlet, cum aliis [including Voltemand and
Cornelius].*

KING
  Though yet of Hamlet our dear brother's death   1
  The memory be green, and that it us befitted
  To bear our hearts in grief, and our whole kingdom
  To be contracted in one brow of woe,
  Yet so far hath discretion fought with nature
  That we with wisest sorrow think on him
  Together with remembrance of ourselves.
  Therefore our sometime sister, now our queen,   8
  Th' imperial jointress to this warlike state,   9
  Have we, as 'twere with a defeated joy,   10
  With an auspicious and a dropping eye,
  With mirth in funeral and with dirge in marriage,
  In equal scale weighing delight and dole,
  Taken to wife. Nor have we herein barred   14
  Your better wisdoms, which have freely gone
  With this affair along. For all, our thanks.
  Now follows, that you know, young Fortinbras,
  Holding a weak supposal of our worth,
  Or thinking by our late dear brother's death
  Our state to be disjoint and out of frame,   20
  Colleaguèd with this dream of his advantage,   21
  He hath not failed to pester us with message
  Importing the surrender of those lands
  Lost by his father, with all bands of law,   24
  To our most valiant brother. So much for him.

I.2 Elsinore **s.d.** *cum aliis* with others **1** *our* my (the royal plural) **8** *sometime sister* former sister-in-law **9** *jointress* widow who has a jointure, or joint tenancy, of an estate (with this word and *imperial,* Claudius acknowledges Gertrude as co-sovereign) **14** *barred* excluded **21** *Colleaguèd* united **24** *bands* bonds

Now for ourself and for this time of meeting.
Thus much the business is: we have here writ
To Norway, uncle of young Fortinbras –
Who, impotent and bedrid, scarcely hears
30 Of this his nephew's purpose – to suppress
31 His further gait herein, in that the levies,
32 The lists, and full proportions are all made
Out of his subject; and we here dispatch
You, good Cornelius, and you, Voltemand,
For bearers of this greeting to old Norway,
Giving to you no further personal power
To business with the king, more than the scope
38 Of these delated articles allow.
Farewell, and let your haste commend your duty.

CORNELIUS, VOLTEMAND
40 In that, and all things, will we show our duty.

KING
We doubt it nothing. Heartily farewell.
                    [Exeunt Voltemand and Cornelius.]
And now, Laertes, what's the news with you?
43 You told us of some suit. What is't, Laertes?
44 You cannot speak of reason to the Dane
45 And lose your voice. What wouldst thou beg, Laertes,
That shall not be my offer, not thy asking?
47 The head is not more native to the heart,
48 The hand more instrumental to the mouth,
Than is the throne of Denmark to thy father.
50 What wouldst thou have, Laertes?

LAERTES   My dread lord,
Your leave and favor to return to France,
From whence though willingly I came to Denmark
To show my duty in your coronation,
Yet now I must confess, that duty done,

---

31 *gait* going   **32** *proportions* amounts of forces and supplies   **38** *delated* (1) expressly stated, (2) conveyed   **43** *suit* request   **44** *Dane* King of Denmark   **45** *lose your voice* speak in vain   **47** *native* joined by nature   **48** *instrumental* serviceable

My thoughts and wishes bend again toward France
And bow them to your gracious leave and pardon.

KING

Have you your father's leave? What says Polonius?

POLONIUS

He hath, my lord, wrung from me my slow leave
By laborsome petition, and at last
Upon his will I sealed my hard consent.   60
I do beseech you give him leave to go.

KING

Take thy fair hour, Laertes. Time be thine,
And thy best graces spend it at thy will.
But now, my cousin Hamlet, and my son –   64

HAMLET   *[Aside]*

A little more than kin, and less than kind!   65

KING

How is it that the clouds still hang on you?

HAMLET

Not so, my lord. I am too much in the sun.   67

QUEEN

Good Hamlet, cast thy nighted color off,
And let thine eye look like a friend on Denmark.
Do not for ever with thy vailèd lids   70
Seek for thy noble father in the dust.
Thou know'st 'tis common. All that lives must die,
Passing through nature to eternity.

HAMLET

Ay, madam, it is common.

QUEEN   If it be,
Why seems it so particular with thee?

HAMLET

Seems, madam? Nay, it is. I know not "seems."
'Tis not alone my inky cloak, good mother,

---

60 *hard* i.e., hard-won   64 *cousin* kinsman more distant than parent, child,
brother, or sister   65 *kin* related as nephew; *kind* (1) natural, (2) kindly, affectionate, (3) related by direct descent, member of the immediate family
67 *sun* sunshine of the king's unwanted favor (with wordplay on "place of a
son")   70 *vailèd* downcast

Nor customary suits of solemn black,
Nor windy suspiration of forced breath,
80 No, nor the fruitful river in the eye,
81 Nor the dejected havior of the visage,
Together with all forms, moods, shapes of grief,
That can denote me truly. These indeed seem,
84 For they are actions that a man might play,
But I have that within which passes show –
These but the trappings and the suits of woe.

KING
'Tis sweet and commendable in your nature, Hamlet,
To give these mourning duties to your father,
But you must know your father lost a father,
90 That father lost, lost his, and the survivor bound
In filial obligation for some term
92 To do obsequious sorrow. But to persever
In obstinate condolement is a course
Of impious stubbornness. 'Tis unmanly grief.
It shows a will most incorrect to heaven,
A heart unfortified, or mind impatient,
An understanding simple and unschooled.
For what we know must be and is as common
As any the most vulgar thing to sense,
100 Why should we in our peevish opposition
Take it to heart? Fie, 'tis a fault to heaven,
A fault against the dead, a fault to nature,
To reason most absurd, whose common theme
Is death of fathers, and who still hath cried,
From the first corpse till he that died today,
"This must be so." We pray you throw to earth
This unprevailing woe, and think of us
As of a father, for let the world take note
109 You are the most immediate to our throne,
110 And with no less nobility of love

___

81 *havior* behavior, demeanor   84 *play* feign, playact   92 *obsequious* proper
to obsequies (funerals); *persever* persevere (accented on the second syllable, as
always in Shakespeare)   109 *most immediate to* i.e., next to inherit

Than that which dearest father bears his son
Do I impart toward you. For your intent
In going back to school in Wittenberg,
It is most retrograde to our desire,   114
And we beseech you, bend you to remain
Here in the cheer and comfort of our eye,
Our chiefest courtier, cousin, and our son.

QUEEN
Let not thy mother lose her prayers, Hamlet.
I pray thee stay with us, go not to Wittenberg.

HAMLET
I shall in all my best obey you, madam.   120

KING
Why, 'tis a loving and a fair reply.
Be as ourself in Denmark. Madam, come.
This gentle and unforced accord of Hamlet
Sits smiling to my heart, in grace whereof
No jocund health that Denmark drinks today
But the great cannon to the clouds shall tell,
And the king's rouse the heaven shall bruit again,   127
Respeaking earthly thunder. Come away.

                      Flourish. Exeunt all but Hamlet.

HAMLET
O that this too too sullied flesh would melt,   129
Thaw, and resolve itself into a dew,   130
Or that the Everlasting had not fixed
His canon 'gainst self-slaughter. O God, God,   132
How weary, stale, flat, and unprofitable
Seem to me all the uses of this world!
Fie on't, ah, fie, 'tis an unweeded garden
That grows to seed. Things rank and gross in nature
Possess it merely. That it should come to this,   137
But two months dead, nay, not so much, not two,
So excellent a king, that was to this

---

114 *retrograde* contrary 127 *rouse* toast drunk in wine; *bruit* echo, make
noise 129 *sullied* dirtied, discolored 130 *resolve* dissolve 132 *canon* law
137 *merely* completely

140   Hyperion to a satyr, so loving to my mother
141   That he might not beteem the winds of heaven
        Visit her face too roughly. Heaven and earth,
        Must I remember? Why, she would hang on him
        As if increase of appetite had grown
        By what it fed on, and yet within a month –
        Let me not think on't; frailty, thy name is woman –
        A little month, or ere those shoes were old
        With which she followed my poor father's body
149   Like Niobe, all tears, why she –
150   O God, a beast that wants discourse of reason
        Would have mourned longer – married with my uncle,
        My father's brother, but no more like my father
        Than I to Hercules. Within a month,
        Ere yet the salt of most unrighteous tears
155   Had left the flushing in her gallèd eyes,
        She married. O, most wicked speed, to post
        With such dexterity to incestuous sheets!
        It is not nor it cannot come to good.
159   But break my heart, for I must hold my tongue.
        Enter Horatio, Marcellus, and Barnardo.

HORATIO
160   Hail to your lordship!
HAMLET   I am glad to see you well.
        Horatio – or I do forget myself.
HORATIO
        The same, my lord, and your poor servant ever.
HAMLET
163   Sir, my good friend, I'll change that name with you.
164   And what make you from Wittenberg, Horatio?
        Marcellus?

---

140 *Hyperion* the sun god   **141** *beteem* allow   **149** *Niobe* (in Greek myth, after Niobe boasted she had more children than Leto, Niobe's children were killed by Apollo and Artemis, Leto's children; Zeus transformed the grieving Niobe into a stone that continually dropped tears)   **150** *discourse* logical power or process   **155** *gallèd* irritated   **159** *But . . . tongue* (Hamlet alludes to a Latin and an English proverb claiming that unspoken griefs crush the heart)   **163** *change* exchange   **164** *make* do

MARCELLUS   My good lord!

HAMLET

    I am very glad to see you. *[To Barnardo]* Good even, sir.
    But what, in faith, make you from Wittenberg?

HORATIO

    A truant disposition, good my lord.

HAMLET

    I would not hear your enemy say so,   *170*
    Nor shall you do my ear that violence
    To make it truster of your own report
    Against yourself. I know you are no truant.
    But what is your affair in Elsinore?
    We'll teach you for to drink ere you depart.   175

HORATIO

    My lord, I came to see your father's funeral.

HAMLET

    I prithee do not mock me, fellow student.
    I think it was to see my mother's wedding.

HORATIO

    Indeed, my lord, it followed hard upon.

HAMLET

    Thrift, thrift, Horatio. The funeral baked meats   *180*
    Did coldly furnish forth the marriage tables.
    Would I had met my dearest foe in heaven   182
    Or ever I had seen that day, Horatio!
    My father – methinks I see my father.

HORATIO

    Where, my lord?

HAMLET   In my mind's eye, Horatio.

HORATIO

    I saw him once. A was a goodly king.   186

HAMLET

    A was a man, take him for all in all,
    I shall not look upon his like again.

---

175 *for to* to (archaic phrase)   **182** *dearest* direst, bitterest   **186, 187** *A* he

HORATIO
My lord, I think I saw him yesternight.

190 HAMLET   Saw? Who?

HORATIO
My lord, the king your father.

HAMLET   The king my father?

HORATIO

192   Season your admiration for a while
193   With an attent ear till I may deliver
       Upon the witness of these gentlemen
       This marvel to you.

HAMLET   For God's love let me hear!

HORATIO
       Two nights together had these gentlemen,
       Marcellus and Barnardo, on their watch
       In the dead waste and middle of the night
       Been thus encountered. A figure like your father,
200   Armèd at point exactly, cap-à-pie,
       Appears before them and with solemn march
       Goes slow and stately by them. Thrice he walked
       By their oppressed and fear-surprisèd eyes
204   Within his truncheon's length, whilst they, distilled
       Almost to jelly with the act of fear,
       Stand dumb and speak not to him. This to me
207   In dreadful secrecy impart they did,
       And I with them the third night kept the watch,
       Where, as they had delivered, both in time,
210   Form of the thing, each word made true and good,
       The apparition comes. I knew your father.
       These hands are not more like.

HAMLET   But where was this?

MARCELLUS
213   My lord, upon the platform where we watched.

---

192 *Season your admiration* control your wonder   193 *attent* attentive, alert
200 *at point* completely; *cap-à-pie* from head to foot   204 *truncheon* military commander's baton   207 *dreadful* full of dread, fearful   213 *platform* battlement

HAMLET
  Did you not speak to it?
HORATIO   My lord, I did,
  But answer made it none. Yet once methought
  It lifted up it head and did address   216
  Itself to motion like as it would speak.
  But even then the morning cock crew loud,
  And at the sound it shrunk in haste away
  And vanished from our sight.   *220*
HAMLET   'Tis very strange.
HORATIO
  As I do live, my honored lord, 'tis true,
  And we did think it writ down in our duty
  To let you know of it.
HAMLET
  Indeed, sirs, but this troubles me.
  Hold you the watch tonight?
ALL   We do, my lord.
HAMLET   Armed, say you?
ALL   Armed, my lord.
HAMLET
  From top to toe?
ALL   My lord, from head to foot.
HAMLET
  Then saw you not his face?
HORATIO
  O, yes, my lord. He wore his beaver up.   230
HAMLET
  What, looked he frowningly?
HORATIO
  A countenance more in sorrow than in anger.
HAMLET   Pale or red?
HORATIO
  Nay, very pale.
HAMLET   And fixed his eyes upon you?

---

216 *it* its (archaic, but common in Shakespeare) **216–17** *did address . . . motion* began to move   **230** *beaver* movable face guard of the helmet

HORATIO
    Most constantly.

HAMLET   I would I had been there.

HORATIO
    It would have much amazed you.

HAMLET
    Very like. Stayed it long?

HORATIO
238   While one with moderate haste might tell a hundred.

BOTH   Longer, longer.

HORATIO
240   Not when I saw't.

HAMLET   His beard was grizzled, no?

HORATIO
    It was as I have seen it in his life,
242   A sable silvered.

HAMLET   I will watch tonight.
    Perchance 'twill walk again.

HORATIO   I warr'nt it will.

HAMLET
    If it assume my noble father's person,
    I'll speak to it though hell itself should gape
    And bid me hold my peace. I pray you all,
    If you have hitherto concealed this sight,
248   Let it be tenable in your silence still,
    And whatsomever else shall hap tonight,
250   Give it an understanding but no tongue.
    I will requite your loves. So fare you well.
    Upon the platform, 'twixt eleven and twelve
    I'll visit you.

ALL   Our duty to your honor.

HAMLET
    Your loves, as mine to you. Farewell.
                     Exeunt [all but Hamlet].
    My father's spirit – in arms? All is not well.

---

238 *tell* count   240 *grizzled* gray   242 *sable silvered* black mixed with white
248 *tenable* held firmly

I doubt some foul play. Would the night were come!   256
Till then sit still, my soul. Foul deeds will rise   257
Though all the earth o'erwhelm them to men's eyes.

                                                   Exit.

                          *

✆ **I.3** *Enter Laertes and Ophelia, his sister.*

LAERTES
My necessaries are embarked. Farewell.
And, sister, as the winds give benefit
And convoy is assistant, do not sleep,   3
But let me hear from you.
OPHELIA   Do you doubt that?
LAERTES
For Hamlet, and the trifling of his favor,
Hold it a fashion and a toy in blood,   6
A violet in the youth of primy nature,   7
Forward, not permanent, sweet, not lasting,   8
The perfume and suppliance of a minute,   9
No more.   10
OPHELIA   No more but so?
LAERTES   Think it no more.
For nature crescent does not grow alone   11
In thews and bulk, but as this temple waxes   12
The inward service of the mind and soul
Grows wide withal. Perhaps he loves you now,
And now no soil nor cautel doth besmirch   15
The virtue of his will, but you must fear,   16
His greatness weighed, his will is not his own.   17
He may not, as unvalued persons do,

---

256 *doubt* suspect, fear 257–58 *Foul . . . eyes* (proverbially, murder cannot be hidden)
    I.3 Elsinore Castle: Polonius's rooms 3 *convoy* means of transport 6 *toy* passing fancy 7 *of primy* of the springtime 8 *Forward* blooming early 9 *perfume and suppliance* filling sweetness 11 *crescent* growing 12 *this temple* the body 15 *cautel* deceit 16 *virtue* (1) strength, (2) virtuousness; *will* desire 17 *greatness weighed* high position considered

19   Carve for himself, for on his choice depends
20   The safety and health of this whole state,
      And therefore must his choice be circumscribed
22   Unto the voice and yielding of that body
      Whereof he is the head. Then if he says he loves you,
      It fits your wisdom so far to believe it
      As he in his particular act and place
      May give his saying deed, which is no further
      Than the main voice of Denmark goes withal.
      Then weigh what loss your honor may sustain
29   If with too credent ear you list his songs,
30   Or lose your heart, or your chaste treasure open
      To his unmastered importunity.
      Fear it, Ophelia, fear it, my dear sister,
33   And keep you in the rear of your affection,
      Out of the shot and danger of desire.
35   The chariest maid is prodigal enough
      If she unmask her beauty to the moon.
      Virtue itself scapes not calumnious strokes.
38   The canker galls the infants of the spring
39   Too oft before their buttons be disclosed,
40   And in the morn and liquid dew of youth
41   Contagious blastments are most imminent.
      Be wary then; best safety lies in fear.
      Youth to itself rebels, though none else near.

OPHELIA
      I shall the effect of this good lesson keep
      As watchman to my heart, but, good my brother,
      Do not as some ungracious pastors do,
      Show me the steep and thorny way to heaven,
      Whiles like a puffed and reckless libertine
      Himself the primrose path of dalliance treads
50   And recks not his own rede.

-----

19 *Carve* choose (with romantic or erotic choice implied)   22 *yielding* assent
29 *credent* credulous; *list* listen to   33 *affection* feelings (which rashly lead
into dangers)   35 *chariest* most careful   38 *canker* rose worm; *galls* injures
39 *buttons* buds   41 *blastments* blights   50 *recks* regards; *rede* counsel

Enter Polonius.

LAERTES　　　　　　　　　　O, fear me not.
　　I stay too long. But here my father comes.
　　A double blessing is a double grace;
　　Occasion smiles upon a second leave.

POLONIUS
　　Yet here, Laertes? Aboard, aboard, for shame!
　　The wind sits in the shoulder of your sail,
　　And you are stayed for. There – my blessing with thee,
　　And these few precepts in thy memory
　　Look thou character. Give thy thoughts no tongue,　58
　　Nor any unproportioned thought his act.　59
　　Be thou familiar, but by no means vulgar.　60
　　Those friends thou hast, and their adoption tried,
　　Grapple them unto thy soul with hoops of steel,
　　But do not dull thy palm with entertainment
　　Of each new-hatched, unfledged courage. Beware　64
　　Of entrance to a quarrel; but being in,
　　Bear't that th' opposèd may beware of thee.
　　Give every man thy ear, but few thy voice;
　　Take each man's censure, but reserve thy judgment.　68
　　Costly thy habit as thy purse can buy,
　　But not expressed in fancy; rich, not gaudy,　70
　　For the apparel oft proclaims the man,
　　And they in France of the best rank and station
　　Are of a most select and generous chief in that.　73
　　Neither a borrower nor a lender be,
　　For loan oft loses both itself and friend,
　　And borrowing dulleth edge of husbandry.　76
　　This above all, to thine own self be true,
　　And it must follow as the night the day
　　Thou canst not then be false to any man.
　　Farewell. My blessing season this in thee!　80

---

58 *character* inscribe, write　59 *unproportioned* distorted from what is right
64 *courage* man of spirit, young blood　68 *censure* judgment　73 *chief* emi-
nence (English prejudice found the French overly fashion-conscious)　76
husbandry thriftiness　80 *season* ripen and make fruitful

LAERTES
Most humbly do I take my leave, my lord.

POLONIUS
82 The time invites you. Go, your servants tend.

LAERTES
Farewell, Ophelia, and remember well
What I have said to you.

OPHELIA   'Tis in my memory locked,
And you yourself shall keep the key of it.

LAERTES   Farewell.   *Exit Laertes.*

POLONIUS
What is't, Ophelia, he hath said to you?

OPHELIA
So please you, something touching the Lord Hamlet.

POLONIUS
89 Marry, well bethought.
90 'Tis told me he hath very oft of late
Given private time to you, and you yourself
Have of your audience been most free and bounteous.
If it be so – as so 'tis put on me,
And that in way of caution – I must tell you
You do not understand yourself so clearly
As it behooves my daughter and your honor.
What is between you? Give me up the truth.

OPHELIA
98 He hath, my lord, of late made many tenders
Of his affection to me.

POLONIUS
100 Affection? Pooh! You speak like a green girl,
101 Unsifted in such perilous circumstance.
Do you believe his tenders, as you call them?

OPHELIA
I do not know, my lord, what I should think.

POLONIUS
Marry, I will teach you. Think yourself a baby

---

82 *tend* wait   89 *Marry* by (the Virgin) Mary (a weak oath)   98 *tenders* offers   101 *Unsifted* untested

That you have ta'en these tenders for true pay   105
Which are not sterling. Tender yourself more dearly,
Or (not to crack the wind of the poor phrase,   107
Running it thus) you'll tender me a fool.

OPHELIA
My lord, he hath importuned me with love
In honorable fashion.   *110*

POLONIUS
Ay, fashion you may call it. Go to, go to.   111

OPHELIA
And hath given countenance to his speech, my lord,
With almost all the holy vows of heaven.

POLONIUS
Ay, springes to catch woodcocks. I do know,   114
When the blood burns, how prodigal the soul
Lends the tongue vows. These blazes, daughter,
Giving more light than heat, extinct in both
Even in their promise, as it is a-making,
You must not take for fire. From this time
Be something scanter of your maiden presence.   *120*
Set your entreatments at a higher rate   121
Than a command to parley. For Lord Hamlet,   122
Believe so much in him that he is young,
And with a larger tether may he walk
Than may be given you. In few, Ophelia,
Do not believe his vows, for they are brokers,   126
Not of that dye which their investments show,   127
But mere implorators of unholy suits,
Breathing like sanctified and pious bawds

105–8 *tenders . . . Tender . . . tender* offers . . . hold in regard . . . present
(wordplay runs through these three meanings; the last use of the word yields
further complexity with its implication that she will show herself to Polonius
as a *fool* [l.108], will show him to the world as a fool, and may go so far as to
present him with a fool, an Elizabethan term of endearment especially ap-
plied to an infant)   **107** *crack . . . of* make wheeze like a horse driven too
hard   **111** *Go to* go away, go on (an expression of impatience)   **114** *springes*
snares; *woodcocks* (birds believed to be foolish)   **121** *entreatments* military
negotiations for surrender   **122** *parley* confer with a besieger   **126** *brokers*
middlemen, panders   **127** *investments* clothes

130   The better to beguile. This is for all:
        I would not, in plain terms, from this time forth
132   Have you so slander any moment leisure
        As to give words or talk with the Lord Hamlet.
        Look to't, I charge you. Come your ways.

OPHELIA
        I shall obey, my lord.   *Exeunt.*

                        ✳

∾ **I.4** *Enter Hamlet, Horatio, and Marcellus.*

HAMLET
1   The air bites shrewdly; it is very cold.
HORATIO
2   It is a nipping and an eager air.
HAMLET
        What hour now?
HORATIO   I think it lacks of twelve.
MARCELLUS   No, it is struck.
HORATIO
        Indeed? I heard it not. It then draws near the season
6   Wherein the spirit held his wont to walk.
            A flourish of trumpets, and two pieces goes off.
        What does this mean, my lord?
HAMLET
8   The king doth wake tonight and takes his rouse,
9   Keeps wassail, and the swaggering upspring reels,
10   And as he drains his draughts of Rhenish down
        The kettledrum and trumpet thus bray out
12   The triumph of his pledge.
HORATIO   Is it a custom?
HAMLET
        Ay, marry, is't,

─────────

132 *slander* use disgracefully; *moment* momentary
    I.4 Elsinore: the battlements 1 *shrewdly* wickedly, bitterly 2 *an eager* a
sharp 6 s.d. *pieces* cannon 8 *rouse* carousal 9 *upspring* German dance
10 *draughts* gulps; *Rhenish* Rhine wine 12 *triumph* achievement, feat (in
downing a cup of wine at one gulp)

But to my mind, though I am native here
And to the manner born, it is a custom
More honored in the breach than the observance.   16
This heavy-headed revel east and west
Makes us traduced and taxed of other nations.   18
They clepe us drunkards and with swinish phrase   19
Soil our addition, and indeed it takes   20
From our achievements, though performed at height,
The pith and marrow of our attribute.   22
So oft it chances in particular men
That (for some vicious mole of nature in them,   24
As in their birth, wherein they are not guilty,
Since nature cannot choose his origin)   26
By the o'ergrowth of some complexion,   27
Oft breaking down the pales and forts of reason,   28
Or by some habit that too much o'erleavens   29
The form of plausive manners – that (these men   30
Carrying, I say, the stamp of one defect,
Being nature's livery, or fortune's star)   32
His virtues else, be they as pure as grace,
As infinite as man may undergo,
Shall in the general censure take corruption
From that particular fault. The dram of evil
Doth all the noble substance often dout,   37
To his own scandal.
          Enter Ghost.
HORATIO   Look, my lord, it comes.
HAMLET
Angels and ministers of grace defend us!
Be thou a spirit of health or goblin damned,   40

---

16 *More . . . observance* better broken than observed   18 *taxed of* censured
by   19 *clepe* call   20 *addition* reputation, title added as a distinction   22
attribute reputation, what is attributed   24 *mole* blemish, flaw   26 *his* its
27 *complexion* part of an individual's human nature   28 *pales* barriers, fences
29 *o'erleavens* works change throughout, as yeast ferments dough   30 *plausive* pleasing   32 *livery* (1) badge or other identifying token, (2) provision,
what *nature* gives us; *star* astrologically determined human nature   37 *dout*
extinguish, put out   40 *of health* sound, good; *goblin* fiend

Bring with thee airs from heaven or blasts from hell,
Be thy intents wicked or charitable,
Thou com'st in such a questionable shape
That I will speak to thee. I'll call thee Hamlet,
King, father, royal Dane. O, answer me!
Let me not burst in ignorance, but tell
47 Why thy canonized bones, hearsèd in death,
48 Have burst their cerements, why the sepulchre
Wherein we saw thee quietly interred
50 Hath oped his ponderous and marble jaws
To cast thee up again. What may this mean
That thou, dead corpse, again in complete steel,
Revisits thus the glimpses of the moon,
54 Making night hideous, and we fools of nature
55 So horridly to shake our disposition
With thoughts beyond the reaches of our souls?
Say, why is this? wherefore? what should we do?
   [Ghost] beckons.

HORATIO
   It beckons you to go away with it,
59 As if it some impartment did desire
60 To you alone.

MARCELLUS   Look with what courteous action
61 It waves you to a more removèd ground.
   But do not go with it.

HORATIO   No, by no means.

HAMLET
   It will not speak. Then I will follow it.

HORATIO
   Do not, my lord.

HAMLET   Why, what should be the fear?
65 I do not set my life at a pin's fee,

---

47 *canonized* buried with the established rites of the church   48 *cerements*
waxed grave cloths   54 *fools of nature* men made conscious of natural limita-
tions by a supernatural manifestation   55 *disposition* mental constitution
59 *some impartment* something to impart, to say   61 *removèd* farther away,
more remote   65 *a pin's fee* the value of a pin (i.e., very little)

And for my soul, what can it do to that,
Being a thing immortal as itself?
It waves me forth again. I'll follow it.

HORATIO
What if it tempt you toward the flood, my lord,
Or to the dreadful summit of the cliff   70
That beetles o'er his base into the sea,   71
And there assume some other horrible form,
Which might deprive your sovereignty of reason   73
And draw you into madness? Think of it.
The very place puts toys of desperation,   75
Without more motive, into every brain
That looks so many fathoms to the sea
And hears it roar beneath.

HAMLET   It waves me still.
Go on. I'll follow thee.

MARCELLUS
You shall not go, my lord.   80

HAMLET   Hold off your hands.

HORATIO
Be ruled. You shall not go.

HAMLET   My fate cries out
And makes each petty artire in this body   82
As hardy as the Nemean lion's nerve.   83
Still am I called. Unhand me, gentlemen.
By heaven, I'll make a ghost of him that lets me!   85
I say, away! Go on. I'll follow thee.

                                        Exit Ghost and Hamlet.

HORATIO
He waxes desperate with imagination.

MARCELLUS
Let's follow. 'Tis not fit thus to obey him.

HORATIO
Have after. To what issue will this come?

---

71 *beetles* juts out   73 *deprive* take away; *sovereignty of reason* state of being
ruled by reason   75 *toys* fancies   82 *artire* artery   83 *Nemean lion* lion Hercules killed in the first of his twelve labors; *nerve* sinew   85 *lets* hinders

MARCELLUS

90   Something is rotten in the state of Denmark.

HORATIO

Heaven will direct it.

MARCELLUS   Nay, let's follow him.   *Exeunt.*

*

∾ **I.5** *Enter Ghost and Hamlet.*

HAMLET

Whither wilt thou lead me? Speak. I'll go no further.

GHOST

2   Mark me.

HAMLET   I will.

GHOST   My hour is almost come,

3   When I to sulph'rous and tormenting flames

Must render up myself.

HAMLET   Alas, poor ghost!

GHOST

Pity me not, but lend thy serious hearing

To what I shall unfold.

HAMLET   Speak. I am bound to hear.

GHOST

So art thou to revenge, when thou shalt hear.

HAMLET   What?

GHOST

I am thy father's spirit,

10   Doomed for a certain term to walk the night,

11   And for the day confined to fast in fires,

Till the foul crimes done in my days of nature

Are burnt and purged away. But that I am forbid

To tell the secrets of my prison house,

I could a tale unfold whose lightest word

Would harrow up thy soul, freeze thy young blood,

I.5 Elsinore: the battlements   **2** *My hour* daybreak   **3** *flames* sufferings in purgatory (not hell)   **11** *fast* do penance

Make thy two eyes like stars start from their spheres,   17
Thy knotted and combinèd locks to part,
And each particular hair to stand an end   19
Like quills upon the fearful porcupine.   20
But this eternal blazon must not be   21
To ears of flesh and blood. List, list, O, list!
If thou didst ever thy dear father love –

HAMLET   O God!

GHOST
Revenge his foul and most unnatural murder.

HAMLET   Murder?

GHOST
Murder most foul, as in the best it is,
But this most foul, strange, and unnatural.

HAMLET
Haste me to know't, that I, with wings as swift
As meditation or the thoughts of love,   30
May sweep to my revenge.

GHOST   I find thee apt,
And duller shouldst thou be than the fat weed
That roots itself in ease on Lethe wharf,   33
Wouldst thou not stir in this. Now, Hamlet, hear.
'Tis given out that, sleeping in my orchard,
A serpent stung me. So the whole ear of Denmark
Is by a forgèd process of my death   37
Rankly abused. But know, thou noble youth,
The serpent that did sting thy father's life
Now wears his crown.   40

HAMLET   O my prophetic soul!
My uncle?

---

17 *spheres* transparent revolving shells in each of which, according to Ptole-
maic astronomy, a planet or other heavenly body was placed   **19** *an* on   **20**
fearful (1) frightened, (2) frightening   **21** *eternal blazon* depiction of eternity   **30** *meditation* thought   **33** *Lethe* a river in Hades (drinking from it
produced forgetfulness of one's past life)   **37** *forgèd process* fabricated official
report

GHOST

42   Ay, that incestuous, that adulterate beast,
With witchcraft of his wit, with traitorous gifts –
O wicked wit and gifts, that have the power
So to seduce! – won to his shameful lust
The will of my most seeming-virtuous queen.
O Hamlet, what a falling off was there
From me, whose love was of that dignity
That it went hand in hand even with the vow
50   I made to her in marriage, and to decline
Upon a wretch whose natural gifts were poor
To those of mine!
But virtue, as it never will be moved,
54   Though lewdness court it in a shape of heaven,
So lust, though to a radiant angel linked,
Will sate itself in a celestial bed
And prey on garbage.
But soft, methinks I scent the morning air.
59   Brief let me be. Sleeping within my orchard,
60   My custom always of the afternoon,
61   Upon my secure hour thy uncle stole
62   With juice of cursed hebona in a vial,
And in the porches of my ears did pour
The leperous distillment, whose effect
Holds such an enmity with blood of man
That swift as quicksilver it courses through
The natural gates and alleys of the body
68   And with a sudden vigor it doth posset
69   And curd, like eager droppings into milk,
70   The thin and wholesome blood. So did it mine,
71   And a most instant tetter barked about
72   Most lazarlike with vile and loathsome crust
All my smooth body.

---

42 *adulterate* adulterous   54 *a shape of heaven* angelic disguise   59 *orchard* garden   61 *secure* carefree, unsuspecting   62 *hebona* poisonous plant   68 *posset* curdle   69 *eager* sour   71 *tetter* eruption; *barked* covered as with bark   72 *lazarlike* leperlike

Thus was I sleeping by a brother's hand
Of life, of crown, of queen at once dispatched,
Cut off even in the blossoms of my sin,
Unhouseled, disappointed, unaneled,   77
No reck'ning made, but sent to my account
With all my imperfections on my head.
O, horrible! O, horrible! most horrible!   80
If thou hast nature in thee, bear it not.
Let not the royal bed of Denmark be
A couch for luxury and damnèd incest.   83
But howsomever thou pursues this act,
Taint not thy mind, nor let thy soul contrive
Against thy mother aught. Leave her to heaven
And to those thorns that in her bosom lodge
To prick and sting her. Fare thee well at once.
The glowworm shows the matin to be near   89
And gins to pale his uneffectual fire.   90
Adieu, adieu, adieu. Remember me.   *[Exit.]*
HAMLET
O all you host of heaven! O earth! What else?
And shall I couple hell? O fie! Hold, hold, my heart,   93
And you, my sinews, grow not instant old,
But bear me stiffly up. Remember thee?
Ay, thou poor ghost, while memory holds a seat
In this distracted globe. Remember thee?   97
Yea, from the table of my memory   98
I'll wipe away all trivial fond records,   99
All saws of books, all forms, all pressures past   100
That youth and observation copied there,
And thy commandment all alone shall live
Within the book and volume of my brain,
Unmixed with baser matter. Yes, by heaven!

---

77 *Unhouseled* without the Christian Eucharist; *disappointed* unprepared
spiritually; *unaneled* without extreme unction (a Christian rite involving
holy oil, given at the end of a believer's life) 83 *luxury* lust 89 *matin*
morning 93 *couple* join with, marry 97 *globe* head 98 *table* writing
tablet, record book 99 *fond* foolish 100 *saws* wise sayings; *forms* mental
images, concepts; *pressures* impressions

O most pernicious woman!
O villain, villain, smiling, damnèd villain!
107   My tables – meet it is I set it down
That one may smile, and smile, and be a villain.
At least I am sure it may be so in Denmark.
    [Writes.]
110   So, uncle, there you are. Now to my word:
It is "Adieu, adieu, remember me."
I have sworn't.
    Enter Horatio and Marcellus.
HORATIO
    My lord, my lord!
MARCELLUS   Lord Hamlet!
HORATIO   Heavens secure him!
HAMLET   So be it!
MARCELLUS
115   Illo, ho, ho, my lord!
HAMLET
    Hillo, ho, ho, boy! Come and come.
MARCELLUS
    How is't, my noble lord?
HORATIO   What news, my lord?
118   HAMLET   O, wonderful!
HORATIO
    Good my lord, tell it.
HAMLET   No, you will reveal it.
HORATIO
120   Not I, my lord, by heaven.
MARCELLUS   Nor I, my lord.
HAMLET
    How say you then? Would heart of man once think it?
    But you'll be secret?
BOTH   Ay, by heaven.
HAMLET
    There's never a villain dwelling in all Denmark

---

107 *meet* appropriate   115 *Illo, ho, ho* (cry of the falconer to summon his
hunting bird)   118 *wonderful* full of wonder, amazing

But he's an arrant knave.

HORATIO
   There needs no ghost, my lord, come from the grave
   To tell us this.

HAMLET   Why, right, you are in the right,
   And so, without more circumstance at all,   127
   I hold it fit that we shake hands and part:
   You, as your business and desire shall point you,
   For every man hath business and desire   130
   Such as it is, and for my own poor part,
   I will go pray.

HORATIO
   These are but wild and whirling words, my lord.

HAMLET
   I am sorry they offend you, heartily;
   Yes, faith, heartily.

HORATIO   There's no offense, my lord.

HAMLET
   Yes, by Saint Patrick, but there is, Horatio,   136
   And much offense too. Touching this vision here,
   It is an honest ghost, that let me tell you.   138
   For your desire to know what is between us,
   O'ermaster't as you may. And now, good friends,   140
   As you are friends, scholars, and soldiers,
   Give me one poor request.

HORATIO
   What is't, my lord? We will.

HAMLET
   Never make known what you have seen tonight.

BOTH   My lord, we will not.

HAMLET   Nay, but swear't.

HORATIO   In faith, my lord, not I.

MARCELLUS   Nor I, my lord – in faith.

HAMLET   Upon my sword.   149

---

127 *circumstance* ceremony   **136** *Saint Patrick* the legendary keeper of purgatory   **138** *an honest ghost* a genuine ghost (not a disguised demon)   **149**
sword i.e., upon the cross formed by the sword hilt

150 MARCELLUS   We have sworn, my lord, already.

HAMLET   Indeed, upon my sword, indeed.

    Ghost cries under the stage.

GHOST   Swear.

HAMLET

153 Ha, ha, boy, say'st thou so? Art thou there, truepenny?
Come on. You hear this fellow in the cellarage.
Consent to swear.

HORATIO   Propose the oath, my lord.

HAMLET

Never to speak of this that you have seen,
Swear by my sword.

GHOST   *[Beneath]* Swear.

HAMLET

159 *Hic et ubique?* Then we'll shift our ground.
160 Come hither, gentlemen,
And lay your hands again upon my sword.
Swear by my sword
Never to speak of this that you have heard.

GHOST   *[Beneath]* Swear by his sword.

HAMLET

Well said, old mole! Canst work i' th' earth so fast?
166 A worthy pioner! Once more remove, good friends.

HORATIO

O day and night, but this is wondrous strange!

HAMLET

And therefore as a stranger give it welcome.
There are more things in heaven and earth, Horatio,
170 Than are dreamt of in your philosophy.
But come:
Here as before, never, so help you mercy,
How strange or odd some'er I bear myself
(As I perchance hereafter shall think meet

---

153 *truepenny* honest old fellow   159 *Hic et ubique* here and everywhere
(Latin)   166 *pioner* pioneer, miner (the archaic spelling is stressed on the
first syllable)   170 *your philosophy* this philosophizing one hears about

To put an antic disposition on),   175
That you, at such times seeing me, never shall,
With arms encumbered thus, or this headshake,   177
Or by pronouncing of some doubtful phrase,
As "Well, well, we know," or "We could, an if we would,"   179
Or "If we list to speak," or "There be, an if they might,"   *180*
Or such ambiguous giving out, to note
That you know aught of me – this do swear,
So grace and mercy at your most need help you.

GHOST   *[Beneath]* Swear.
    [They swear.]

HAMLET
Rest, rest, perturbèd spirit! So, gentlemen,
With all my love I do commend me to you,   186
And what so poor a man as Hamlet is
May do t' express his love and friending to you,
God willing, shall not lack. Let us go in together,
And still your fingers on your lips, I pray.   190
The time is out of joint. O cursèd spite
That ever I was born to set it right!
Nay, come, let's go together.   *Exeunt.*

               *

∾ **II.1** *Enter old Polonius, with his man [Reynaldo].*

POLONIUS
Give him this money and these notes, Reynaldo.
REYNALDO
I will, my lord.
POLONIUS
You shall do marvelous wisely, good Reynaldo,
Before you visit him, to make inquire
Of his behavior.

---

175 *antic* grotesque, mad   **177** *encumbered* folded   **179** *an if* if   **186** *commend* entrust   **190** *still* always
   II.1 Polonius's rooms in Elsinore

REYNALDO   My lord, I did intend it.

POLONIUS
   Marry, well said, very well said. Look you, sir,
7   Inquire me first what Danskers are in Paris,
8   And how, and who, what means, and where they keep,
   What company, at what expense; and finding
10 By this encompassment and drift of question
   That they do know my son, come you more nearer
12 Than your particular demands will touch it.
   Take you as 'twere some distant knowledge of him,
   As thus, "I know his father and his friends,
   And in part him" – do you mark this, Reynaldo?

REYNALDO
   Ay, very well, my lord.

POLONIUS
   "And in part him, but," you may say, "not well,
   But if't be he I mean, he's very wild,
   Addicted so and so." And there put on him
20 What forgeries you please; marry, none so rank
   As may dishonor him – take heed of that –
   But, sir, such wanton, wild, and usual slips
   As are companions noted and most known
   To youth and liberty.

REYNALDO   As gaming, my lord.

POLONIUS
   Ay, or drinking, fencing, swearing, quarreling,
26 Drabbing. You may go so far.

REYNALDO
   My lord, that would dishonor him.

POLONIUS
28 Faith, as you may season it in the charge.
   You must not put another scandal on him,
30 That he is open to incontinency.

---

7 *Danskers* Danes   8 *what means* what their wealth; *keep* dwell   10 *encompassment* roundabout means   12 *particular demands* definite questions   20 *forgeries* invented wrongdoings; *rank* exaggerated, terrible   26 *Drabbing* whoring   28 *Faith* (a mild oath; F reads "Faith, no,"); *season* soften   30 *incontinency* extreme promiscuity

That's not my meaning. But breathe his faults so quaintly   31
That they may seem the taints of liberty,
The flash and outbreak of a fiery mind,
A savageness in unreclaimèd blood,   34
Of general assault.   35

REYNALDO   But, my good lord –

POLONIUS
Wherefore should you do this?

REYNALDO   Ay, my lord,
I would know that.

POLONIUS   Marry, sir, here's my drift,
And I believe it is a fetch of wit.   38
You laying these slight sullies on my son
As 'twere a thing a little soiled with working,   40
Mark you,
Your party in converse, him you would sound,
Having ever seen in the prenominate crimes   43
The youth you breathe of guilty, be assured
He closes with you in this consequence: 45
"Good sir," or so, or "friend," or "gentleman" –
According to the phrase or the addition   47
Of man and country –

REYNALDO   Very good, my lord.

POLONIUS
And then, sir, does a this – a does –   49
What was I about to say? By the mass, I was about to   50
say something! Where did I leave?

REYNALDO   At "closes in the consequence."

POLONIUS
At "closes in the consequence" – Ay, marry!
He closes thus: "I know the gentleman;
I saw him yesterday, or th' other day,
Or then, or then, with such or such, and, as you say,

---

31 *quaintly* artfully   **34** *unreclaimèd* untamed   **35** *Of general assault* assailing all young men   **38** *fetch of wit* clever trick   **43** *Having ever* if he has ever; *prenominate* aforementioned   **45** *closes with* agrees with; *consequence* following way   **47** *addition* title   **49** *a* he

57 There was a gaming, there o'ertook in's rouse,
58 There falling out at tennis"; or perchance,
"I saw him enter such a house of sale,"
60 Videlicet, a brothel, or so forth.
See you now —
Your bait of falsehood takes this carp of truth,
63 And thus do we of wisdom and of reach,
64 With windlasses and with assays of bias,
65 By indirections find directions out.
So, by my former lecture and advice,
67 Shall you my son. You have me, have you not?

REYNALDO
68 My lord, I have.

POLONIUS   God buy ye, fare ye well.

REYNALDO   Good my lord.

POLONIUS
70 Observe his inclination in yourself.

REYNALDO   I shall, my lord.

POLONIUS
And let him ply his music.

REYNALDO   Well, my lord.

POLONIUS
Farewell.   *Exit Reynaldo.*
    Enter Ophelia.
              How now, Ophelia, what's the matter?

OPHELIA
O my lord, my lord, I have been so affrighted!

POLONIUS
With what, i' th' name of God?

OPHELIA
76 My lord, as I was sewing in my closet,

---

57 *a* he; *o'ertook* overcome with drunkenness; *rouse* carousal   58 *falling out* quarreling   60 *Videlicet* namely (Latin)   63 *reach* far-reaching comprehension   64 *windlasses* roundabout courses; *assays of bias* devious attacks (metaphors from the game of bowls, in which balls are weighted or "biased")   65 *directions* ways of procedure   67 *have me* understand me   68 *God buy ye* God be with you, good-bye   76 *closet* private room

Lord Hamlet, with his doublet all unbraced, 77
No hat upon his head, his stockings fouled,
Ungartered, and down-gyvèd to his ankle, 79
Pale as his shirt, his knees knocking each other, 80
And with a look so piteous in purport
As if he had been loosèd out of hell
To speak of horrors – he comes before me.

POLONIUS
  Mad for thy love?

OPHELIA   My lord, I do not know,
  But truly I do fear it.

POLONIUS   What said he?

OPHELIA
  He took me by the wrist and held me hard.
  Then goes he to the length of all his arm,
  And with his other hand thus o'er his brow
  He falls to such perusal of my face
  As a would draw it. Long stayed he so. 90
  At last, a little shaking of mine arm
  And thrice his head thus waving up and down,
  He raised a sigh so piteous and profound
  As it did seem to shatter all his bulk
  And end his being. That done, he lets me go,
  And with his head over his shoulder turned
  He seemed to find his way without his eyes,
  For out o' doors he went without their helps
  And to the last bended their light on me.

POLONIUS
  Come, go with me. I will go seek the king. 100
  This is the very ecstasy of love, 101
  Whose violent property fordoes itself 102
  And leads the will to desperate undertakings
  As oft as any passion under heaven

---

77 *doublet* jacket; *unbraced* unlaced 79 *down-gyvèd* fallen down like gyves (chains) on a prisoner's legs 101 *ecstasy* madness 102 *property* quality; *fordoes* destroys

That does afflict our natures. I am sorry.
What, have you given him any hard words of late?

OPHELIA
No, my good lord; but as you did command
I did repel his letters and denied
His access to me.

POLONIUS   That hath made him mad.

110   I am sorry that with better heed and judgment
111   I had not quoted him. I feared he did but trifle
112   And meant to wrack thee; but beshrew my jealousy.
        By heaven, it is as proper to our age
114   To cast beyond ourselves in our opinions
        As it is common for the younger sort
        To lack discretion. Come, go we to the king.
117   This must be known, which, being kept close, might
        move
118   More grief to hide than hate to utter love.
        Come.   *Exeunt.*

*

∾ **II.2** *Flourish. Enter King and Queen, Rosencrantz,
and Guildenstern [with others].*

KING
        Welcome, dear Rosencrantz and Guildenstern.
2   Moreover that we much did long to see you,
        The need we have to use you did provoke
        Our hasty sending. Something have you heard
        Of Hamlet's transformation – so call it,
6   Sith nor th' exterior nor the inward man
        Resembles that it was. What it should be,

---

111 *quoted* observed   112 *wrack* ruin (by sexual seduction); *beshrew* curse
114 *cast beyond ourselves* pay more attention to (or, suppose more signifi-
cance in) something than we ought to   117 *close* secret; *move* cause   118 *to
hide . . . love* i.e., more grief will come from concealing Hamlet's supposed
love for Ophelia than hate will come from making that love public
   II.2 Elsinore   2 *Moreover* besides; *we* (the royal plural)   6 *Sith* since

More than his father's death, that thus hath put him
So much from th' understanding of himself,
I cannot dream of. I entreat you both   10
That, being of so young days brought up with him,
And sith so neighbored to his youth and havior,   12
That you vouchsafe your rest here in our court   13
Some little time, so by your companies
To draw him on to pleasures, and to gather
So much as from occasion you may glean,
Whether aught to us unknown afflicts him thus,
That opened lies within our remedy.   18

QUEEN
Good gentlemen, he hath much talked of you,
And sure I am two men there is not living   20
To whom he more adheres. If it will please you   21
To show us so much gentry and good will   22
As to expend your time with us a while
For the supply and profit of our hope,
Your visitation shall receive such thanks
As fits a king's remembrance.

ROSENCRANTZ   Both your majesties
Might, by the sovereign power you have of us,
Put your dread pleasures more into command
Than to entreaty.

GUILDENSTERN   But we both obey,
And here give up ourselves in the full bent   30
To lay our service freely at your feet,
To be commanded.

KING
Thanks, Rosencrantz and gentle Guildenstern.

QUEEN
Thanks, Guildenstern and gentle Rosencrantz.

---

10 *dream of* imagine   12 *youth and havior* youthful ways of life ("behavior")
13 *vouchsafe your rest* agree to stay   18 *opened* revealed   20 *is* (a singular
verb with a plural subject is common in Shakespeare's period)   21 *more adheres* is more attached   22 *gentry* courtesy   30 *in the full bent* to full capac-
ity (a metaphor from the *bent* bow)

And I beseech you instantly to visit
My too much changèd son. – Go, some of you,
And bring these gentlemen where Hamlet is.

GUILDENSTERN
Heavens make our presence and our practices
Pleasant and helpful to him!

QUEEN   Ay, amen!

Exeunt Rosencrantz and Guildenstern
[with some Attendants].

Enter Polonius.

POLONIUS
40   Th' ambassadors from Norway, my good lord,
Are joyfully returned.

KING
42   Thou still hast been the father of good news.

POLONIUS
Have I, my lord? I assure my good liege
I hold my duty as I hold my soul,
Both to my God and to my gracious king,
And I do think – or else this brain of mine
Hunts not the trail of policy so sure
As it hath used to do – that I have found
The very cause of Hamlet's lunacy.

KING
50   O, speak of that! That do I long to hear.

POLONIUS
Give first admittance to th' ambassadors.
52   My news shall be the fruit to that great feast.

KING
53   Thyself do grace to them and bring them in.

[Exit Polonius.]

He tells me, my dear Gertrude, he hath found
The head and source of all your son's distemper.

QUEEN
56   I doubt it is no other but the main,
His father's death and our o'erhasty marriage.

---

42 *still* always   52 *fruit* dessert   53 *grace* honor   56 *doubt* suspect

KING
    Well, we shall sift him.
      Enter Ambassadors [Voltemand and Cornelius, with
      Polonius].
                        Welcome, my good friends.
    Say, Voltemand, what from our brother Norway?
VOLTEMAND
    Most fair return of greetings and desires.   60
    Upon our first, he sent out to suppress   61
    His nephew's levies, which to him appeared
    To be a preparation 'gainst the Polack,
    But better looked into, he truly found
    It was against your highness, whereat grieved,
    That so his sickness, age, and impotence
    Was falsely borne in hand, sends out arrests   67
    On Fortinbras, which he in brief obeys,
    Receives rebuke from Norway, and in fine   69
    Makes vow before his uncle never more   70
    To give th' assay of arms against your majesty.   71
    Whereon old Norway, overcome with joy,
    Gives him threescore thousand crowns in annual fee
    And his commission to employ those soldiers,   74
    So levied as before, against the Polack,
    With an entreaty, herein further shown,
      [Gives a paper.]
    That it might please you to give quiet pass
    Through your dominions for this enterprise,
    On such regards of safety and allowance   79
    As therein are set down.   80
KING   It likes us well;
    And at our more considered time we'll read,   81
    Answer, and think upon this business.
    Meantime we thank you for your well-took labor.

---

61 *our first* our first words about the matter   **67** *borne in hand* deceived   **69**
in fine in the end   **71** *assay* trial, test   **74–80** *And his . . . well* (see IV.4)   **79**
regards terms   **81** *considered time* convenient time for consideration

Go to your rest; at night we'll feast together.
Most welcome home!   *Exeunt Ambassadors.*
POLONIUS   This business is well ended.
86   My liege and madam, to expostulate
What majesty should be, what duty is,
Why day is day, night night, and time is time,
Were nothing but to waste night, day, and time.
90   Therefore, since brevity is the soul of wit,
And tediousness the limbs and outward flourishes,
I will be brief. Your noble son is mad.
Mad call I it, for, to define true madness,
What is't but to be nothing else but mad?
But let that go.
QUEEN   .   More matter, with less art.
POLONIUS
Madam, I swear I use no art at all.
That he's mad, 'tis true: 'tis true 'tis pity,
98   And pity 'tis 'tis true – a foolish figure.
But farewell it, for I will use no art.
100   Mad let us grant him then, and now remains
That we find out the cause of this effect –
Or rather say, the cause of this defect,
For this effect defective comes by cause.
Thus it remains, and the remainder thus.
105   Perpend.
I have a daughter (have while she is mine),
Who in her duty and obedience, mark,
Hath given me this. Now gather and surmise.
    [Reads the] letter.
"To the celestial, and my soul's idol, the most beauti-
110   fied Ophelia" –
That's an ill phrase, a vile phrase; "beautified" is a vile
phrase. But you shall hear. Thus:
    [Reads.]

---

86 *expostulate* discuss   90 *wit* understanding   98 *figure* figure of speech
105 *Perpend* consider, think about (this)

"In her excellent white bosom, these, etc."   113

QUEEN
Came this from Hamlet to her?

POLONIUS
Good madam, stay a while. I will be faithful.   115
  [Reads.]
            "Doubt thou the stars are fire;   116
              Doubt that the sun doth move;
            Doubt truth to be a liar;
            But never doubt I love.
O dear Ophelia, I am ill at these numbers. I have not   120
art to reckon my groans, but that I love thee best, O
most best, believe it. Adieu.
            Thine evermore, most dear lady,
              whilst this machine is to him, Hamlet."   124

This in obedience hath my daughter shown me,
And more above hath his solicitings,   126
As they fell out by time, by means, and place,   127
All given to mine ear.

KING   But how hath she
Received his love?

POLONIUS   What do you think of me?

KING
As of a man faithful and honorable.   *130*

POLONIUS
I would fain prove so. But what might you think,   131
When I had seen this hot love on the wing
(As I perceived it, I must tell you that,
Before my daughter told me), what might you,
Or my dear majesty your queen here, think,

---

113 *etc.* (i.e., other conventional words of greeting: early modern letters
often include "etc." for such common, formalized greetings) 115 *faithful*
i.e., true to the text 116 *Doubt* suspect 120 *numbers* verses 124 *machine*
body; *to* attached to 126 *above* besides 127 *fell out* came about 131 *fain*
wish to, prefer to

136   If I had played the desk or table book,
137   Or given my heart a winking, mute and dumb,
      Or looked upon this love with idle sight?
139   What might you think? No, I went round to work
140   And my young mistress thus I did bespeak:
141   "Lord Hamlet is a prince, out of thy star.
142   This must not be." And then I prescripts gave her
      That she should lock herself from his resort,
      Admit no messengers, receive no tokens.
      Which done, she took the fruits of my advice,
      And he, repelled, a short tale to make,
      Fell into a sadness, then into a fast,
148   Thence to a watch, thence into a weakness,
149   Thence to a lightness, and, by this declension,
150   Into the madness wherein now he raves,
      And all we mourn for.
KING   Do you think this?
QUEEN
      It may be, very like.
POLONIUS
      Hath there been such a time – I would fain know
        that –
      That I have positively said " 'Tis so,"
      When it proved otherwise?
KING   Not that I know.
POLONIUS
156   Take this from this, if this be otherwise.
      If circumstances lead me, I will find
      Where truth is hid, though it were hid indeed
159   Within the center.
KING   How may we try it further?

---

136 *desk or table book* i.e., silent receptacle   137 *winking* closing of the eyes
139 *round* plainly   140 *mistress* i.e., "miss" (a dismissive term for his daughter)   141 *star* status determined by stellar influence   142 *prescripts* instructions   148 *watch* sleepless state   149 *lightness* light-headedness   156
Take . . . from this i.e., behead me (traditionally the actor is directed to ges-
ture to head and neck or shoulder)   159 *center* center of the earth

POLONIUS

   You know sometimes he walks four hours together   *160*
   Here in the lobby.

QUEEN   So he does indeed.

POLONIUS

   At such a time I'll loose my daughter to him.   *162*
   Be you and I behind an arras then.   *163*
   Mark the encounter. If he love her not,
   And be not from his reason fallen thereon,   *165*
   Let me be no assistant for a state
   But keep a farm and carters.

KING   We will try it.

   Enter Hamlet [reading on a book].

QUEEN

   But look where sadly the poor wretch comes reading.   *168*

POLONIUS

   Away, I do beseech you both, away.

              Exit King and Queen [with Attendants].

   I'll board him presently. O, give me leave.   *170*
   How does my good Lord Hamlet?

HAMLET   Well, God-a-mercy.   *172*

POLONIUS   Do you know me, my lord?

HAMLET   Excellent well. You are a fishmonger.   *174*

POLONIUS   Not I, my lord.

HAMLET   Then I would you were so honest a man.

POLONIUS   Honest, my lord?

HAMLET   Ay, sir. To be honest, as this world goes, is to be
one man picked out of ten thousand.

POLONIUS   That's very true, my lord.   *180*

HAMLET   For if the sun breed maggots in a dead dog,
being a good kissing carrion – Have you a daughter?   *182*

---

162 *loose* release (the word refers specifically to the breeding of domesticated animals and hence is coarse when used of humans, much less one's daughter) 163 *an arras* a hanging tapestry 165 *thereon* on that account 168 *sadly* seriously 170 *board* greet; *presently* at once 172 *God-a-mercy* thank you (literally, "God have mercy!") 174 *fishmonger* seller of fish (but also slang for procurer: Ophelia is "bait") 182 *a good kissing carrion* flesh good for kissing

POLONIUS   I have, my lord.

HAMLET   Let her not walk i' th' sun. Conception is a
blessing, but as your daughter may conceive, friend,
look to't.

POLONIUS   *[Aside]* How say you by that? Still harping on
my daughter. Yet he knew me not at first. A said I was a
fishmonger. A is far gone. And truly in my youth I suf-
190   fered much extremity for love, very near this. I'll speak
to him again. – What do you read, my lord?

HAMLET   Words, words, words.

POLONIUS   What is the matter, my lord?

194   HAMLET   Between who?

POLONIUS   I mean the matter that you read, my lord.

HAMLET   Slanders, sir, for the satirical rogue says here
that old men have gray beards, that their faces are wrin-
kled, their eyes purging thick amber and plum-tree
199   gum, and that they have a plentiful lack of wit, together
200   with most weak hams. All which, sir, though I most
powerfully and potently believe, yet I hold it not hon-
202   esty to have it thus set down, for yourself, sir, shall grow
old as I am if, like a crab, you could go backward.

POLONIUS   *[Aside]* Though this be madness, yet there is
method in't. – Will you walk out of the air, my lord?

HAMLET   Into my grave.

POLONIUS   Indeed, that's out of the air. *[Aside]* How
208   pregnant sometimes his replies are! a happiness that
often madness hits on, which reason and sanity could
210   not so prosperously be delivered of. I will leave him
211   [and suddenly contrive the means of meeting between
him] and my daughter. – My lord, I will take my leave
of you.

---

194 *Between who* (Hamlet jokingly misunderstands *matter* as the subject of a
quarrel or a lawsuit)   199 *gum* resin (?)   200 *hams* legs   202–3 *shall . . .
backward* you will be as old as I am if you could age backward   208 *pregnant*
full of meaning; *a happiness* an aptness of expression   211–12 *and . . . him*
(this phrase from F was probably omitted accidentally from Q2 when the
compositor's eye skipped from *him* to *him*)

HAMLET   You cannot take from me anything that I will   214
  not more willingly part withal – except my life, except   215
  my life, except my life.
  Enter Guildenstern and Rosencrantz.
POLONIUS   Fare you well, my lord.
HAMLET   These tedious old fools!
POLONIUS   You go to seek the Lord Hamlet. There he is.
ROSENCRANTZ   *[To Polonius]* God save you, sir.   220
                                    [Exit Polonius.]
GUILDENSTERN   My honored lord!
ROSENCRANTZ   My most dear lord!
HAMLET   My excellent good friends! How dost thou,
  Guildenstern? Ah, Rosencrantz! Good lads, how do
  you both?
ROSENCRANTZ
  As the indifferent children of the earth.   226
GUILDENSTERN   Happy in that we are not overhappy on
  Fortune's cap. We are not the very button.
HAMLET   Nor the soles of her shoe?
ROSENCRANTZ   Neither, my lord.   230
HAMLET   Then you live about her waist or in the middle
  of her favors?
GUILDENSTERN   Faith, her privates we.   233
HAMLET   In the secret parts of Fortune? O, most true;
  she is a strumpet. What news?
ROSENCRANTZ   None, my lord, but the world's grown
  honest.
HAMLET   Then is doomsday near. But your news is not
  true. But in the beaten way of friendship, what make   239
  you at Elsinore?   240
ROSENCRANTZ   To visit you, my lord; no other occasion.

214–15 *cannot . . . not* (a common double negative)   **215** *withal* with   **226**
indifferent average   **233** *privates* ordinary men in private, not public, life
(with wordplay on "private parts," which Hamlet emphasizes with *secret
parts*)   **239** *true* (after this word F includes a substantial passage not in Q2:
see Folio-only Passages in Note on the Text); *beaten* well-trodden, well-worn;
make do

HAMLET   Beggar that I am, I am ever poor in thanks, but
I thank you; and sure, dear friends, my thanks are too
244   dear a halfpenny. Were you not sent for? Is it your own
inclining? Is it a free visitation? Come, come, deal justly
with me. Come, come. Nay, speak.

GUILDENSTERN   What should we say, my lord?

HAMLET   Anything but to th' purpose. You were sent for,
and there is a kind of confession in your looks, which
250   your modesties have not craft enough to color. I know
the good king and queen have sent for you.

ROSENCRANTZ   To what end, my lord?

HAMLET   That you must teach me. But let me conjure
254   you by the rights of our fellowship, by the consonancy
of our youth, by the obligation of our ever-preserved
256   love, and by what more dear a better proposer can
257   charge you withal, be even and direct with me whether
you were sent for or no.

ROSENCRANTZ   *[Aside to Guildenstern]* What say you?

260   HAMLET   *[Aside]* Nay then, I have an eye of you. – If you
love me, hold not off.

GUILDENSTERN   My lord, we were sent for.

HAMLET   I will tell you why. So shall my anticipation
264   prevent your discovery, and your secrecy to the king
265   and queen molt no feather. I have of late – but wherefore I know not – lost all my mirth, forgone all custom
of exercises; and indeed, it goes so heavily with my disposition that this goodly frame the earth seems to me a
sterile promontory; this most excellent canopy, the air,
270   look you, this brave o'erhanging firmament, this majes-
271   tical roof fretted with golden fire – why, it appeareth

---

244 *a halfpenny* at a halfpenny   **250** *color* conceal, cover up with deceptive
colorings   **254** *consonancy* accord (in sameness of age)   **256** *proposer* pro-
pounder   **257** *withal* with; *even* straight   **264** *prevent* forestall; *discovery* dis-
closure   **265** *molt no feather* let fall no feather (i.e., be left whole)   **270**
firmament sky   **271** *fretted* decorated with fretwork (it is traditionally supposed that the original actor of Hamlet here gestured toward the roof of the
Globe's stage, which was painted with *golden fire,* the zodiac and stars)

nothing to me but a foul and pestilent congregation of
vapors. What piece of work is a man, how noble in reason, how infinite in faculties, in form and moving how
express and admirable, in action how like an angel, in   275
apprehension how like a god: the beauty of the world,
the paragon of animals! And yet to me what is this
quintessence of dust? Man delights not me – nor   278
woman neither, though by your smiling you seem to
say so.   280

ROSENCRANTZ   My lord, there was no such stuff in my
thoughts.

HAMLET   Why did ye laugh then, when I said "Man delights not me"?

ROSENCRANTZ   To think, my lord, if you delight not in
man, what Lenten entertainment the players shall re-   286
ceive from you. We coted them on the way, and hither   287
are they coming to offer you service.

HAMLET   He that plays the king shall be welcome – his
majesty shall have tribute of me –, the adventurous   290
knight shall use his foil and target, the lover shall not   291
sigh gratis, the humorous man shall end his part in   292
peace, [the clown shall make those laugh whose lungs   293
are tickle o' th' sere,] and the lady shall say her mind   294
freely, or the blank verse shall halt for't. What players   295
are they?

ROSENCRANTZ   Even those you were wont to take such
delight in, the tragedians of the city.

_____

275 *express* well-framed   278 *quintessence* fifth (*quint-*) and finest essence
(an alchemical term for something superior to the four essences or
elements – fire, air, earth, water – that constituted all earthly life); *dust* the
earth of which humankind is created according to the Judeo-Christian Scrip-
tures (see V.1.187 ff.)   286 *Lenten* scanty (from "Lent," the forty-day period
of abstinence and repentance before the Christian Easter)   287 *coted* overtook   291 *foil and target* sword and shield   292 *the humorous man* an ec-
centric character   293–94 *the clown . . . sere,* (versions of this phrase appear
in Q1 and F; it seems accidentally absent from Q2)   294 *tickle o' th' sere*
hair-triggered for the discharge of laughter (*sere* = part of a gunlock)   295
halt go lame (a joke on metrical "feet" in verse)

299 HAMLET   How chances it they travel? Their residence,
300   both in reputation and profit, was better both ways.

ROSENCRANTZ   I think their inhibition comes by the
302   means of the late innovation.

HAMLET   Do they hold the same estimation they did
304   when I was in the city? Are they so followed?

305 ROSENCRANTZ   No indeed, are they not.

HAMLET   It is not very strange, for my uncle is King of
307   Denmark, and those that would make mouths at him
   while my father lived give twenty, forty, fifty, a hundred
309   ducats apiece for his picture in little. 'Sblood, there is
310   something in this more than natural, if philosophy
   could find it out.

   A flourish.

GUILDENSTERN   There are the players.

HAMLET   Gentlemen, you are welcome to Elsinore. Your
   hands, come then. Th' appurtenance of welcome is
   fashion and ceremony. Let me comply with you in this
316   garb, lest my extent to the players (which I tell you
   must show fairly outwards) should more appear like
   entertainment than yours. You are welcome. But my
   uncle-father and aunt-mother are deceived.

320 GUILDENSTERN   In what, my dear lord?

HAMLET   I am but mad north-northwest. When the
322   wind is southerly I know a hawk from a handsaw.

   Enter Polonius.

POLONIUS   Well be with you, gentlemen.

----

299 *residence* (for Shakespeare and his audience, this word would evoke the theatrical center, London)   **302** *late innovation* new fashion (possibly the companies of boy actors who had reappeared circa 1601 as competitors for adult companies such as Shakespeare's; possibly a reference to political upheaval)   **304** *city* (as in l. 298, presumably *city* = London for Shakespeare's original audiences)   **305** *not* (after this word F has a lengthy passage: see Folio-only Passages in Note on the Text)   **307** *make mouths at him* make faces at him, ridicule him   **309** *his picture in little* a miniature; *'Sblood* by God's [i.e., Christ's] blood   **316** *garb* manner; *extent* showing, behavior   **322** *hawk* mattock or pickax (also called "hack"; here used apparently with a play on *hawk*, the bird); *handsaw* carpenter's tool (apparently with a play on some form of "hernshaw," the heron)

HAMLET Hark you, Guildenstern – and you too – at each ear a hearer. That great baby you see there is not yet out of his swaddling clouts.   326

ROSENCRANTZ Happily he is the second time come to them, for they say an old man is twice a child.   327

HAMLET I will prophesy he comes to tell me of the players. Mark it. – You say right, sir; a Monday morning, 'twas then indeed.   330

POLONIUS My lord, I have news to tell you.

HAMLET My lord, I have news to tell you. When Roscius was an actor in Rome –   333

POLONIUS The actors are come hither, my lord.

HAMLET Buzz, buzz.

POLONIUS Upon my honor –

HAMLET Then came each actor on his ass –

POLONIUS The best actors in the world, either for tragedy, comedy, history, pastoral, pastoral-comical,   340
historical-pastoral; scene individable, or poem unlim-   341
ited. Seneca cannot be too heavy, nor Plautus too light.   342
For the law of writ and the liberty, these are the only   343
men.

HAMLET O Jephthah, judge of Israel, what a treasure   345
hadst thou!

POLONIUS What a treasure had he, my lord?

HAMLET Why,
      "One fair daughter, and no more,
      The which he lovèd passing well."   350

POLONIUS *[Aside]* Still on my daughter.

HAMLET Am I not i' th' right, old Jephthah?

---

326 *clouts* clothes 327 *Happily* haply, perhaps 333 *Roscius* a legendary Roman comic actor 341 *scene individable* drama observing the unity of place (?) 341–42 *poem unlimited* drama not observing the unity of place (?) 342 *Seneca* classical Roman writer of tragedies; *heavy* serious; *Plautus* classical Roman writer of comedies; *light* unserious 343 *law of writ* drama written (as Shakespeare's was not) according to classical or neoclassical rules; *liberty* freedom from such rule-based orthodoxy 345 *Jephthah* biblical father whose rash vow compelled him to sacrifice his beloved daughter (Judges 11:30–40) 350 *passing* surpassingly (the verses are from a surviving ballad on Jephthah)

POLONIUS If you call me Jephthah, my lord, I have a
  daughter that I love passing well.
HAMLET Nay, that follows not.
POLONIUS What follows then, my lord?
HAMLET Why,
      "As by lot, God wot,"
  and then, you know,
360   "It came to pass, as most like it was."
361 The first row of the pious chanson will show you more,
362 for look where my abridgment comes.
      Enter the Players.
  You are welcome, masters, welcome, all. – I am glad to
  see thee well. – Welcome, good friends. – O, old friend,
365 why, thy face is valanced since I saw thee last. Com'st
366 thou to beard me in Denmark? – What, my young lady
  and mistress? By'r Lady, your ladyship is nearer to heaven
368 than when I saw you last by the altitude of a chopine.
369 Pray God your voice, like a piece of uncurrent gold, be
370 not cracked within the ring. – Masters, you are all welcome. We'll e'en to't like French falconers, fly at anything we see. We'll have a speech straight. Come, give
  us a taste of your quality. Come, a passionate speech.
PLAYER What speech, my good lord?
HAMLET I heard thee speak me a speech once, but it was
  never acted, or if it was, not above once, for the play, I
  remember, pleased not the million; 'twas caviar to the
378 general, but it was (as I received it, and others, whose
379 judgments in such matters cried in the top of mine) an
380 excellent play, well digested in the scenes, set down

---

361 *row* stanza; *chanson* song (French) **362** *my abridgment* something that
shortens my talk **365** *valanced* fringed (with a *beard*) **366** *young lady* boy
who plays women's parts **368** *chopine* woman's thick-soled shoe **369–70** *a
piece . . . cracked within the ring* i.e., literally, a coin that has had precious
metal removed from within the *ring* surrounding the sovereign's image; figu-
ratively, the boy actor's voice, which has *cracked,* making him unsuitable for
women's roles; finally there is bawdy wordplay on the *ring* of a woman's (or
female character's) vagina, *cracked* by sexual intercourse **369** *uncurrent* not
legal tender **378** *general* multitude **379** *in the top of* more authoritatively
than

with as much modesty as cunning. I remember one said
there were no sallets in the lines to make the matter sa-   382
vory, nor no matter in the phrase that might indict the
author of affection, but called it an honest method, as   384
wholesome as sweet, and by very much more hand-
some than fine. One speech in't I chiefly loved. 'Twas
Aeneas' tale to Dido, and thereabout of it especially
when he speaks of Priam's slaughter. If it live in your   388
memory, begin at this line – let me see, let me see:
    "The rugged Pyrrhus, like th' Hyrcanian beast –"   390
'Tis not so; it begins with Pyrrhus:
    "The rugged Pyrrhus, he whose sable arms,   392
    Black as his purpose, did the night resemble
    When he lay couchèd in the ominous horse,   394
    Hath now this dread and black complexion smeared
    With heraldry more dismal. Head to foot   396
    Now is he total gules, horridly tricked   397
    With blood of fathers, mothers, daughters, sons,
    Baked and impasted with the parching streets,   399
    That lend a tyrannous and a damnèd light   400
    To their lord's murder. Roasted in wrath and fire,
    And thus o'ersizèd with coagulate gore,   402
    With eyes like carbuncles, the hellish Pyrrhus
    Old grandsire Priam seeks."
So, proceed you.

POLONIUS   'Fore God, my lord, well spoken, with good
accent and good discretion.

PLAYER   "Anon he finds him,

---

382 *sallets* salads (metaphorically: highly seasoned literary passages) **384**
affection affectation **388** *Priam's slaughter* i.e., at the fall of Troy (Virgil,
Aeneid II, 506 ff.; *Priam* was King of Troy, *Aeneas* his son-in-law, *Hecuba* his
wife; after Troy's fall, Aeneas wandered the Mediterranean Sea and visited
Carthage, whose queen was *Dido*) **390** *Hyrcanian beast* tiger (Hyrcania is
on the southern shores of the Caspian Sea) **392** *sable* black **394** *ominous*
fateful; *horse* wooden horse by which the Greeks gained entrance to Troy
396 *dismal* ill-omened **397** *gules* red (a heraldic term); *tricked* decorated in
color (another heraldic term) **399** *parching* drying (i.e., because Troy is
burning) **402** *o'ersizèd* covered as with "size," a glutinous material used for
filling, for example, pores of plaster or gaps in cloth; *coagulate* clotted

Striking too short at Greeks. His antique sword,
410 Rebellious to his arm, lies where it falls,
Repugnant to command. Unequal matched,
Pyrrhus at Priam drives, in rage strikes wide,
413 But with the whiff and wind of his fell sword
414 Th' unnervèd father falls. [Then senseless Ilium,]
Seeming to feel this blow, with flaming top
416 Stoops to his base, and with a hideous crash
Takes prisoner Pyrrhus' ear. For lo! his sword,
Which was declining on the milky head
Of reverend Priam, seemed i' th' air to stick.
420 So as a painted tyrant Pyrrhus stood,
421 And like a neutral to his will and matter
Did nothing.
423 But as we often see, against some storm,
424 A silence in the heavens, the rack stand still,
The bold winds speechless, and the orb below
As hush as death, anon the dreadful thunder
427 Doth rend the region, so after Pyrrhus' pause,
Arousèd vengeance sets him new awork,
429 And never did the Cyclops' hammers fall
430 On Mars's armor, forged for proof eterne,
431 With less remorse than Pyrrhus' bleeding sword
Now falls on Priam.
Out, out, thou strumpet Fortune! All you gods,
In general synod take away her power,
435 Break all the spokes and fellies from her wheel,
436 And bowl the round nave down the hill of heaven,
As low as to the fiends."
POLONIUS   This is too long.

---

413 *But* even (i.e., with only the sword's movement); *fell* cruel   414 *senseless* without feeling   416 *his* its   420 *painted* pictured   421 *will and matter* desire and aim (between which he stands *neutral,* motionless)   423 *against* just before   424 *rack* clouds   427 *region* sky   429 *Cyclops* giant workmen who made armor in Vulcan's forge   430 *proof eterne* eternal protection   431 *remorse* pity, compassion   435 *fellies* segments of the rim of a wheel   436 *nave* hub of a wheel

HAMLET   It shall to the barber's, with your beard. –
Prithee say on. He's for a jig or a tale of bawdry, or he   440
sleeps. Say on; come to Hecuba.

PLAYER
"But who (ah woe!) had seen the mobled queen –"   442

HAMLET   "The mobled queen"?

POLONIUS   That's good.

PLAYER
"Run barefoot up and down, threat'ning the flames
With bisson rheum; a clout upon that head   446
Where late the diadem stood, and for a robe,
About her lank and all o'erteemèd loins,   448
A blanket in the alarm of fear caught up –
Who this had seen, with tongue in venom steeped   450
'Gainst Fortune's state would treason have pro-   451
nounced.
But if the gods themselves did see her then,
When she saw Pyrrhus make malicious sport
In mincing with his sword her husband's limbs,
The instant burst of clamor that she made
(Unless things mortal move them not at all)
Would have made milch the burning eyes of heaven   457
And passion in the gods."

POLONIUS   Look, where he has not turned his color, and   459
has tears in's eyes. Prithee no more.   460

HAMLET   'Tis well. I'll have thee speak out the rest of this
soon. – Good my lord, will you see the players well be-   462
stowed? Do you hear? Let them be well used, for they
are the abstract and brief chronicles of the time. After   464
your death you were better have a bad epitaph than
their ill report while you live.

---

440 *a jig* comic singing and dancing often performed following a play in the
public theaters   442 *mobled* muffled (the archaic word's pronunciation is
uncertain, "mobled" or "mobbled," short or long *o*)   446 *bisson rheum*
blinding tears; *clout* cloth   448 *o'erteemèd* overproductive of children   451
state government of worldly events   457 *milch* tearful (milk-giving); *eyes* i.e.,
stars   459 *where* whether   462–63 *bestowed* lodged   464 *they . . . time* i.e.,
the players tell the stories of our times

POLONIUS My lord, I will use them according to their desert.

469
470
HAMLET God's bodkin, man, much better! Use every man after his desert, and who shall scape whipping? Use them after your own honor and dignity. The less they deserve, the more merit is in your bounty. Take them in.

POLONIUS Come, sirs.

HAMLET Follow him, friends. We'll hear a play tomorrow. *[Aside to Player]* Dost thou hear me, old friend? Can you play "The Murder of Gonzago"?

PLAYER Ay, my lord.

479
480
HAMLET We'll ha't tomorrow night. You could for a need study a speech of some dozen or sixteen lines which I would set down and insert in't, could you not?

PLAYER Ay, my lord.

HAMLET Very well. Follow that lord, and look you mock him not. – My good friends, I'll leave you till night. You are welcome to Elsinore.   *Exeunt Polonius and Players.*

ROSENCRANTZ Good my lord.
                              Exeunt [Rosencrantz and Guildenstern].

HAMLET
  Ay, so, God buy to you. – Now I am alone.
  O, what a rogue and peasant slave am I!
  Is it not monstrous that this player here,
490 But in a fiction, in a dream of passion,
491 Could force his soul so to his own conceit
492 That from her working all his visage wanned,
  Tears in his eyes, distraction in his aspect,
494 A broken voice, and his whole function suiting
  With forms to his conceit? And all for nothing,
  For Hecuba!
  What's Hecuba to him, or he to her,

---

469 *God's bodkin* by God's little body (an oath)   **479** *for a need* if necessary
491 *conceit* conception, idea   **492** *wanned* paled   **494** *function* action of bodily powers

That he should weep for her? What would he do
Had he the motive and the cue for passion
That I have? He would drown the stage with tears   *500*
And cleave the general ear with horrid speech,
Make mad the guilty and appall the free,
Confound the ignorant, and amaze indeed
The very faculties of eyes and ears.
Yet I,
A dull and muddy-mettled rascal, peak   506
Like John-a-dreams, unpregnant of my cause,   507
And can say nothing. No, not for a king,
Upon whose property and most dear life   509
A damned defeat was made. Am I a coward?   *510*
Who calls me villain? breaks my pate across?   511
Plucks off my beard and blows it in my face?
Tweaks me by the nose? gives me the lie i' th' throat
As deep as to the lungs? Who does me this?
Ha, 'swounds, I should take it, for it cannot be   515
But I am pigeon-livered and lack gall   516
To make oppression bitter, or ere this
I should ha' fatted all the region kites   518
With this slave's offal. Bloody, bawdy villain!   519
Remorseless, treacherous, lecherous, kindless villain! 520
Why, what an ass am I! This is most brave,
That I, the son of a dear father murdered,
Prompted to my revenge by heaven and hell,
Must like a whore unpack my heart with words
And fall a-cursing like a very drab,
A stallion! Fie upon't, foh! About, my brains.   526
Hum –

---

506 *muddy-mettled* dull-spirited; *peak* mope   507 *John-a-dreams* a lazy
dawdler; *unpregnant* barren of realization   509 *property* proper (own) person
(?)   511 *pate* head   515 *'swounds* by God's [i.e., Christ's] wounds (an oath)
516 *pigeon-livered* unaggressive (pigeons were supposed to lack a *gall* bladder
and hence to be meek)   518 *region kites* kites (scavenging birds) of the air
519 *offal* guts   520 *kindless* unnatural   526 *stallion* (slang for "prostitute,"
male or female); *About* get working, get going

528   I have heard that guilty creatures sitting at a play
       Have by the very cunning of the scene
530   Been struck so to the soul that presently
       They have proclaimed their malefactions.
       For murder, though it have no tongue, will speak
       With most miraculous organ. I'll have these players
       Play something like the murder of my father
       Before mine uncle. I'll observe his looks.
536   I'll tent him to the quick. If a do blench,
       I know my course. The spirit that I have seen
       May be a devil, and the devil hath power
       T' assume a pleasing shape, yea, and perhaps
540   Out of my weakness and my melancholy,
       As he is very potent with such spirits,
542   Abuses me to damn me. I'll have grounds
543   More relative than this. The play's the thing
       Wherein I'll catch the conscience of the king.   *Exit.*

                              *

❧ **III.1** *Enter King, Queen, Polonius, Ophelia,*
       Rosencrantz, Guildenstern, Lords.

KING
1   And can you by no drift of conference
       Get from him why he puts on this confusion,
       Grating so harshly all his days of quiet
       With turbulent and dangerous lunacy?
ROSENCRANTZ
       He does confess he feels himself distracted,
6   But from what cause a will by no means speak.
GUILDENSTERN
7   Nor do we find him forward to be sounded,
       But with a crafty madness keeps aloof

528–31 *guilty . . . malefactions* (popular belief held that such incidents oc-
curred) 530 *presently* immediately 536 *tent* probe; *a* he; *blench* flinch
542 *Abuses* deludes 543 *relative* cogent
    III.1 Elsinore 1 *drift of conference* course of conversation 6 *a* he 7 *for-*
ward . . . sounded willing to be (thoroughly) understood

When we would bring him on to some confession
Of his true state.   *10*

QUEEN   Did he receive you well?

ROSENCRANTZ
Most like a gentleman.

GUILDENSTERN
But with much forcing of his disposition.

ROSENCRANTZ
Niggard of question, but of our demands   *13*
Most free in his reply.   *14*

QUEEN   Did you assay him
To any pastime?

ROSENCRANTZ
Madam, it so fell out that certain players
We o'erraught on the way. Of these we told him,   *17*
And there did seem in him a kind of joy
To hear of it. They are here about the court,
And, as I think, they have already order   *20*
This night to play before him.

POLONIUS   'Tis most true,
And he beseeched me to entreat your majesties
To hear and see the matter.

KING
With all my heart, and it doth much content me
To hear him so inclined.
Good gentlemen, give him a further edge   *26*
And drive his purpose into these delights.

ROSENCRANTZ
We shall, my lord.

            Exeunt Rosencrantz and Guildenstern.

KING   Sweet Gertrude, leave us too,
For we have closely sent for Hamlet hither,   *29*
That he, as 'twere by accident, may here   *30*
Affront Ophelia.   *31*

---

13 *Niggard of* chary of, not forthcoming with   **14** *assay* try to win   **17** *o'erraught* overtook   **26** *edge* keen desire   **29** *closely* privately   **31** *Affront* come
face to face with

32   Her father and myself, lawful espials,
We'll so bestow ourselves that, seeing unseen,
We may of their encounter frankly judge
And gather by him, as he is behaved,
If't be th' affliction of his love or no
That thus he suffers for.
QUEEN   I shall obey you. –
And for your part, Ophelia, I do wish
That your good beauties be the happy cause
40   Of Hamlet's wildness. So shall I hope your virtues
Will bring him to his wonted way again,
To both your honors.
OPHELIA   Madam, I wish it may.
                       [Exit Queen.]

POLONIUS
Ophelia, walk you here. – Gracious, so please you,
We will bestow ourselves.
   [To Ophelia]   Read on this book,
45   That show of such an exercise may color
46   Your loneliness. We are oft to blame in this,
'Tis too much proved, that with devotion's visage
48   And pious action we do sugar o'er
The devil himself.
KING   *[Aside]*   O, 'tis too true.
50   How smart a lash that speech doth give my conscience!
The harlot's cheek, beautied with plast'ring art,
52   Is not more ugly to the thing that helps it
Than is my deed to my most painted word.
O heavy burden!
POLONIUS
I hear him coming. Let's withdraw, my lord.
                  [Exeunt King and Polonius.]
   Enter Hamlet.

---

32 *espials* spies   **45** *an exercise* a religious exercise (the *book* is apparently a devotional text); *color* give an appearance of naturalness to   **46** *loneliness* solitude   **48** *sugar o'er* conceal beneath sweetness   **52** *to* compared to

HAMLET

    To be, or not to be – that is the question:
    Whether 'tis nobler in the mind to suffer
    The slings and arrows of outrageous fortune
    Or to take arms against a sea of troubles
    And by opposing end them. To die, to sleep   *60*
    No more, and by a sleep to say we end
    The heartache, and the thousand natural shocks
    That flesh is heir to. 'Tis a consummation
    Devoutly to be wished. To die, to sleep,
    To sleep – perchance to dream – ay, there's the rub,   *65*
    For in that sleep of death what dreams may come
    When we have shuffled off this mortal coil   *67*
    Must give us pause. There's the respect   *68*
    That makes calamity of so long life.   *69*
    For who would bear the whips and scorns of time,   *70*
    Th' oppressor's wrong, the proud man's contumely,   *71*
    The pangs of despised love, the law's delay,
    The insolence of office, and the spurns
    That patient merit of th' unworthy takes,
    When he himself might his quietus make   *75*
    With a bare bodkin? Who would fardels bear,   *76*
    To grunt and sweat under a weary life,
    But that the dread of something after death,
    The undiscovered country, from whose bourn   *79*
    No traveler returns, puzzles the will,   *80*
    And makes us rather bear those ills we have
    Than fly to others that we know not of?
    Thus conscience does make cowards of us all,   *83*
    And thus the native hue of resolution

---

65 *rub* obstacle (literally, obstruction encountered by a lawn bowler's ball) **67** *shuffled* cast; *coil* to-do, turmoil **68** *respect* consideration, regard **69** *of so long life* so long-lived (but also, perhaps, *long life* as a *calamity*) **70** *time* the world as we experience it **71** *contumely* rudeness, contempt **75** *quietus* settlement (literally, release, "quit," from debt) **76** *bodkin* short dagger; *fardels* burdens **79** *bourn* region **83** *conscience* (1) inner moral sense, (2) consciousness

Is sicklied o'er with the pale cast of thought,
86   And enterprises of great pitch and moment
87   With this regard their currents turn awry
88   And lose the name of action. – Soft you now,
89   The fair Ophelia! – Nymph, in thy orisons
90   Be all my sins remembered.

OPHELIA   Good my lord,
How does your honor for this many a day?

HAMLET
I humbly thank you, well.

OPHELIA
My lord, I have remembrances of yours
That I have longèd long to redeliver.
I pray you, now receive them.

HAMLET   No, not I,
I never gave you aught.

OPHELIA
My honored lord, you know right well you did,
And with them words of so sweet breath composed
As made the things more rich. Their perfume lost,
100   Take these again, for to the noble mind
Rich gifts wax poor when givers prove unkind.
There, my lord.

103 HAMLET   Ha, ha! Are you honest?

OPHELIA   My lord?

HAMLET   Are you fair?

OPHELIA   What means your lordship?

HAMLET   That if you be honest and fair, your honesty
should admit no discourse to your beauty.

109 OPHELIA   Could beauty, my lord, have better commerce
110   than with honesty?

HAMLET   Ay, truly; for the power of beauty will sooner
transform honesty from what it is to a bawd than the

---

86 *pitch* height (of a soaring falcon's flight)   87 *regard* consideration   88
Soft you now be quiet, stop talking   89 *orisons* prayers   103 *honest* (1) truthful, (2) chaste   109 *commerce* intercourse

force of honesty can translate beauty into his likeness.
This was sometime a paradox, but now the time gives it   114
proof. I did love you once.

OPHELIA   Indeed, my lord, you made me believe so.

HAMLET   You should not have believed me, for virtue
cannot so inoculate our old stock but we shall relish of   118
it. I loved you not.

OPHELIA   I was the more deceived.   120

HAMLET   Get thee to a nunnery. Why wouldst thou be a   121
breeder of sinners? I am myself indifferent honest, but   122
yet I could accuse me of such things that it were better
my mother had not borne me: I am very proud, re-
vengeful, ambitious, with more offenses at my beck
than I have thoughts to put them in, imagination to
give them shape, or time to act them in. What should
such fellows as I do crawling between earth and
heaven? We are arrant knaves all; believe none of us. Go
thy ways to a nunnery. Where's your father?   130

OPHELIA   At home, my lord.

HAMLET   Let the doors be shut upon him, that he may
play the fool nowhere but in's own house. Farewell.

OPHELIA   O, help him, you sweet heavens!

HAMLET   If thou dost marry, I'll give thee this plague for
thy dowry: be thou as chaste as ice, as pure as snow,
thou shalt not escape calumny. Get thee to a nunnery,
farewell. Or if thou wilt needs marry, marry a fool, for
wise men know well enough what monsters you make   139
of them. To a nunnery, go, and quickly too. Farewell.   140

OPHELIA   Heavenly powers, restore him!

HAMLET   I have heard of your paintings well enough.
God hath given you one face, and you make yourselves
another. You jig and amble, and you lisp; you nick-

---

114 *a paradox* an idea contrary to common opinion   118 *inoculate* graft (in
horticulture); *relish* have a flavor   121 *nunnery* house of nuns (but also
slang, by opposition, for "whorehouse")   122 *indifferent honest* moderately
respectable   139 *monsters* cuckolds (?)

145   name God's creatures and make your wantonness your
        ignorance. Go to, I'll no more on't; it hath made me
        mad. I say we will have no more marriage. Those that
        are married already – all but one – shall live. The rest
        shall keep as they are. To a nunnery, go.   *Exit.*

OPHELIA
150   O, what a noble mind is here o'erthrown!
        The courtier's, soldier's, scholar's, eye, tongue, sword,
152   Th' expectancy and rose of the fair state,
153   The glass of fashion and the mold of form,
        Th' observed of all observers, quite, quite down!
        And I, of ladies most deject and wretched,
        That sucked the honey of his music vows,
        Now see that noble and most sovereign reason
        Like sweet bells jangled, out of time and harsh,
159   That unmatched form and feature of blown youth
160   Blasted with ecstasy. O, woe is me
        T' have seen what I have seen, see what I see.
            Enter King and Polonius.

KING
162   Love? his affections do not that way tend,
        Nor what he spake, though it lacked form a little,
        Was not like madness. There's something in his soul
        O'er which his melancholy sits on brood,
166   And I do doubt the hatch and the disclose
        Will be some danger; which for to prevent,
        I have in quick determination
        Thus set it down: he shall with speed to England
170   For the demand of our neglected tribute.
        Haply the seas, and countries different,
        With variable objects, shall expel

---

145 *wantonness* affectation   145–46 *your ignorance* something you pretend
you don't know better than to do   152 *expectancy and rose* fair hope   153
glass mirror   159 *blown* in full flower   160 *Blasted* destroyed (as of a de-
cayed flower); *ecstasy* madness   162 *affections* emotions   166 *doubt* fear;
hatch and the disclose revealing, outcome (as of birds emerging from eggs)

This something-settled matter in his heart,   173
Whereon his brains still beating puts him thus   174
From fashion of himself. What think you on't?   175
POLONIUS
    It shall do well. But yet do I believe
    The origin and commencement of his grief
    Sprung from neglected love. – How now, Ophelia?
    You need not tell us what Lord Hamlet said.
    We heard it all. – My lord, do as you please,   180
    But if you hold it fit, after the play
    Let his queen mother all alone entreat him
    To show his grief. Let her be round with him,   183
    And I'll be placed, so please you, in the ear
    Of all their conference. If she find him not,
    To England send him, or confine him where
    Your wisdom best shall think.
KING   It shall be so.
    Madness in great ones must not unwatched go.
                                            Exeunt.

                        *

❧ **III.2** *Enter Hamlet and three of the Players.*

HAMLET   Speak the speech, I pray you, as I pronounced
it to you, trippingly on the tongue. But if you mouth it,   2
as many of our players do, I had as lief the town crier
spoke my lines. Nor do not saw the air too much with
your hand, thus, but use all gently, for in the very tor-
rent, tempest, and (as I may say) whirlwind of your
passion, you must acquire and beget a temperance that
may give it smoothness. O, it offends me to the soul to
hear a robustious periwig-pated fellow tear a passion to   9

---

173 *something-settled* somewhat settled   174 *still* constantly   175 *fashion of
himself* Hamlet's normal behavior   183 *round* plainspoken
    III.2 Elsinore   2 *trippingly* easily   9 *robustious* boisterous; *periwig-pated*
wig-wearing (as contemporary actors were)

10 tatters, to very rags, to split the ears of the groundlings,
who for the most part are capable of nothing but inex-
12 plicable dumb shows and noise. I would have such a
13 fellow whipped for o'erdoing Termagant. It out-Herods
14 Herod. Pray you avoid it.

PLAYER   I warrant your honor.

HAMLET   Be not too tame neither, but let your own discretion be your tutor. Suit the action to the word, the
word to the action, with this special observance, that
you o'erstep not the modesty of nature. For anything
20 so overdone is from the purpose of playing, whose
end, both at the first and now, was and is, to hold, as
'twere, the mirror up to nature, to show virtue her feature, scorn her own image, and the very age and body
24 of the time his form and pressure. Now this overdone,
25 or come tardy off, though it makes the unskillful laugh,
26 cannot but make the judicious grieve, the censure of
the which one must in your allowance o'erweigh a
whole theater of others. O, there be players that I have
seen play, and heard others praise, and that highly (not
30 to speak it profanely), that neither having th' accent of
Christians, nor the gait of Christian, pagan, nor man,
have so strutted and bellowed that I have thought some
33 of Nature's journeymen had made men, and not made
them well, they imitated humanity so abominably.

35 PLAYER   I hope we have reformed that indifferently with
us.

HAMLET   O, reform it altogether! And let those that play
38 your clowns speak no more than is set down for them,

---

10 *groundlings* spectators who paid least and stood in the yard of the open-air
theater   **12** *dumb shows* brief pantomimes sketching dramatic matter to follow   **13** *Termagant* a Saracen "god" in medieval romance and drama   **14**
Herod a stereotypical tyrant, based on the biblical kings of that name and a
common character in pre-Shakespearean religious plays   **20** *from* apart from
24 *pressure* impression (as of a stamp in wax or on a coin)   **25** *come tardy off*
brought off slowly and badly   **26–27** *the censure of the which one* the judgment of even one of whom (note Hamlet's elitist streak)   **33** *journeymen*
workmen not yet masters of their trade   **35** *indifferently* fairly well   **38**
clowns comic actors

for there be of them that will themselves laugh, to set   39
on some quantity of barren spectators to laugh too,   40
though in the meantime some necessary question of
the play be then to be considered. That's villainous and
shows a most pitiful ambition in the fool that uses it.
Go make you ready.   *[Exeunt Players.]*
     Enter Polonius, Guildenstern, and Rosencrantz.
How now, my lord? Will the king hear this piece of
work?

POLONIUS   And the queen too, and that presently.   47

HAMLET   Bid the players make haste.   *[Exit Polonius.]*
Will you two help to hasten them?

ROSENCRANTZ   Ay, my lord.   *Exeunt they two.*   50

HAMLET   What, ho, Horatio!
     Enter Horatio.

HORATIO
Here, sweet lord, at your service.

HAMLET
Horatio, thou art e'en as just a man   53
As e'er my conversation coped withal.   54

HORATIO
O, my dear lord –

HAMLET   Nay, do not think I flatter.
For what advancement may I hope from thee,
That no revenue hast but thy good spirits
To feed and clothe thee? Why should the poor be flat-
   tered?
No, let the candied tongue lick absurd pomp,
And crook the pregnant hinges of the knee   60
Where thrift may follow fawning. Dost thou hear?   61
Since my dear soul was mistress of her choice
And could of men distinguish her election,
S' hath sealed thee for herself, for thou hast been   64

---

39 *of them* some of them **47** *presently* at once **53** *just* well-balanced **54**
conversation coped withal dealings (not just talk) with men encountered **60**
pregnant quick to move **61** *thrift* profit **64** *S' hath sealed* she (the soul) has
marked

As one in suff'ring all that suffers nothing,
A man that Fortune's buffets and rewards
Hast ta'en with equal thanks; and blessed are those
68   Whose blood and judgment are so well commeddled
69   That they are not a pipe for Fortune's finger
70   To sound what stop she please. Give me that man
That is not passion's slave, and I will wear him
In my heart's core, ay, in my heart of heart,
As I do thee. Something too much of this —
There is a play tonight before the king.
One scene of it comes near the circumstance
Which I have told thee, of my father's death.
I prithee, when thou seest that act afoot,
78   Even with the very comment of thy soul
79   Observe my uncle. If his occulted guilt
80   Do not itself unkennel in one speech,
81   It is a damnèd ghost that we have seen,
And my imaginations are as foul
83   As Vulcan's stithy. Give him heedful note,
For I mine eyes will rivet to his face,
And after we will both our judgments join
86   In censure of his seeming.

HORATIO   Well, my lord.
87   If a steal aught the whilst this play is playing,
And scape detecting, I will pay the theft.

    Enter Trumpets and Kettledrums, King, Queen,
    Polonius, Ophelia [, Rosencrantz, Guildenstern, and
    other Lords attendant].

89   HAMLET   They are coming to the play. I must be idle.
90   Get you a place.

---

68 *blood* passion; *commeddled* mingled **69** *a pipe* an instrument like a recorder or flute **78** *the very . . . soul* thy deepest consideration **79** *occulted* hidden **80** *unkennel* dislodge, come out (literally, *unkennel* = to drive a fox from its hole; *kennel* also means "gutter") **81** *a damnèd ghost* an evil spirit, a devil (as thought of in II.2.537 ff.) **83** *stithy* smithy (hence, "black," "hellish") **86** *censure of* sentence upon **87–88** *If . . . theft* (Horatio analogizes Claudius with the pickpockets who haunted the Elizabethan public theater) **87** *a* he **89** *be idle* be foolish, act like the madman

KING   How fares our cousin Hamlet?   91

HAMLET   Excellent, i' faith, of the chameleon's dish. I eat   92
the air, promise-crammed. You cannot feed capons so.

KING   I have nothing with this answer, Hamlet. These
words are not mine.   95

HAMLET   No, nor mine now. *[To Polonius]* My lord, you
played once i' th' university, you say?

POLONIUS   That did I, my lord, and was accounted a
good actor.

HAMLET   What did you enact?   100

POLONIUS   I did enact Julius Caesar. I was killed i' th'
Capitol; Brutus killed me.   102

HAMLET   It was a brute part of him to kill so capital a calf
there. Be the players ready?

ROSENCRANTZ   Ay, my lord. They stay upon your pa-   105
tience.

QUEEN   Come hither, my dear Hamlet, sit by me.

HAMLET   No, good mother. Here's metal more attractive.

POLONIUS   *[To the King]* O ho! do you mark that?

HAMLET   Lady, shall I lie in your lap?   110

OPHELIA   No, my lord.

HAMLET   Do you think I meant country matters?   112

OPHELIA   I think nothing, my lord.

HAMLET   That's a fair thought to lie between maids' legs.

OPHELIA   What is, my lord?

HAMLET   Nothing.

OPHELIA   You are merry, my lord.

HAMLET   Who, I?

OPHELIA   Ay, my lord.

---

91 *cousin* nephew   **92** *chameleon's dish* i.e., air (which was believed the
chameleon's food; Hamlet jokingly misunderstands *fares*)   **95** *not mine* not
for me as the asker of my question   **102** *Capitol* (it was on the summit of the
Capitoline hill, overlooking classical Rome's Forum)   **105–6** *stay upon your
patience* await your indulgence   **110** *lie . . . lap* have sexual intercourse with
you   **112** *country* rustic (with a bawdy pun on the first syllable: "cunt-try")

120 HAMLET   O God, your only jig-maker! What should a
man do but be merry? For look you how cheerfully my
mother looks, and my father died within's two hours.

OPHELIA   Nay, 'tis twice two months, my lord.

HAMLET   So long? Nay then, let the devil wear black, for
125 I'll have a suit of sables. O heavens! die two months
ago, and not forgotten yet? Then there's hope a great
man's memory may outlive his life half a year. But, by'r
Lady, a must build churches then, or else shall a suffer
129 not thinking on, with the hobbyhorse, whose epitaph is
130 "For O, for O, the hobbyhorse is forgot!"

The trumpets sounds. Dumb show follows.
Enter a King and a Queen [very lovingly], the Queen
embracing him, and he her. [She kneels; and makes show of
protestation unto him.] He takes her up, and declines his
head upon her neck. He lies him down upon a bank of
flowers. She, seeing him asleep, leaves him. Anon come in
another man: takes off his crown, kisses it, pours poison in
the sleeper's ears, and leaves him. The Queen returns, finds
the King dead, makes passionate action. The poisoner, with
some three or four, come in again, seem to condole with her.
The dead body is carried away. The poisoner woos the Queen
with gifts; she seems harsh awhile, but in the end accepts love.
[Exeunt.]

OPHELIA   What means this, my lord?

132 HAMLET   Marry, this is miching mallecho; it means mis-
chief.

134 OPHELIA   Belike this show imports the argument of the
play.
Enter Prologue.

---

120 *jig-maker* writer of jigs (see II.2.440)   **125** *sables* black furs (luxurious
garb, not for mourning)   **129** *hobbyhorse* (an imitation horse worn by a performer in May games and morris dances so the performer appeared to ride
the horse suspended from his own shoulders)   **132** *miching mallecho* sneak-
ing iniquity   **134** *argument* (1) subject, (2) plot outline

HAMLET   We shall know by this fellow. The players cannot keep counsel; they'll tell all.

OPHELIA   Will a tell us what this show meant?

HAMLET   Ay, or any show that you will show him. Be not you ashamed to show, he'll not shame to tell you what   *140* it means.

OPHELIA   You are naught, you are naught. I'll mark the   *142* play.

PROLOGUE

　　　　　For us and for our tragedy,
　　　　　Here stooping to your clemency,
　　　　　We beg your hearing patiently.   *[Exit.]*

HAMLET   Is this a prologue, or the posy of a ring?   *147*

OPHELIA   'Tis brief, my lord.

HAMLET   As woman's love.

　　　Enter [two Players as] King and Queen.

PLAYER KING

Full thirty times hath Phoebus' cart gone round   *150*
Neptune's salt wash and Tellus' orbèd ground,   *151*
And thirty dozen moons with borrowed sheen   *152*
About the world have times twelve thirties been,   *153*
Since love our hearts, and Hymen did our hands,   *154*
Unite commutual in most sacred bands.   *155*

PLAYER QUEEN

So many journeys may the sun and moon
Make us again count o'er ere love be done!
But woe is me, you are so sick of late,
So far from cheer and from your former state,
That I distrust you. Yet, though I distrust,   *160*
Discomfort you, my lord, it nothing must.
For women fear too much, even as they love,
And women's fear and love hold quantity,   *163*

---

142 *naught* indecent, offensive   147 *posy* brief motto in rhyme often engraved inside a *ring*   150 *Phoebus' cart* the sun's chariot   151 *Tellus* Roman goddess of the earth   152 *borrowed* i.e., taken from the sun   153 *twelve thirties* i.e., thirty years   154 *Hymen* the Greek god of marriage   155 *commutual* mutually   160 *distrust you* fear for you   163 *quantity* proportion

In neither aught, or in extremity.
Now what my love is, proof hath made you know,
And as my love is sized, my fear is so.
Where love is great, the littlest doubts are fear;
Where little fears grow great, great love grows there.

PLAYER KING

. Faith, I must leave thee, love, and shortly too;

170   My operant powers their functions leave to do.
And thou shalt live in this fair world behind,
Honored, beloved, and haply one as kind
For husband shalt thou —

PLAYER QUEEN   O, confound the rest!
Such love must needs be treason in my breast.
In second husband let me be accurst!

176   None wed the second but who killed the first.

177   HAMLET   *[Aside]* That's wormwood.

PLAYER QUEEN

178   The instances that second marriage move
   Are base respects of thrift, but none of love.

180   A second time I kill my husband dead
When second husband kisses me in bed.

PLAYER KING

I do believe you think what now you speak,
But what we do determine oft we break.

184   Purpose is but the slave to memory,

185   Of violent birth, but poor validity,

186   Which now, the fruit unripe, sticks on the tree,
But fall unshaken when they mellow be.
Most necessary 'tis that we forget
To pay ourselves what to ourselves is debt.

190   What to ourselves in passion we propose,

---

170 *operant powers* active bodily forces   **176** *None . . . first* (a general statement: *None* is plural)   **177** *wormwood* a bitter herb   **178** *instances* motives **184** *Purpose . . . memory* i.e., fulfilling our intentions depends upon our remembering them, and memory may be faulty (see ll. 190–91, 209); *slave to* i.e., dependent on   **185** *validity* strength   **186–87** *Which . . . be* i.e., as time passes, the *fruit* ripens and falls, just as *purpose* fails when not sustained by *memory*

The passion ending, doth the purpose lose.
The violence of either grief or joy
Their own enactures with themselves destroy.   193
Where joy most revels, grief doth most lament;
Grief joys, joy grieves, on slender accident.
This world is not for aye, nor 'tis not strange
That even our loves should with our fortunes change,
For 'tis a question left us yet to prove,   198
Whether love lead fortune, or else fortune love.
The great man down, you mark his favorite flies,   *200*
The poor advanced makes friends of enemies;
And hitherto doth love on fortune tend,
For who not needs shall never lack a friend,
And who in want a hollow friend doth try,
Directly seasons him his enemy.   205
But, orderly to end where I begun,
Our wills and fates do so contrary run   207
That our devices still are overthrown;   208
Our thoughts are ours, their ends none of our own.
So think thou wilt no second husband wed,   *210*
But die thy thoughts when thy first lord is dead.

PLAYER QUEEN
  Nor earth to me give food, nor heaven light,
  Sport and repose lock from me day and night,
  To desperation turn my trust and hope,
  An anchor's cheer in prison be my scope,   215
  Each opposite that blanks the face of joy   216
  Meet what I would have well, and it destroy,
  Both here and hence pursue me lasting strife,   218
  If, once a widow, ever I be wife!

HAMLET   If she should break it now!   *220*

PLAYER KING
  'Tis deeply sworn. Sweet, leave me here a while.

---

193 *enactures* fulfillments   198 *prove* test   205 *seasons him* ripens him into
207 *wills* desires, intentions   208 *still* always   215 *An anchor's cheer* a hermit's way of life (*anchor* = anchorite – i.e., hermit); *scope* limit, all I may have
216 *blanks* blanches, makes pale   218 *hence* in the next world

My spirits grow dull, and fain I would beguile
The tedious day with sleep.

PLAYER QUEEN   Sleep rock thy brain, *[He sleeps.]*
And never come mischance between us twain!   *[Exit.]*

HAMLET   Madam, how like you this play?

QUEEN   The lady doth protest too much, methinks.

HAMLET   O, but she'll keep her word.

228   KING   Have you heard the argument? Is there no offense
in't?

230   HAMLET   No, no, they do but jest, poison in jest; no offense i' th' world.

KING   What do you call the play?

233   HAMLET   "The Mousetrap." Marry, how? Tropically.
This play is the image of a murder done in Vienna.
Gonzago is the duke's name; his wife, Baptista. You
shall see anon. 'Tis a knavish piece of work, but what of
237   that? Your majesty, and we that have free souls, it
238   touches us not. Let the galled jade wince; our withers
are unwrung.

    Enter [a Player as] Lucianus.

240   This is one Lucianus, nephew to the king.

241   OPHELIA   You are as good as a chorus, my lord.

HAMLET   I could interpret between you and your love, if
243   I could see the puppets dallying.

244   OPHELIA   You are keen, my lord, you are keen.

HAMLET   It would cost you a groaning to take off mine
edge.

OPHELIA   Still better, and worse.

HAMLET   So you mis-take your husbands. – Begin, murderer. Leave thy damnable faces and begin. Come, the
250   croaking raven doth bellow for revenge.

---

228 *argument* (1) subject, (2) plot outline **233** *Tropically* in the way of a
"trope" or rhetorical figure (with a play on "trapically" – as in *Mousetrap*)
237 *free* guiltless **238** *galled* sore-backed; *jade* horse; *withers* shoulders (of a
horse) **241** *a chorus* one in a play who explains the action **243** *puppets* i.e.,
you and your lover as in a puppet show **244–46** *keen . . . edge* (Hamlet
turns *keen* wit into the bite of sexual desire whose gratification might bring
groaning in sexual pleasure and/or pain in childbirth)

PLAYER LUCIANUS
   Thoughts black, hands apt, drugs fit, and time agreeing,
   Confederate season, else no creature seeing,   252
   Thou mixture rank, of midnight weeds collected,
   With Hecate's ban thrice blasted, thrice infected,   254
   Thy natural magic and dire property
   On wholesome life usurps immediately.
    [Pours the poison in his ears.]

HAMLET   A poisons him i' th' garden for his estate. His   257
name's Gonzago. The story is extant, and written in
very choice Italian. You shall see anon how the murderer gets the love of Gonzago's wife.   *260*

OPHELIA   The king rises.

QUEEN   How fares my lord?

POLONIUS   Give o'er the play.

KING   Give me some light. Away!

POLONIUS   Lights, lights, lights!
                  Exeunt all but Hamlet and Horatio.

HAMLET
     Why, let the stricken deer go weep,
       The hart ungallèd play.
     For some must watch, while some must sleep;   268
       Thus runs the world away.
   Would not this, sir, and a forest of feathers – if the rest   270
of my fortunes turn Turk with me – with Provincial   271
roses on my razed shoes, get me a fellowship in a cry of   272
players?

HORATIO   Half a share.

HAMLET   A whole one, I.

---

252 *Confederate season* the moment agreeing with my plan   **254** *Hecate* the
goddess of magic arts; *ban* curse   **257** *A* he   **268** *watch* stay awake at night
270 *feathers* plumes for actors' costumes   **271** *turn Turk* turn renegade, like
a Christian turning Muslim   **271–72** *Provincial roses* rosettes that covered
shoelaces in fashionable garb (the Provençal rose is a large-blossomed cab-
bage rose)   **272** *razed* decorated with slashed patterns; *fellowship* financial
partnership (such as Shakespeare had) in a theatrical company, a *share* (l.
274); *cry* pack (of hounds)

276   For thou dost know, O Damon dear,
                   This realm dismantled was
               Of Jove himself; and now reigns here
279   A very, very – pajock.

280 HORATIO   You might have rhymed.

HAMLET   O good Horatio, I'll take the ghost's word for a
thousand pound. Didst perceive?

HORATIO   Very well, my lord.

HAMLET   Upon the talk of the poisoning?

HORATIO   I did very well note him.

286 HAMLET   Aha! Come, some music! Come, the recorders!
287   For if the king like not the comedy,
288   Why then, belike he likes it not, perdy.
       Come, some music!
           Enter Rosencrantz and Guildenstern.

290 GUILDENSTERN   Good my lord, vouchsafe me a word
with you.

292 HAMLET   Sir, a whole history.

GUILDENSTERN   The king, sir –

HAMLET   Ay, sir, what of him?

295 GUILDENSTERN   Is in his retirement marvelous distempered.

HAMLET   With drink, sir?

298 GUILDENSTERN   No, my lord, with choler.

HAMLET   Your wisdom should show itself more richer to
300 signify this to the doctor, for for me to put him to his
purgation would perhaps plunge him into more choler.

GUILDENSTERN   Good my lord, put your discourse into
303 some frame, and start not so wildly from my affair.

304 HAMLET   I am tame, sir; pronounce.

---

276 *Damon* (conventional name for a shepherd-friend in classical Greco-Roman and early modern pastoral literature)   279 *pajock* patchock, disreputable fellow   286 *recorders* wind instruments (cf. l. 69)   287 *comedy* i.e., any drama (Latin: *comoedia*), not just one meant to amuse   288 *perdy* by God (French: *pardieu*)   292 *history* lengthy discourse   295–96 *distempered* out of temper, vexed (twisted by Hamlet into "drunk")   298 *choler* anger   303 *frame* logical order   304 *tame* calm (i.e., quietly awaiting your speech)

GUILDENSTERN   The queen, your mother, in most great affliction of spirit hath sent me to you.

HAMLET   You are welcome.

GUILDENSTERN   Nay, good my lord, this courtesy is not of the right breed. If it shall please you to make me a wholesome answer, I will do your mother's command-   310
ment. If not, your pardon and my return shall be the end of my business.

HAMLET   Sir, I cannot.

ROSENCRANTZ   What, my lord?

HAMLET   Make you a wholesome answer; my wit's dis-eased. But, sir, such answer as I can make, you shall command, or rather, as you say, my mother. Therefore no more, but to the matter. My mother, you say –

ROSENCRANTZ   Then thus she says: your behavior hath struck her into amazement and admiration.   320

HAMLET   O wonderful son, that can so stonish a mother! But is there no sequel at the heels of this mother's ad-miration? Impart.

ROSENCRANTZ   She desires to speak with you in her closet ere you go to bed.   325

HAMLET   We shall obey, were she ten times our mother. Have you any further trade with us?   327

ROSENCRANTZ   My lord, you once did love me.

HAMLET   And do still, by these pickers and stealers.   329

ROSENCRANTZ   Good my lord, what is your cause of dis-   330
temper? You do surely bar the door upon your own lib-erty, if you deny your griefs to your friend.

HAMLET   Sir, I lack advancement.

ROSENCRANTZ   How can that be, when you have the voice of the king himself for your succession in Den-   335
mark?

---

310 *wholesome* i.e., rational   320 *admiration* wonder, astonishment (cf. *stonish*, l. 321)   325 *closet* private room   327 *trade* business   329 *pickers and stealers* i.e., hands (a quotation from the Anglican catechism)   330 *Good my lord* my good lord   335 *voice . . . succession* (cf. I.2.109)

337   HAMLET Ay, sir, but "while the grass grows" – the
proverb is something musty.
       Enter the Players with recorders.
339   O, the recorders. Let me see one. To withdraw with
340   you – why do you go about to recover the wind of me,
341   as if you would drive me into a toil?
       GUILDENSTERN O my lord, if my duty be too bold, my
343   love is too unmannerly.
       HAMLET I do not well understand that. Will you play
upon this pipe?
       GUILDENSTERN My lord, I cannot.
       HAMLET I pray you.
       GUILDENSTERN Believe me, I cannot.
       HAMLET I do beseech you.
350   GUILDENSTERN I know no touch of it, my lord.
351   HAMLET It is as easy as lying. Govern these ventages
with your fingers and thumb, give it breath with your
mouth, and it will discourse most eloquent music.
Look you, these are the stops.
       GUILDENSTERN But these cannot I command to any ut-
terance of harmony. I have not the skill.
       HAMLET Why, look you now, how unworthy a thing
you make of me! You would play upon me, you would
seem to know my stops, you would pluck out the heart
360   of my mystery, you would sound me from my lowest
361   note to the top of my compass; and there is much
music, excellent voice, in this little organ, yet cannot
you make it speak. 'Sblood, do you think I am easier to
be played on than a pipe? Call me what instrument you
365   will, though you can fret me, you cannot play upon me.
       Enter Polonius.
       God bless you, sir!

---

337 *while the grass grows* (a proverb, ending: "the horse starves") 339 *withdraw* step aside 340 *recover the wind* come up to windward (as a hunter
might in order to drive game into the *toil*) 341 *toil* snare 343 *is too unmannerly* leads me beyond the restraint of good manners 351 *ventages*
holes, vents 361 *compass* range 365 *fret* irritate (with wordplay on the fin-
gering of some stringed musical instruments)

POLONIUS   My lord, the queen would speak with you, and presently.   368

HAMLET   Do you see yonder cloud that's almost in shape of a camel?   370

POLONIUS   By th' mass and 'tis, like a camel indeed.

HAMLET   Methinks it is like a weasel.

POLONIUS   It is backed like a weasel.

HAMLET   Or like a whale.

POLONIUS   Very like a whale.

HAMLET   Then I will come to my mother by and by.   376
     [Aside] They fool me to the top of my bent. – I will   377
     come by and by.

POLONIUS   I will say so.   *[Exit.]*

HAMLET   "By and by" is easily said. Leave me, friends.   380
                                  [Exeunt all but Hamlet.]
'Tis now the very witching time of night,   381
When churchyards yawn, and hell itself breathes out
Contagion to this world. Now could I drink hot blood
And do such bitter business as the day
Would quake to look on. Soft, now to my mother.
O heart, lose not thy nature; let not ever   386
The soul of Nero enter this firm bosom.   387
Let me be cruel, not unnatural;
I will speak daggers to her, but use none.
My tongue and soul in this be hypocrites: 390
How in my words somever she be shent,   391
To give them seals never, my soul, consent!   *Exit.*   392
                         *

∾ **III.3** *Enter King, Rosencrantz, and Guildenstern.*

KING
     I like him not, nor stands it safe with us

---

368 *presently* at once   **376** *by and by* immediately   **377** *bent* (see II.2.30 n.)
381 *witching* i.e., associated with witches   **386** *nature* filial love   **387** *Nero*
Roman emperor and murderer of his mother, Agrippina   **391** *shent* re-
proved   **392** *seals* authentications in actions; *never* may never
     III.3 Elsinore

To let his madness range. Therefore prepare you.
3   I your commission will forthwith dispatch,
    And he to England shall along with you.
5   The terms of our estate may not endure
    Hazard so near's as doth hourly grow
7   Out of his brows.

GUILDENSTERN   We will ourselves provide.
    Most holy and religious fear it is
    To keep those many many bodies safe
10 That live and feed upon your majesty.

ROSENCRANTZ
11 The single and peculiar life is bound
    With all the strength and armor of the mind
13 To keep itself from noyance, but much more
14 That spirit upon whose weal depends and rests
15 The lives of many. The cess of majesty
16 Dies not alone, but like a gulf doth draw
    What's near it with it; or it is a massy wheel
    Fixed on the summit of the highest mount,
    To whose huge spokes ten thousand lesser things
20 Are mortised and adjoined, which when it falls,
    Each small annexment, petty consequence,
22 Attends the boist'rous ruin. Never alone
    Did the king sigh, but with a general groan.

KING
24 Arm you, I pray you, to this speedy voyage,
    For we will fetters put about this fear,
    Which now goes too free-footed.

ROSENCRANTZ   We will haste us.
                                   Exeunt Gentlemen.

    Enter Polonius.

POLONIUS
    My lord, he's going to his mother's closet.

---

3 *commission* written order **5** *terms* circumstances; *estate* royal position
7 *brows* (1) frowns (?), (2) head (i.e., Hamlet's plans) (?) **11** *peculiar* individual **13** *noyance* harm **14** *weal* health **15** *cess* decease, cessation **16**
gulf whirlpool **22** *Attends* joins in (like a royal attendant) **24** *Arm* prepare;
speedy immediate

Behind the arras I'll convey myself   28
To hear the process. I'll warrant she'll tax him home,   29
And, as you said, and wisely was it said,   30
'Tis meet that some more audience than a mother,
Since nature makes them partial, should o'erhear
The speech, of vantage. Fare you well, my liege.   33
I'll call upon you ere you go to bed
And tell you what I know.   35
KING   Thanks, dear my lord.
                                    Exit [Polonius].

O, my offense is rank, it smells to heaven;
It hath the primal eldest curse upon't,   37
A brother's murder. Pray can I not,
Though inclination be as sharp as will.
My stronger guilt defeats my strong intent,   40
And like a man to double business bound
I stand in pause where I shall first begin,
And both neglect. What if this cursèd hand
Were thicker than itself with brother's blood,
Is there not rain enough in the sweet heavens   45
To wash it white as snow? Whereto serves mercy
But to confront the visage of offense?   47
And what's in prayer but this twofold force,
To be forestallèd ere we come to fall,
Or pardoned being down? Then I'll look up.   50
My fault is past, but, O, what form of prayer
Can serve my turn? "Forgive me my foul murder"?
That cannot be, since I am still possessed
Of those effects for which I did the murder,   54
My crown, mine own ambition, and my queen.
May one be pardoned and retain th' offense?   56

---

28 *arras* cloth wall hanging   **29** *process* proceedings; *tax him home* reprimand
him severely   **33** *of vantage* from an advantageous position   **35** *dear my lord*
my dear lord   **37** *primal eldest curse* God's curse on the biblical Cain, who
also murdered a brother (Genesis 4:11–12)   **45** *rain* i.e., heavenly mercy
(see Ecclesiasticus 35:20 and *The Merchant of Venice*, IV.1.182–83)   **47** *offense* sin   **54** *effects* things I acquired   **56** *offense* i.e., what Claudius has
gained by murdering old Hamlet

In the corrupted currents of this world
58   Offense's gilded hand may shove by justice,
      And oft 'tis seen the wicked prize itself
60   Buys out the law. But 'tis not so above.
61   There is no shuffling; there the action lies
      In his true nature, and we ourselves compelled,
63   Even to the teeth and forehead of our faults,
      To give in evidence. What then? What rests?
      Try what repentance can. What can it not?
      Yet what can it when one cannot repent?
      O wretched state! O bosom black as death!
68   O limèd soul, that struggling to be free
69   Art more engaged! Help, angels! Make assay.
70   Bow, stubborn knees, and, heart with strings of steel,
      Be soft as sinews of the newborn babe.
      All may be well.
          [He kneels.]
          Enter Hamlet.

HAMLET
73   Now might I do it pat, now a is a-praying,
      And now I'll do't. And so a goes to heaven,
75   And so am I revenged. That would be scanned.
      A villain kills my father, and for that
      I, his sole son, do this same villain send
      To heaven.
      Why, this is [hire and salary,] not revenge.
80   A took my father grossly, full of bread,
81   With all his crimes broad blown, as flush as May;
82   And how his audit stands, who knows save heaven?
      But in our circumstance and course of thought,
      'Tis heavy with him; and am I then revenged,

---

58 *gilded* gold-laden   61 *shuffling* cheating; *action* legal proceeding (in heaven's court)   63 *to the teeth and forehead* face-to-face   68 *limèd* caught in birdlime, a gluey material spread as a bird snare   69 *engaged* embedded; *assay* essay, attempt   73 *pat* opportunely   73, 74 *a* he   75 *scanned* studied, thought about   80 *grossly* morally unprepared; *full of bread* i.e., sensually gratified (hence not ready for a purified death)   81 *broad blown* fully blossomed; *flush* vigorous   82 *audit* account

To take him in the purging of his soul,
When he is fit and seasoned for his passage?
No.
Up, sword, and know thou a more horrid hent.   88
When he is drunk asleep, or in his rage,
Or in th' incestuous pleasure of his bed,   90
At game a-swearing, or about some act
That has no relish of salvation in't –   92
Then trip him, that his heels may kick at heaven,
And that his soul may be as damned and black
As hell, whereto it goes. My mother stays.
This physic but prolongs thy sickly days.   *Exit.*
KING   *[Rises.]*
My words fly up, my thoughts remain below.
Words without thoughts never to heaven go.   *Exit.*

                              *

∾ **III.4** *Enter [Queen] Gertrude and Polonius.*

POLONIUS
A will come straight. Look you lay home to him.   1
Tell him his pranks have been too broad to bear with,   2
And that your grace hath screened and stood between
Much heat and him. I'll silence me even here.
Pray you be round.   5
QUEEN   I'll warrant you; fear me not. Withdraw; I hear
him coming.
      [Polonius hides behind the arras.]
      Enter Hamlet.
HAMLET
Now, mother, what's the matter?
QUEEN
Hamlet, thou hast thy father much offended.

---

88 *hent* occasion   92 *relish* flavor
    III.4 Elsinore: Gertrude's private rooms   1 *A* he; *lay home to* tax (see
III.3.29)   2 *broad* unrestrained   5 *round* plainspoken

HAMLET

10   Mother, you have my father much offended.

QUEEN

11   Come, come, you answer with an idle tongue.

HAMLET

Go, go, you question with a wicked tongue.

QUEEN

13   Why, how now, Hamlet?

HAMLET   What's the matter now?

QUEEN

14   Have you forgot me?

HAMLET   No, by the rood, not so!
You are the queen, your husband's brother's wife,
And (would it were not so) you are my mother.

QUEEN

Nay, then I'll set those to you that can speak.

HAMLET

Come, come, and sit you down. You shall not budge.

19   You go not till I set you up a glass

20   Where you may see the inmost part of you.

QUEEN

What wilt thou do? Thou wilt not murder me?
Help, ho!

23   POLONIUS   *[Behind]* What, ho! help!

HAMLET   *[Draws.]*

How now? a rat? Dead for a ducat, dead!
    [Thrusts through the arras and kills Polonius.]

POLONIUS   *[Behind]*

O, I am slain!

QUEEN   O me, what hast thou done?

HAMLET

Nay, I know not. Is it the king?

QUEEN

O, what a rash and bloody deed is this!

---

11 *an idle* a foolish   13 *matter* subject, point of our discussion   14 *rood*
cross   19 *glass* mirror   23 s.d. *Behind* (for the action here, see IV.1.8–12)

HAMLET
  A bloody deed – almost as bad, good mother,
  As kill a king, and marry with his brother.
QUEEN
  As kill a king?   *30*
HAMLET   Ay, lady, it was my word.
    [Looks behind the arras and sees Polonius.]
  Thou wretched, rash, intruding fool, farewell!
  I took thee for thy better. Take thy fortune.
  Thou find'st to be too busy is some danger. –
  Leave wringing of your hands. Peace, sit you down
  And let me wring your heart, for so I shall
  If it be made of penetrable stuff,
  If damnèd custom have not brazed it so   *37*
  That it be proof and bulwark against sense.   *38*
QUEEN
  What have I done that thou dar'st wag thy tongue
  In noise so rude against me?   *40*
HAMLET   Such an act
  That blurs the grace and blush of modesty,
  Calls virtue hypocrite, takes off the rose
  From the fair forehead of an innocent love,
  And sets a blister there, makes marriage vows   *44*
  As false as dicers' oaths. O, such a deed
  As from the body of contraction plucks   *46*
  The very soul, and sweet religion makes   *47*
  A rhapsody of words! Heaven's face does glow,   *48*
  O'er this solidity and compound mass,   *49*
  With heated visage, as against the doom,   *50*
  Is thought-sick at the act.

---

37 *custom* habit; *brazed* hardened like brass   38 *proof* armor; *sense* feeling
44 *blister* brand (in the early modern period, convicted prostitutes were
sometimes branded on the forehead; see IV.5.118–19)   46 *contraction* the
category, contract-making, of which marriage is an instance   47 *religion* i.e.,
sacred marriage vows   48 *rhapsody* confused heap   49 *compound mass* the
earth as compounded of the four elements (see II.2.278 n.)   50 *against* in
expectation of; *doom* Day of Judgment

QUEEN   Ay me, what act,
52   That roars so loud and thunders in the index?
HAMLET
     Look here upon this picture, and on this,
54   The counterfeit presentment of two brothers.
     See what a grace was seated on this brow:
56   Hyperion's curls, the front of Jove himself,
     An eye like Mars, to threaten and command,
58   A station like the herald Mercury
     New lighted on a heaven-kissing hill –
60   A combination and a form indeed
     Where every god did seem to set his seal
     To give the world assurance of a man.
     This was your husband. Look you now what follows.
     Here is your husband, like a mildewed ear
     Blasting his wholesome brother. Have you eyes?
     Could you on this fair mountain leave to feed,
67   And batten on this moor? Ha! have you eyes?
     You cannot call it love, for at your age
69   The heyday in the blood is tame, it's humble,
70   And waits upon the judgment, and what judgment
71   Would step from this to this? Sense sure you have,
72   Else could you not have motion, but sure that sense
73   Is apoplexed, for madness would not err,
74   Nor sense to ecstasy was ne'er so thralled
     But it reserved some quantity of choice
76   To serve in such a difference. What devil was't
77   That thus hath cozened you at hoodman-blind?
     Eyes without feeling, feeling without sight,

---

52 *index* table of contents preceding the body of a book, prefatory matter
54 *counterfeit presentment* representation in a portrait   56 *Hyperion* the sun god; *front* forehead   58 *station* stance; *herald Mercury* messenger of the Olympian gods, typifying grace   67 *batten* feed greedily   69 *heyday* excitement of passion   70 *waits upon* yields to   71 *Sense* feeling   72 *motion* desire, impulse   73 *apoplexed* paralyzed   74 *ecstasy* madness   76 *serve . . . difference* i.e., make a choice where there is such great difference   77 *cozened* cheated; *hoodman-blind* blindman's buff

Ears without hands or eyes, smelling sans all,   79
Or but a sickly part of one true sense   *80*
Could not so mope.   81
O shame, where is thy blush? Rebellious hell,
If thou canst mutine in a matron's bones,   83
To flaming youth let virtue be as wax
And melt in her own fire. Proclaim no shame
When the compulsive ardor gives the charge,   86
Since frost itself as actively doth burn,
And reason panders will.   88
QUEEN   O Hamlet, speak no more.
Thou turn'st my eyes into my very soul,
And there I see such black and grainèd spots   90
As will leave there their tinct.   91
HAMLET   Nay, but to live
In the rank sweat of an enseamèd bed,   92
Stewed in corruption, honeying and making love
Over the nasty sty —
QUEEN   O, speak to me no more.
These words like daggers enter in my ears.
No more, sweet Hamlet.
HAMLET   A murderer and a villain,
A slave that is not twentieth part the tithe   97
Of your precedent lord, a vice of kings,   98
A cutpurse of the empire and the rule,   99
That from a shelf the precious diadem stole   *100*
And put it in his pocket —   101
QUEEN   No more.
    Enter [the] Ghost [in his nightgown].

---

79 *sans* without (French)   81 *mope* be in a daze   83 *mutine* mutiny   86
compulsive compelling; *gives the charge* delivers the attack   88 *panders will*
acts as procurer for desire (implied: *reason* should control *will* — desire in
general, sexual desire in particular)   90 *grainèd* indelibly dyed ("grain" =
dye)   91 *leave there* (F reads "not leave," which amounts to the same thing);
tinct color   92 *enseamèd* grease-laden ("seam" = grease)   97 *tithe* tenth part
98 *vice* clownish rogue (like the Vice, a staple character of the earlier moral-
ity plays)   99 *cutpurse* skulking thief   101 s.d. *nightgown* dressing gown

HAMLET
    A king of shreds and patches –
103   Save me and hover o'er me with your wings,
    You heavenly guards! What would your gracious figure?

QUEEN
    Alas, he's mad.

HAMLET
    Do you not come your tardy son to chide,
107   That, lapsed in time and passion, lets go by
    Th' important acting of your dread command?
    O, say!

GHOST
110   Do not forget. This visitation
    Is but to whet thy almost blunted purpose.
112   But look, amazement on thy mother sits.
    O, step between her and her fighting soul!
114   Conceit in weakest bodies strongest works.
    Speak to her, Hamlet.

HAMLET   How is it with you, lady?

QUEEN
    Alas, how is't with you,
    That you do bend your eye on vacancy,
118   And with th' incorporal air do hold discourse?
    Forth at your eyes your spirits wildly peep,
120   And as the sleeping soldiers in th' alarm
121   Your bedded hair, like life in excrements,
122   Start up and stand an end. O gentle son,
123   Upon the heat and flame of thy distemper
    Sprinkle cool patience. Whereon do you look?

HAMLET
    On him, on him! Look you, how pale he glares!
    His form and cause conjoined, preaching to stones,

103–4 *Save . . . guards* (cf. 1.4.39)   **107** *lapsed . . . passion* having let both the moment and passionate purpose slip   **112** *amazement* bewilderment (literally, "in a maze")   **114** *Conceit* imagination   **118** *incorporal* bodiless   **120** *alarm* call to arms   **121** *excrements* outgrowths   **122** *an* on   **123** *distemper* mental disorder

Would make them capable. – Do not look upon me,   127
Lest with this piteous action you convert
My stern effects. Then what I have to do   129
Will want true color – tears perchance for blood.   130

QUEEN
To whom do you speak this?

HAMLET   Do you see nothing there?

QUEEN
Nothing at all; yet all that is I see.

HAMLET
Nor did you nothing hear?

QUEEN   No, nothing but ourselves.

HAMLET
Why, look you there! Look how it steals away!
My father, in his habit as he lived!
Look where he goes even now out at the portal!

                                               Exit Ghost.

QUEEN
This is the very coinage of your brain.
This bodiless creation ecstasy   138
Is very cunning in.

HAMLET
My pulse as yours doth temperately keep time   *140*
And makes as healthful music. It is not madness
That I have uttered. Bring me to the test,
And I the matter will reword, which madness
Would gambol from. Mother, for love of grace,   144
Lay not that flattering unction to your soul,   145
That not your trespass but my madness speaks.
It will but skin and film the ulcerous place
Whiles rank corruption, mining all within,   148
Infects unseen. Confess yourself to heaven,

---

127 *capable* responsive, able to comprehend   129 *effects* planned actions
130 *want* lack; *color* (1) character, distinguishing quality, (2) tincture (i.e.,
red *blood* rather than colorless *tears*)   138 *ecstasy* madness   144 *gambol* shy
(like a startled horse)   145 *unction* ointment   148 *mining* undermining

150 Repent what's past, avoid what is to come,
And do not spread the compost on the weeds
To make them ranker. Forgive me this my virtue.
153 For in the fatness of these pursy times
Virtue itself of vice must pardon beg,
155 Yea, curb and woo for leave to do him good.

QUEEN
O Hamlet, thou hast cleft my heart in twain.

HAMLET
O, throw away the worser part of it,
And live the purer with the other half.
Good night – but go not to my uncle's bed.
160 Assume a virtue, if you have it not.
161 That monster custom, who all sense doth eat
Of habits evil, is angel yet in this,
That to the use of actions fair and good
164 He likewise gives a frock or livery
That aptly is put on. Refrain tonight,
And that shall lend a kind of easiness
To the next abstinence; the next more easy;
168 For use almost can change the stamp of nature,
169 And either [lodge] the devil, or throw him out
170 With wondrous potency. Once more, good night,
And when you are desirous to be blessed,
I'll blessing beg of you. – For this same lord,
I do repent; but heaven hath pleased it so,
To punish me with this, and this with me,
That I must be their scourge and minister.
176 I will bestow him and will answer well
The death I gave him. So again, good night.
I must be cruel only to be kind.

---

153 *fatness* grossness (physical and moral); *pursy* corpulent (derived from "purse") **155** *curb* bow to **161–62** *custom . . . evil* i.e., long continuance (*custom*) deprives us of knowing that our behavior is *evil* (the next lines explain that we may also become habituated to good behavior) **164** *livery* characteristic dress **168** *use* habit; *stamp* impression, form **169** *lodge* (a conjectural addition to Q2, which lacks a verb to parallel *throw*) **176** *bestow* stow, hide; *answer* be responsible for

This bad begins, and worse remains behind.   179
One word more, good lady.   *180*

QUEEN   What shall I do?

HAMLET
Not this, by no means, that I bid you do:
Let the bloat king tempt you again to bed,   182
Pinch wanton on your cheek, call you his mouse,
And let him, for a pair of reechy kisses,   184
Or paddling in your neck with his damned fingers,
Make you to ravel all this matter out,   186
That I essentially am not in madness,
But mad in craft. 'Twere good you let him know,
For who that's but a queen, fair, sober, wise,
Would from a paddock, from a bat, a gib,   190
Such dear concernings hide? Who would do so?   191
No, in despite of sense and secrecy,
Unpeg the basket on the house's top,
Let the birds fly, and like the famous ape,   194
To try conclusions, in the basket creep   195
And break your own neck down.

QUEEN
Be thou assured, if words be made of breath,
And breath of life, I have no life to breathe
What thou hast said to me.

HAMLET
I must to England; you know that?   *200*

QUEEN   Alack,
I had forgot. 'Tis so concluded on.

HAMLET
There's letters sealed, and my two schoolfellows,
Whom I will trust as I will adders fanged,
They bear the mandate; they must sweep my way   204
And marshal me to knavery. Let it work.   205

---

179 *This* i.e., the killing of Polonius; *behind* to come   182 *bloat* flabby   184
reechy filthy (i.e., "reeky")   186 *ravel . . . out* disentangle   190 *paddock* toad;
gib tomcat   191 *dear concernings* matters so personally important   194 *famous ape* (the story, if there was one, is now unknown)   195 *conclusions* ex-
periments   204 *mandate* order   205 *marshal* conduct, lead

206   For 'tis the sport to have the enginer
207   Hoist with his own petard, and 't shall go hard
       But I will delve one yard below their mines
       And blow them at the moon. O, 'tis most sweet
210   When in one line two crafts directly meet.
211   This man shall set me packing.
       I'll lug the guts into the neighbor room.
       Mother, good night. Indeed, this counselor
214   Is now most still, most secret, and most grave,
       Who was in life a foolish prating knave.
       Come, sir, to draw toward an end with you.
       Good night, mother.

                    [Exit the Queen. Then] exit [Hamlet,
                    lugging in Polonius].

                    *

∾ **IV.1** *Enter King and Queen, with Rosencrantz and*
       Guildenstern.

KING
       There's matter in these sighs. These profound heaves
       You must translate; 'tis fit we understand them.
       Where is your son?
QUEEN
4   Bestow this place on us a little while.
                    [Exeunt Rosencrantz and Guildenstern.]
       Ah, mine own lord, what have I seen tonight!
KING
       What, Gertrude? How does Hamlet?
QUEEN
       Mad as the sea and wind when both contend
       Which is the mightier. In his lawless fit,

---

206 *enginer* maker of military engines (the spelling, from Q2, indicates stress
on the first syllable)   207 *Hoist* blown up; *petard* bomb or mine   211 *packing* (1) traveling in a hurry, (2) carrying Polonius's body, (3) plotting, con-
triving   214 *grave* (a bad pun)
    IV.1 Elsinore (the act break here is not in Q2 or F, and Gertrude remains
onstage)   4 *Bestow this place on us* give us privacy (a polite formula)

Behind the arras hearing something stir,
Whips out his rapier, cries "A rat, a rat!"   10
And in this brainish apprehension kills   11
The unseen good old man.
KING   O heavy deed!
It had been so with us, had we been there.   13
His liberty is full of threats to all,
To you yourself, to us, to every one.
Alas, how shall this bloody deed be answered?
It will be laid to us, whose providence   17
Should have kept short, restrained, and out of haunt   18
This mad young man. But so much was our love
We would not understand what was most fit,   20
But, like the owner of a foul disease,
To keep it from divulging, let it feed   22
Even on the pith of life. Where is he gone?
QUEEN
To draw apart the body he hath killed;
O'er whom his very madness, like some ore   25
Among a mineral of metals base,   26
Shows itself pure. A weeps for what is done.   27
KING
O Gertrude, come away!
The sun no sooner shall the mountains touch
But we will ship him hence, and this vile deed   30
We must with all our majesty and skill   31
Both countenance and excuse. Ho, Guildenstern!
     Enter Rosencrantz and Guildenstern.
Friends both, go join you with some further aid.
Hamlet in madness hath Polonius slain,
And from his mother's closet hath he dragged him.
Go seek him out; speak fair, and bring the body

---

11 *brainish* deluded, crazed   13 *us* me (the royal plural and so throughout the scene)   17 *providence* foresight   18 *short* i.e., on a short leash; *haunt* association with others   22 *divulging* becoming known   25 *some* (the printer's manuscript might have read "fine");   *ore* vein of gold   26 *mineral* mine   27 *A* he   31–32 *majesty . . . excuse* i.e., royal power will *countenance,* make publicly acceptable, and *skill,* political savvy, will make palatable

Into the chapel. I pray you haste in this.
                    [Exeunt Rosencrantz and Guildenstern.]
Come, Gertrude, we'll call up our wisest friends
And let them know both what we mean to do
40   And what's untimely done.
Whose whisper o'er the world's diameter,
42   As level as the cannon to his blank
Transports his poisoned shot, may miss our name
And hit the woundless air. O, come away!
My soul is full of discord and dismay.   *Exeunt.*

                    *

∾ **IV.2** *Enter Hamlet.*

1   HAMLET   Safely stowed. *[Calling within]* But soft, what
noise? Who calls on Hamlet? O, here they come.
                    [Enter] Rosencrantz, [Guildenstern,] and others.
ROSENCRANTZ
What have you done, my lord, with the dead body?
HAMLET
4   Compounded it with dust, whereto 'tis kin.
ROSENCRANTZ
Tell us where 'tis, that we may take it thence
And bear it to the chapel.
HAMLET   Do not believe it.
ROSENCRANTZ   Believe what?
HAMLET   That I can keep your counsel and not mine
10   own. Besides, to be demanded of a sponge, what repli-
cation should be made by the son of a king?
ROSENCRANTZ   Take you me for a sponge, my lord?

---

40 *And . . . done* (some words seem to be missing after this partial line; two
editorial guesses: "So, haply, slander" [Capell]; "So envious slander" [Jenkins])
42 *As level* with as direct aim; *blank* mark, central white spot on a target
    IV.2 Elsinore   **1** s.d. *Calling within* (in F, "Gentlemen within" call Ham-
let's name after *stowed*)   **4** *dust . . . kin* (see Genesis 3:19: ". . . dust thou art,
and unto dust shalt thou return")   **10** *sponge* i.e., something that absorbs
(e.g., *counsel*) and may also be squeezed dry (i.e., by Claudius)   **10–11**
replication reply (a legal term)

HAMLET　Ay, sir, that soaks up the king's countenance,　13
his rewards, his authorities. But such officers do the
king best service in the end. He keeps them, like an
ape, in the corner of his jaw, first mouthed, to be last
swallowed. When he needs what you have gleaned, it is
but squeezing you and, sponge, you shall be dry again.

ROSENCRANTZ　I understand you not, my lord.

HAMLET　I am glad of it. A knavish speech sleeps in a　20
foolish ear.

ROSENCRANTZ　My lord, you must tell us where the body
is and go with us to the king.

HAMLET　The body is with the king, but the king is not
with the body. The king is a thing —

GUILDENSTERN　A thing, my lord?

HAMLET　Of nothing. Bring me to him.　　　　*Exeunt.*　27

❋

❧　**IV.3**　*Enter King, and two or three.*

KING
I have sent to seek him and to find the body.
How dangerous is it that this man goes loose!
Yet must not we put the strong law on him;
He's loved of the distracted multitude,　　　　　　4
Who like not in their judgment, but their eyes,
And where 'tis so, th' offender's scourge is weighed,　6
But never the offense. To bear all smooth and even,
This sudden sending him away must seem
Deliberate pause. Diseases desperate grown　　　9
By desperate appliance are relieved,　　　　　　10
Or not at all.
　　　Enter Rosencrantz [, Guildenstern,] and all the rest.
　　　　　How now? What hath befallen?

---

13 *countenance* favor　20 *sleeps in* means nothing to　27 *Of nothing* (cf. the
Anglican Book of Common Prayer, Psalm 144:4, "Man is like a thing of
naught: his time passeth away like a shadow")
　IV.3 Elsinore　4 *distracted* confused　6 *scourge* punishment　9 *Deliberate pause* i.e., something thoughtfully deliberated　10 *appliance* treatment

ROSENCRANTZ
Where the dead body is bestowed, my lord,
We cannot get from him.

KING   But where is he?

ROSENCRANTZ
Without, my lord; guarded, to know your pleasure.

KING
Bring him before us.

ROSENCRANTZ   Ho! Bring in the lord.
They enter [with Hamlet].

KING   Now, Hamlet, where's Polonius?

HAMLET   At supper.

KING   At supper? Where?

19 HAMLET   Not where he eats, but where a is eaten. A cer-
20 tain convocation of politic worms are e'en at him. Your
21 worm is your only emperor for diet. We fat all creatures
    else to fat us, and we fat ourselves for maggots. Your fat
23 king and your lean beggar is but variable service – two
    dishes, but to one table. That's the end.

KING   Alas, alas!

26 HAMLET   A man may fish with the worm that hath eat of
    a king, and eat of the fish that hath fed of that worm.

KING   What dost thou mean by this?

HAMLET   Nothing but to show you how a king may go a
30 progress through the guts of a beggar.

KING   Where is Polonius?

HAMLET   In heaven. Send thither to see. If your messen-
    ger find him not there, seek him i' th' other place your-
    self. But if indeed you find him not within this month,
    you shall nose him as you go up the stairs into the
    lobby.

---

19 *a* he 20 *politic worms* craftily scheming worms (just as Polonius was a
schemer) 21 *diet* food and drink (perhaps with a play upon a famous *convocation,* the Diet [Council] of Worms opened by Charles V on 28 January
1521, before which the Protestant reformer Martin Luther appeared) 23
variable service different servings of one food 26 *eat* (past tense, pronounced "et") 30 *progress* royal journey through the hinterlands

KING   *[To Attendants]* Go seek him there.

HAMLET   A will stay till you come. *[Exeunt Attendants.]*

KING
Hamlet, this deed, for thine especial safety,
Which we do tender as we dearly grieve   40
For that which thou hast done, must send thee hence
With fiery quickness. Therefore prepare thyself.
The bark is ready and the wind at help,   43
Th' associates tend, and everything is bent   44
For England.

HAMLET   For England?

KING   Ay, Hamlet.

HAMLET   Good.

KING
So is it, if thou knew'st our purposes.

HAMLET   I see a cherub that sees them. But come, for   47
England! Farewell, dear mother.

KING   Thy loving father, Hamlet.

HAMLET   My mother – father and mother is man and   50
wife, man and wife is one flesh; so, my mother. Come,   51
for England!   *Exit.*

KING
Follow him at foot; tempt him with speed aboard.   53
Delay it not; I'll have him hence tonight.
Away! for everything is sealed and done
That else leans on th' affair. Pray you make haste.   56
                    [Exeunt all but the King.]
And, England, if my love thou hold'st at aught –   57
As my great power thereof may give thee sense,
Since yet thy cicatrice looks raw and red   59
After the Danish sword, and thy free awe   60

---

40 *tender* hold dear; *dearly* intensely   **43** *bark* ship   **44** *tend* wait; *bent* set in
readiness (like a bent bow)   **47** *cherub* one of the cherubim, second in the
nine orders of angels   **51** *one flesh* (many biblical passages endorse this
claim; see Genesis 2:24, Matthew 19:5–6, Mark 10:8)   **53** *at foot* closely
56 *else* otherwise; *leans on* is connected with   **57** *England* King of England;
aught anything, any value   **59** *cicatrice* scar   **60** *free awe* voluntary respect

61 Pays homage to us – thou mayst not coldly set
62 Our sovereign process, which imports at full
63 By letters congruing to that effect
64 The present death of Hamlet. Do it, England,
65 For like the hectic in my blood he rages,
    And thou must cure me. Till I know 'tis done,
67 Howe'er my haps, my joys will ne'er begin.   *Exit.*

*

❧ **IV.4** *Enter Fortinbras with his Army [including a
Norwegian Captain, marching] over the stage.*

FORTINBRAS
    Go, captain, from me greet the Danish king.
    Tell him that by his license Fortinbras
3   Craves the conveyance of a promised march
    Over his kingdom. You know the rendezvous.
    If that his majesty would aught with us,
6   We shall express our duty in his eye;
    And let him know so.
NORWEGIAN CAPTAIN   I will do't, my lord.
FORTINBRAS
8   Go softly on.   *[Exeunt all but the Captain.]*
        *Enter Hamlet, Rosencrantz, [Guildenstern,]
        and others.*
HAMLET
9   Good sir, whose powers are these?
NORWEGIAN CAPTAIN
10 They are of Norway, sir.
HAMLET
    How purposed, sir, I pray you?
NORWEGIAN CAPTAIN
    Against some part of Poland.

---

61 *set* esteem   **62** *process* formal command   **63** *congruing* agreeing   **64** *present* instant   **65** *the hectic* a continuous fever   **67** *haps* fortunes
    IV.4 Somewhere in Denmark's territories   **3** *conveyance* escort; *promised* i.e., agreed upon by diplomats (see II.2.77–80)   **6** *eye* presence   **8** *softly* slowly   **9** *powers* forces

HAMLET
  Who commands them, sir?
NORWEGIAN CAPTAIN
  The nephew to old Norway, Fortinbras.
HAMLET
  Goes it against the main of Poland, sir,   15
  Or for some frontier?
NORWEGIAN CAPTAIN
  Truly to speak, and with no addition,   17
  We go to gain a little patch of ground
  That hath in it no profit but the name.
  To pay five ducats, five, I would not farm it,   20
  Nor will it yield to Norway or the Pole
  A ranker rate, should it be sold in fee.   22
HAMLET
  Why, then the Polack never will defend it.
NORWEGIAN CAPTAIN
  Yes, it is already garrisoned.   24
HAMLET
  Two thousand souls and twenty thousand ducats
  Will not debate the question of this straw.
  This is th' imposthume of much wealth and peace,   27
  That inward breaks, and shows no cause without
  Why the man dies. I humbly thank you, sir.
NORWEGIAN CAPTAIN
  God buy you, sir.   *[Exit.]*   30
ROSENCRANTZ   Will't please you go, my lord?
HAMLET
  I'll be with you straight. Go a little before.
                              [Exeunt all but Hamlet.]
  How all occasions do inform against me   32
  And spur my dull revenge! What is a man,
  If his chief good and market of his time   34
  Be but to sleep and feed? A beast, no more.

---

15 *main* main body   17 *addition* exaggeration   20 *To pay* (i.e., as rent)   22
ranker more lavish; *in fee* outright   24 *garrisoned* guarded by soldiers   27
imposthume abscess   32 *inform* take shape   34 *market of* compensation for

36 Sure he that made us with such large discourse,
    Looking before and after, gave us not
    That capability and godlike reason
39 To fust in us unused. Now, whether it be
40 Bestial oblivion, or some craven scruple
41 Of thinking too precisely on th' event –
42 A thought which, quartered, hath but one part wisdom
    And ever three parts coward – I do not know
    Why yet I live to say "This thing's to do,"
    Sith I have cause, and will, and strength, and means'
46 To do't. Examples gross as earth exhort me.
47 Witness this army of such mass and charge,
    Led by a delicate and tender prince,
    Whose spirit, with divine ambition puffed,
50 Makes mouths at the invisible event,
    Exposing what is mortal and unsure
    To all that fortune, death, and danger dare,
    Even for an eggshell. Rightly to be great
    Is not to stir without great argument,
55 But greatly to find quarrel in a straw
    When honor's at the stake. How stand I then,
    That have a father killed, a mother stained,
    Excitements of my reason and my blood,
    And let all sleep, while to my shame I see
60 The imminent death of twenty thousand men
61 That for a fantasy and trick of fame
    Go to their graves like beds, fight for a plot
63 Whereon the numbers cannot try the cause,
    Which is not tomb enough and continent
    To hide the slain? O, from this time forth,
    My thoughts be bloody, or be nothing worth!   *Exit.*

*

---

36 *discourse* power of thought **39** *fust* mold **40** *oblivion* forgetfulness **41** *event* outcome (see l. 50) **42** *quartered* divided in four (see the many earlier mathematical divisions: e.g., III.4.97) **46** *gross* large and evident **47** *charge* expense **50** *Makes mouths* makes scornful faces **55** *greatly . . . straw* to recognize the *great argument* even in some small matter **61** *fantasy* fanciful image; *trick* something negligible **63** *try the cause* fight to a conclusion the issue in contention

∾ **IV.5** *Enter Horatio, [Queen] Gertrude, and*
   a Gentleman.

QUEEN
   I will not speak with her.
GENTLEMAN
   She is importunate, indeed distract.   2
   Her mood will needs be pitied.
QUEEN   What would she have?
GENTLEMAN
   She speaks much of her father, says she hears
   There's tricks i' th' world, and hems, and beats her heart,   5
   Spurns enviously at straws, speaks things in doubt   6
   That carry but half sense. Her speech is nothing,
   Yet the unshapèd use of it doth move   8
   The hearers to collection; they aim at it,   9
   And botch the words up fit to their own thoughts,   10
   Which, as her winks and nods and gestures yield them,
   Indeed would make one think there might be thought,
   Though nothing sure, yet much unhappily.
HORATIO
   'Twere good she were spoken with, for she may strew
   Dangerous conjectures in ill-breeding minds.
QUEEN
   Let her come in.   *[Exit Gentleman.]*
      [Aside]
   To my sick soul (as sin's true nature is)   17
   Each toy seems prologue to some great amiss.   18
   So full of artless jealousy is guilt   19
   It spills itself in fearing to be spilt.   20
      Enter Ophelia [distracted].

IV.5 Elsinore **2** *distract* insane **5** *tricks* deceits **6** *Spurns enviously* kicks
spitefully, takes offense; *straws* trifles **8** *unshapèd use* disordered manner
9 *collection* attempts at making her *speech* coherent; *aim* guess **10** *botch*
patch **17–20** *To my . . . spilt* (in Q2, each of these lines begins with a quotation mark, indicating sententious sayings) **18** *toy* trifle; *amiss* misdeed,
evil deed **19** *artless* unskillfully managed; *jealousy* suspicion **20** *spills* destroys

OPHELIA
Where is the beauteous majesty of Denmark?
QUEEN   How now, Ophelia?
OPHELIA
She sings.

How should I your truelove know
From another one?
25   By his cockle hat and staff
26   And his sandal shoon.

QUEEN
Alas, sweet lady, what imports this song?
OPHELIA   Say you? Nay, pray you mark.

Song.
He is dead and gone, lady,
30   He is dead and gone;
At his head a grass-green turf,
At his heels a stone.

O, ho!
QUEEN   Nay, but Ophelia –
OPHELIA   Pray you mark.
[Sings.]
White his shroud as the mountain snow –
Enter King.
QUEEN   Alas, look here, my lord.
OPHELIA
Song.
38   Larded all with sweet flowers;
Which bewept to the ground did not go
40   With truelove showers.

KING   How do you, pretty lady?

---

25 *cockle hat* hat bearing a cockleshell, worn by a pilgrim who had been to
the shrine of Saint James of Compostela in northwestern Spain   26 *shoon*
shoes   38 *Larded* bedecked

OPHELIA   Well, good dild you! They say the owl was a   42
   baker's daughter. Lord, we know what we are, but
   know not what we may be. God be at your table!

KING   Conceit upon her father.   45

OPHELIA   Pray let's have no words of this, but when they
   ask you what it means, say you this:

                    Song.
          Tomorrow is Saint Valentine's day.
             All in the morning betime,   49
          And I a maid at your window,   50
             To be your Valentine.
          Then up he rose and donned his clo'es
             And dupped the chamber door,   53
          Let in the maid, that out a maid
             Never departed more.

KING   Pretty Ophelia!

OPHELIA   Indeed without an oath, I'll make an end on't:
   [Sings.]
          By Gis and by Saint Charity,   58
             Alack, and fie for shame!
          Young men will do't if they come to't.   60
             By Cock, they are to blame.   61
          Quoth she, "Before you tumbled me,
             You promised me to wed."
   He answers:
          "So would I 'a' done, by yonder sun,
             And thou hadst not come to my bed."

KING   How long hath she been thus?

OPHELIA   I hope all will be well. We must be patient, but
   I cannot choose but weep to think they would lay him

---

42 *good dild* (a colloquial form of "God yield," or repay); *the owl* (according
to a folktale, a baker's daughter was transformed into an owl because she
wasn't generous when Christ asked for bread) 45 *Conceit upon* fantasies
about 49 *betime* early 53 *dupped* opened 58 *Gis* Jesus; *Saint Charity* (not
a recognized saint, but a common saying) 61 *Cock* (1) God (a common ver-
bal corruption), (2) penis (?)

70   i' th' cold ground. My brother shall know of it; and so I
thank you for your good counsel. Come, my coach!
Good night, ladies, good night. Sweet ladies, good
night, good night.   *[Exit.]*

KING
    Follow her close; give her good watch, I pray you.
                                    [Exit Horatio.]
    O, this is the poison of deep grief; it springs
    All from her father's death and now behold,
    O Gertrude, Gertrude,
78   When sorrows come, they come not single spies,
    But in battalions: first, her father slain;
80   Next, your son gone, and he most violent author
81   Of his own just remove; the people muddied,
    Thick and unwholesome in their thoughts and whispers
83   For good Polonius' death, and we have done but greenly
84   In hugger-mugger to inter him; poor Ophelia
    Divided from herself and her fair judgment,
86   Without the which we are pictures or mere beasts;
    Last, and as much containing as all these,
    Her brother is in secret come from France,
89   Feeds on this wonder, keeps himself in clouds,
90   And wants not buzzers to infect his ear
    With pestilent speeches of his father's death,
92   Wherein necessity, of matter beggared,
93   Will nothing stick our person to arraign
    In ear and ear. O my dear Gertrude, this,
95   Like to a murd'ring piece, in many places
96   Gives me superfluous death.
            A noise within.   Attend!
97   Where is my Switzers? Let them guard the door.

---

78 *spies* scouts (the entire idea is proverbial; cf. IV.7.161–62)   **81** *muddied*
stirred up and confused   **83** *greenly* foolishly   **84** *hugger-mugger* secrecy   **86**
pictures soulless images, vacant forms; *mere* solely   **89** *clouds* obscurity   **90**
wants lacks; *buzzers* rumor bearers   **92** *of matter beggared* unprovided with
facts   **93** *Will nothing stick* doesn't hesitate; *arraign* accuse   **95** *murd'ring
piece* cannon loaded with shot meant to scatter   **96** *superfluous* (since one
death would suffice)   **97** *Switzers* Swiss mercenaries

What is the matter?
   Enter a Messenger.

MESSENGER   Save yourself, my lord.
  The ocean, overpeering of his list,   99
  Eats not the flats with more impetuous haste   100
  Than young Laertes, in a riotous head,   101
  O'erbears your officers. The rabble call him lord,
  And, as the world were now but to begin,
  Antiquity forgot, custom not known,
  The ratifiers and props of every word,   105
  They cry, "Choose we! Laertes shall be king!"
  Caps, hands, and tongues applaud it to the clouds,
  "Laertes shall be king! Laertes king!"
    A noise within.

QUEEN
  How cheerfully on the false trail they cry!   109
  O, this is counter, you false Danish dogs!   110

KING
  The doors are broke.
    Enter Laertes with others.

LAERTES
  Where is this king? – Sirs, stand you all without.

ALL
  No, let's come in.

LAERTES   I pray you give me leave.

ALL   We will, we will.

LAERTES
  I thank you. Keep the door.   *[Exeunt his Followers.]*
                  O thou vile king,
  Give me my father.

QUEEN   Calmly, good Laertes.

LAERTES
  That drop of blood that's calm proclaims me bastard,

---

99 *overpeering of* rising above; *list* boundary   **100** *impetuous* violent (Q2's "impitious" is an old spelling, not a different modern word)   **101** *head* armed force   **105** *word* motto, slogan   **109** *cry* bellow (i.e., like a pack of hounds)   **110** *counter* hunting the scent backward

Cries cuckold to my father, brands the harlot
Even here between the chaste unsmirchèd brow
120 Of my true mother.

KING   What is the cause, Laertes,
121 That thy rebellion looks so giantlike?
122 Let him go, Gertrude. Do not fear our person.
123 There's such divinity doth hedge a king
124 That treason can but peep to what it would,
Acts little of his will. Tell me, Laertes,
Why thou art thus incensed. – Let him go, Gertrude. –
Speak, man.

LAERTES
Where is my father?

KING   Dead.

QUEEN   But not by him.

KING
Let him demand his fill.

LAERTES
130 How came he dead? I'll not be juggled with.
To hell allegiance, vows to the blackest devil,
Conscience and grace to the profoundest pit!
I dare damnation. To this point I stand,
134 That both the worlds I give to negligence,
Let come what comes, only I'll be revenged
136 Most throughly for my father.

KING   Who shall stay you?

LAERTES
My will, not all the world's.
And for my means, I'll husband them so well
They shall go far with little.

KING   Good Laertes,

---

121 *giantlike* (an allusion to the war the giants made on Olympus: see Ovid, *Metamorphoses* I, and mentions of Pelion and Ossa here at V.1.243 and 273) 122 *fear* fear for 123 *divinity . . . king* (an allusion to the contemporary theory that God appointed and protected earthly monarchs) 124 *peep to* i.e., through the barrier 134 *both the worlds* this world and the next; *give to negligence* disregard 136 *throughly* thoroughly

If you desire to know the certainty   140
Of your dear father, is't writ in your revenge
That sweepstake you will draw both friend and foe,   142
Winner and loser?
LAERTES
None but his enemies.
KING   Will you know them then?
LAERTES
To his good friends thus wide I'll ope my arms
And like the kind life-rend'ring pelican   146
Repast them with my blood.
KING   Why, now you speak
Like a good child and a true gentleman.
That I am guiltless of your father's death,
And am most sensibly in grief for it,   150
It shall as level to your judgment 'pear   151
As day does to your eye.
    A noise within [: "Let her come in."]
LAERTES
How now? What noise is that?
    Enter Ophelia.
O heat, dry up my brains; tears seven times salt
Burn out the sense and virtue of mine eye!
By heaven, thy madness shall be paid with weight
Till our scale turn the beam. O rose of May,   157
Dear maid, kind sister, sweet Ophelia!
O heavens, is't possible a young maid's wits
Should be as mortal as an old man's life?   160
OPHELIA
                    Song.
        They bore him barefaced on the bier
        And in his grave rained many a tear –
        Fare you well, my dove!

---

142 *sweepstake* taking all stakes on the gambling table   146 *life-rend'ring*
life-yielding (fable held that the mother pelican took blood from her breast
to feed her young)   150 *sensibly* feelingly   151 *level* plain   157 *beam* bar of
a balance

LAERTES
    Hadst thou thy wits, and didst persuade revenge,
    It could not move thus.
OPHELIA   You must sing "A-down a-down, and you call
167   him a-down-a." O, how the wheel becomes it! It is the
    false steward, that stole his master's daughter.
169 LAERTES   This nothing's more than matter.
170 OPHELIA   There's rosemary, that's for remembrance. Pray
171   you, love, remember. And there is pansies, that's for
    thoughts.
173 LAERTES   A document in madness, thoughts and remem-
    brance fitted.
175 OPHELIA There's fennel for you, and columbines.
176   There's rue for you, and here's some for me. We may
    call it herb of grace o' Sundays. You must wear your rue
178   with a difference. There's a daisy. I would give you
179   some violets, but they withered all when my father
180   died. They say a made a good end.
    [Sings.]
         For bonny sweet Robin is all my joy.
LAERTES
    Thought and afflictions, passion, hell itself,
183   She turns to favor and to prettiness.
OPHELIA

               Song.
        And will a not come again?
        And will a not come again?
          No, no, he is dead;
          Go to thy deathbed;
        He never will come again.

---

167 *wheel* refrain   **169** *more than matter* more meaningful than sane speech
170–79 *rosemary . . . violets* (to whom Ophelia distributes which flowers and
herbs is uncertain; perhaps: rosemary and pansies to Laertes, fennel and
columbines to Gertrude, rue to Claudius, with daisy kept for herself)
171–72 *pansies . . . for thoughts* (*pansies* derives from French *pensées* – i.e.,
thoughts)   **173** *document* lesson   **175** *fennel* (symbol of flattery or deceit);
columbines (symbol of infidelity)   **176** *rue* (symbol of regret)   **178** *daisy*
(symbol of dissembling [?])   **179** *violets* (symbol of faithfulness; see
V.1.229–30)   **183** *favor* charm

> His beard was as white as snow,
> Flaxen was his poll.   190
>   He is gone, he is gone,
>   And we cast away moan.
> God 'a' mercy on his soul.
> And of all Christian souls, God buy you.   *[Exit.]*   194

LAERTES
Do you see this, O God?

KING
Laertes, I must commune with your grief,
Or you deny me right. Go but apart,
Make choice of whom your wisest friends you will,
And they shall hear and judge 'twixt you and me.
If by direct or by collateral hand   200
They find us touched, we will our kingdom give,   201
Our crown, our life, and all that we call ours,
To you in satisfaction; but if not,
Be you content to lend your patience to us,
And we shall jointly labor with your soul
To give it due content.

LAERTES   Let this be so.
His means of death, his obscure funeral –
No trophy, sword, nor hatchment o'er his bones,   208
No noble rite nor formal ostentation –   209
Cry to be heard, as 'twere from heaven to earth,   *210*
That I must call't in question.   211

KING   So you shall;
And where th' offense is, let the great ax fall.
I pray you go with me.   *Exeunt.*

                              *

___

190 *poll* head   194 *of* on   200 *collateral* indirect   201 *touched* i.e., with the
crime   208 *trophy* memorial; *hatchment* coat of arms (hung up as a memorial)   209 *ostentation* ceremony   211 *That* so that

∽ **IV.6** *Enter Horatio and others.*

HORATIO   What are they that would speak with me?

GENTLEMAN   Seafaring men, sir. They say they have letters for you.

HORATIO   Let them come in.   *[Exit Attendant.]*
I do not know from what part of the world
I should be greeted, if not from Lord Hamlet.
    Enter Sailors.

SAILOR   God bless you, sir.

HORATIO   Let him bless thee too.

9   SAILOR   A shall, sir, and't please him. There's a letter for
10 you, sir – it came from th' ambassador that was bound
for England – if your name be Horatio, as I am let to
know it is.

HORATIO   *[Reads the letter.]* "Horatio, when thou shalt
14 have overlooked this, give these fellows some means to
the king. They have letters for him. Ere we were two
16 days old at sea, a pirate of very warlike appointment
gave us chase. Finding ourselves too slow of sail, we put
on a compelled valor, and in the grapple I boarded
them. On the instant they got clear of our ship; so I
20 alone became their prisoner. They have dealt with me
21 like thieves of mercy, but they knew what they did: I
22 am to do a turn for them. Let the king have the letters I
have sent, and repair thou to me with as much speed as
thou wouldest fly death. I have words to speak in thine
25 ear will make thee dumb; yet are they much too light
26 for the bore of the matter. These good fellows will bring
thee where I am. Rosencrantz and Guildenstern hold
their course for England. Of them I have much to tell
thee. Farewell.

30   He that thou knowest thine, Hamlet."

IV.6 Elsinore   **9** *A* he   **14** *overlooked* scanned; *means* i.e., of access   **16** *pirate* i.e., pirate ship; *appointment* equipment   **21** *thieves of mercy* merciful thieves   **22** *turn* i.e., an act responding to the sailors' (good) act   **25** *dumb* silent, dumbstruck   **26** *bore* caliber (as of a gun)

Come, I will give you way for these your letters,
And do't the speedier that you may direct me
To him from whom you brought them.   *Exeunt.*

✳

∾ **IV.7** *Enter King and Laertes.*

KING
Now must your conscience my acquittance seal,
And you must put me in your heart for friend,
Sith you have heard, and with a knowing ear,
That he which hath your noble father slain
Pursued my life.
LAERTES   It well appears. But tell me
Why you proceeded not against these feats   6
So criminal and so capital in nature,   7
As by your safety, wisdom, all things else,
You mainly were stirred up.   9
KING   O, for two special reasons,
Which may to you perhaps seem much unsinewed,   10
But yet to me th' are strong. The queen his mother
Lives almost by his looks, and for myself –
My virtue or my plague, be it either which –
She is so conjunctive to my life and soul   14
That, as the star moves not but in his sphere,   15
I could not but by her. The other motive
Why to a public count I might not go   17
Is the great love the general gender bear him,   18
Who, dipping all his faults in their affection,
Work like the spring that turneth wood to stone,   20
Convert his gyves to graces; so that my arrows,   21
Too slightly timbered for so loud a wind,
Would have reverted to my bow again,
But not where I had aimed them.

IV.7 Elsinore **6** *feats* acts **7** *capital* punishable by death **9** *mainly* powerfully **14** *conjunctive* closely united **15** *his* its **17** *count* trial, accounting
18 *general gender* ordinary people **21** *gyves* chains

LAERTES

And so have I a noble father lost,

26   A sister driven into desp'rate terms,

27   Whose worth, if praises may go back again,

28   Stood challenger on mount of all the age

For her perfections. But my revenge will come.

KING

30   Break not your sleeps for that. You must not think

That we are made of stuff so flat and dull

That we can let our beard be shook with danger,

And think it pastime. You shortly shall hear more.

I loved your father, and we love ourself,

And that, I hope, will teach you to imagine –

Enter a Messenger with letters.

MESSENGER

These to your majesty, this to the queen.

KING

From Hamlet? Who brought them?

MESSENGER

Sailors, my lord, they say; I saw them not.

They were given me by Claudio; he received them

40   Of him that brought them.

KING   Laertes, you shall hear them. –

Leave us.   *[Exit Messenger.]*

[Reads.] "High and mighty, you shall know I am set

43   naked on your kingdom. Tomorrow shall I beg leave to

see your kingly eyes; when I shall (first asking your par-

don thereunto) recount the occasion of my sudden

return."

What should this mean? Are all the rest come back?

48   Or is it some abuse, and no such thing?

LAERTES

49   Know you the hand?

---

26 *terms* circumstances   **27** *back again* i.e., to her former (sane) self   **28** *on mount* on a height   **43** *naked* i.e., without a princely entourage (cf. *rest,* l. 47)   **48** *abuse* deception   **49** *hand* handwriting

KING   'Tis Hamlet's character. "Naked"!
  And in a postscript here, he says "alone."   50
  Can you devise me?   51
LAERTES
  I am lost in it, my lord. But let him come.
  It warms the very sickness in my heart
  That I shall live and tell him to his teeth,
  "Thus didest thou."
KING   If it be so, Laertes –
  As how should it be so? how otherwise? –
  Will you be ruled by me?
LAERTES   Ay, my lord,
  So you will not o'errule me to a peace.
KING
  To thine own peace. If he be now returned,
  As checking at his voyage, and that he means   60
  No more to undertake it, I will work him
  To an exploit now ripe in my device,
  Under the which he shall not choose but fall;
  And for his death no wind of blame shall breathe,
  But even his mother shall uncharge the practice   65
  And call it accident.
LAERTES   My lord, I will be ruled;
  The rather if you could devise it so
  That I might be the organ.   68
KING   It falls right.
  You have been talked of since your travel much,
  And that in Hamlet's hearing, for a quality   70
  Wherein they say you shine. Your sum of parts
  Did not together pluck such envy from him
  As did that one, and that, in my regard,
  Of the unworthiest siege.   74
LAERTES   What part is that, my lord?

---

49 *character* handwriting   51 *devise* explain to   60 *checking* shying   65 *uncharge the practice* acquit the stratagem of being a plot   68 *organ* instrument
74 *siege* status, rank

KING

75 A very ribbon in the cap of youth,
    Yet needful too, for youth no less becomes
77 The light and careless livery that it wears
78 Than settled age his sables and his weeds
79 Importing health and graveness. Two months since
80 Here was a gentleman of Normandy.
    I have seen myself and served against the French,
82 And they can well on horseback, but this gallant
    Had witchcraft in't. He grew unto his seat,
    And to such wondrous doing brought his horse
85 As had he been incorpsed and deminatured
86 With the brave beast. So far he topped my thought
87 That I, in forgery of shapes and tricks,
    Come short of what he did.

LAERTES   A Norman was't?

KING   A Norman.

LAERTES

90 Upon my life, Lamord.

KING   The very same.

LAERTES

91 I know him well. He is the brooch indeed
    And gem of all the nation.

KING

93 He made confession of you,
    And gave you such a masterly report
    For art and exercise in your defense
    And for your rapier most especial,
    That he cried out 'twould be a sight indeed
98 If one could match you. The scrimers of their nation

---

75 *ribbon* decoration   77 *livery* distinctive attire   78 *sables* richly furred
robes; *weeds* garments   79 *health* prosperity   82 *well* perform well   85 *incorpsed* made one body; *deminatured* made sharer of nature half and half (as
man shares with horse in the centaur)   86 *topped* excelled; *thought* imagination of possibilities   87 *forgery* invention; *shapes and tricks* i.e., various show-
stopping exercises   90 *Lamord* i.e., "the death" (French: *la mort*)   91 *brooch*
jewel, decorative ornament   93 *made confession of* testified to   98 *scrimers*
fencers

He swore had neither motion, guard, nor eye,
If you opposed them. Sir, this report of his   *100*
Did Hamlet so envenom with his envy
That he could nothing do but wish and beg
Your sudden coming o'er to play with you.
Now, out of this –
LAERTES   What out of this, my lord?
KING
Laertes, was your father dear to you?
Or are you like the painting of a sorrow,   *106*
A face without a heart?
LAERTES   Why ask you this?
KING
Not that I think you did not love your father,
But that I know love is begun by time,   *109*
And that I see, in passages of proof,   *110*
Time qualifies the spark and fire of it.   *111*
There lives within the very flame of love
A kind of wick or snuff that will abate it,   *113*
And nothing is at a like goodness still,   *114*
For goodness, growing to a plurisy,   *115*
Dies in his own too-much. That we would do
We should do when we would, for this "would" changes,
And hath abatements and delays as many
As there are tongues, are hands, are accidents,
And then this "should" is like a spendthrift sigh,   *120*
That hurts by easing. But to the quick of th' ulcer –   *121*
Hamlet comes back; what would you undertake
To show yourself in deed your father's son
More than in words?
LAERTES   To cut his throat i' th' church!

106–7 *painting . . . heart* (cf. IV.5.86 and n.) **109–11** *But . . . it* (cf.
III.2.178 ff.) **110** *passages of proof* experience **111** *qualifies* weakens **113**
snuff unconsumed portion of burned *wick* **114** *still* always **115** *a plurisy*
an excess **121** *hurts* i.e., shortens life by drawing blood from the heart (as
was believed); *quick* sensitive flesh

KING

125   No place indeed should murder sanctuarize;
       Revenge should have no bounds. But, good Laertes,
       Will you do this? Keep close within your chamber.
       Hamlet returned shall know you are come home.
129   We'll put on those shall praise your excellence
130   And set a double varnish on the fame
131   The Frenchman gave you, bring you in fine together
132   And wager o'er your heads. He, being remiss,
       Most generous, and free from all contriving,
134   Will not peruse the foils, so that with ease,
       Or with a little shuffling, you may choose
136   A sword unbated, and, in a pass of practice,
       Requite him for your father.

LAERTES   I will do't,
       And for that purpose I'll anoint my sword.
139   I bought an unction of a mountebank,
140   So mortal that, but dip a knife in it,
141   Where it draws blood no cataplasm so rare,
142   Collected from all simples that have virtue
       Under the moon, can save the thing from death
144   That is but scratched withal. I'll touch my point
145   With this contagion, that, if I gall him slightly,
       It may be death.

KING   Let's further think of this,
       Weigh what convenience both of time and means
148   May fit us to our shape. If this should fail,
149   And that our drift look through our bad performance,
150   'Twere better not assayed. Therefore this project
       Should have a back or second, that might hold

---

125 *sanctuarize* protect from punishment   129 *put on* instigate   131 *in fine* at the end (*fine* derives from Latin *finis,* the end; cf. the jokes on *fine* at V.1.99 ff.)   132 *remiss* negligent   134 *peruse* examine   136 *unbated* not blunted; *pass of practice* thrust made effective by trickery   139 *unction* ointment; *mountebank* snake oil salesman, quack   141 *cataplasm* poultice   142 *simples* herbs   144 *withal* with it   145 *gall* scratch   148 *shape* plan   149 *drift* scheme; *look* be seen

If this did blast in proof. Soft, let me see.   152
We'll make a solemn wager on your cunnings –   153
I ha't!
When in your motion you are hot and dry –
As make your bouts more violent to that end –
And that he calls for drink, I'll have prepared him
A chalice for the nonce, whereon but sipping,   158
If he by chance escape your venomed stuck,   159
Our purpose may hold there. – But stay, what noise?   160
   Enter Queen.

QUEEN
One woe doth tread upon another's heel,
So fast they follow. Your sister's drowned, Laertes.

LAERTES   Drowned! O, where?

QUEEN
There is a willow grows askant the brook,   164
That shows his hoary leaves in the glassy stream.   165
Therewith fantastic garlands did she make
Of crowflowers, nettles, daisies, and long purples,
That liberal shepherds give a grosser name,   168
But our cold maids do dead-men's-fingers call them.
There on the pendent boughs her crownet weeds   170
Clamb'ring to hang, an envious sliver broke,
When down her weedy trophies and herself
Fell in the weeping brook. Her clothes spread wide,
And mermaidlike awhile they bore her up,
Which time she chanted snatches of old lauds,   175
As one incapable of her own distress,   176
Or like a creature native and indued   177
Unto that element. But long it could not be
Till that her garments, heavy with their drink,
Pulled the poor wretch from her melodious lay   *180*

---

152 *blast in proof* blow up during trial (like a faulty cannon?)   153 *cunnings*
respective skills (i.e., how you do and how he does)   158 *nonce* occasion
159 *stuck* thrust   164 *askant* alongside   165 *his* its; *hoary* gray   168 *liberal*
free-spoken, licentious   170 *crownet* coronet (a small crown)   175 *lauds*
hymns   176 *incapable of* insensible to   177 *indued* endowed

    To muddy death.

LAERTES   Alas, then she is drowned?

QUEEN   Drowned, drowned.

LAERTES

    Too much of water hast thou, poor Ophelia,
    And therefore I forbid my tears; but yet

185   It is our trick; nature her custom holds,
    Let shame say what it will. When these are gone,
    The woman will be out. Adieu, my lord.
    I have a speech o' fire, that fain would blaze
    But that this folly drowns it.   *Exit.*

KING   Let's follow, Gertrude.

190   How much I had to do to calm his rage!
    Now fear I this will give it start again;
    Therefore let's follow.   *Exeunt.*

                         *

❧ **V.1** *Enter two Clowns [, one a gravedigger].*

1 CLOWN   Is she to be buried in Christian burial when she
    willfully seeks her own salvation?

OTHER   I tell thee she is. Therefore make her grave

4   straight. The crowner hath sat on her, and finds it
    Christian burial.

CLOWN   How can that be, unless she drowned herself in
    her own defense?

OTHER   Why, 'tis found so.

9 CLOWN   It must be *se offendendo;* it cannot be else. For

10   here lies the point: if I drown myself wittingly, it argues

---

185 *trick* (human) way (i.e., to shed tears when sorrowful)
   V.1 A churchyard **s.d.** *Clowns* humble rural folk (the gravedigger probably here carries a spade and pickax; see l. 88)   **1** *Christian burial* consecrated
ground with the prescribed service of the church (a burial denied to suicides)
4 *straight* straightaway, at once; *crowner* coroner   **9** *se offendendo* (a mis-
speaking of Latin *se defendendo,* in "self-defense")

an act, and an act hath three branches – it is to act, to   12
do, to perform. Argal, she drowned herself wittingly.

OTHER   Nay, but hear you, Goodman Delver.   14

CLOWN   Give me leave. Here lies the water – good. Here
stands the man – good. If the man go to this water and
drown himself, it is, will he nill he, he goes, mark you   17
that. But if the water come to him and drown him, he
drowns not himself. Argal, he that is not guilty of his
own death shortens not his own life.   20

OTHER   But is this law?

CLOWN   Ay marry, is't – crowner's quest law.   22

OTHER   Will you ha' the truth on't? If this had not been a
gentlewoman, she should have been buried out o'
Christian burial.

CLOWN   Why, there thou say'st. And the more pity that   26
great folk should have countenance in this world   27
to drown or hang themselves more than their even-   28
Christian. Come, my spade. There is no ancient gentlemen but gard'ners, ditchers, and gravemakers. They   30
hold up Adam's profession.

OTHER   Was he a gentleman?

CLOWN   A was the first that ever bore arms. I'll put an-   33
other question to thee. If thou answerest me not to the
purpose, confess thyself –

OTHER   Go to.

CLOWN   What is he that builds stronger than either the
mason, the shipwright, or the carpenter?

OTHER   The gallowsmaker, for that frame outlives a
thousand tenants.   40

CLOWN   I like thy wit well, in good faith. The gallows
does well. But how does it well? It does well to those
that do ill. Now thou dost ill to say the gallows is built

---

12 *Argal* (a comic [?] mispronunciation of Latin *ergo*, "therefore")   **14**
Delver Digger (spoken as if the gravedigger's occupation was also his family
name)   **17** *will he nill he* willy-nilly   **22** *quest* inquest   **26** *thou say'st* you're
right   **27** *countenance* privilege   **28–29** *even-Christian* fellow Christians
33 *A* he

stronger than the church. Argal, the gallows may do well to thee. To't again, come.

OTHER   Who builds stronger than a mason, a ship-wright, or a carpenter?

48   CLOWN   Ay, tell me that, and unyoke.

OTHER   Marry, now I can tell.

50   CLOWN   To't.

51   OTHER   Mass, I cannot tell.

CLOWN   Cudgel thy brains no more about it, for your dull ass will not mend his pace with beating. And when you are asked this question next, say "a gravemaker." The houses he makes lasts till doomsday. Go, get thee

56   in, and fetch me a stoup of liquor.

[Exit Other Clown.]
Enter Hamlet and Horatio [as Clown digs and sings].

Song.
In youth when I did love, did love,
   Methought it was very sweet

59   To contract – O – the time for – a –
     my behove,

60   O, methought there – a – was nothing –
     a – meet.

61   HAMLET   Has this fellow no feeling of his business? A sings in gravemaking.

63   HORATIO   Custom hath made it in him a property of eas-iness.

HAMLET   'Tis e'en so. The hand of little employment

66   hath the daintier sense.

CLOWN

Song.
But age with his stealing steps
   Hath clawed me in his clutch,

---

48 *unyoke* i.e., unharness your powers of thought after a good day's work **51** *Mass* by the mass **56** *stoup* tankard **59** *behove* behoof, advantage **61** *A* he **63–64** *property of easiness* matter of indifference **66** *daintier sense* more delicate feeling (because the *hand* is less callused)

And hath shipped me into the land,
    As if I had never been such.   70

[Throws up a skull.]

HAMLET   That skull had a tongue in it, and could sing
once. How the knave jowls it to the ground, as if 'twere   72
Cain's jawbone, that did the first murder! This might   73
be the pate of a politician, which this ass now o'er-   74
reaches; one that would circumvent God, might it not?

HORATIO   It might, my lord.

HAMLET   Or of a courtier, which could say "Good mor-
row, sweet lord! How dost thou, sweet lord?" This
might be my Lord Such-a-one, that praised my Lord
Such-a-one's horse when a meant to beg it, might it   80
not?

HORATIO   Ay, my lord.

HAMLET   Why, e'en so, and now my Lady Worm's, chop-   83
less, and knocked about the mazard with a sexton's   84
spade. Here's fine revolution, an we had the trick to
see't. Did these bones cost no more the breeding but to
play at loggets with them? Mine ache to think on't.   87

CLOWN

Song.
A pickax and a spade, a spade,
    For and a shrouding sheet;   89
O, a pit of clay for to be made   90
    For such a guest is meet.

[Throws up another skull.]

HAMLET   There's another. Why may not that be the skull
of a lawyer? Where be his quiddities now, his quillities,   93

---

72 *jowls* hurls **73** *Cain's jawbone* (according to Genesis 4, Cain killed his
brother Abel – traditionally, but not biblically, using the jawbone of an ass)
74 *politician* crafty schemer; *o'erreaches* gets the better of (with a play on the
literal meaning) **80** *a* he **83–84** *chopless* lacking the lower chop, or jaw
84 *mazard* head (a jocular, slangy word) **87** *loggets* small pieces of wood
thrown in a game **89** *For and* and moreover **93** *quiddities* subtleties (from
medieval scholastic terminology, "quidditas," meaning the distinctive nature
of anything); *quillities* nice distinctions (variant of *quiddities*)

94   his cases, his tenures, and his tricks? Why does he suffer
95   this mad knave now to knock him about the sconce
with a dirty shovel, and will not tell him of his action of
battery? Hum! This fellow might be in's time a great
98   buyer of land, with his statutes, his recognizances, his
99   fines, his double vouchers, his recoveries. [Is this the
100   fine of his fines, and the recovery of his recoveries,] to
have his fine pate full of fine dirt? Will his vouchers
vouch him no more of his purchases, and double ones
103   too, than the length and breadth of a pair of inden-
104   tures? The very conveyances of his lands will scarcely lie
in this box, and must th' inheritor himself have no
more, ha?

HORATIO   Not a jot more, my lord.

HAMLET   Is not parchment made of sheepskins?

HORATIO   Ay, my lord, and of calfskins too.

110   HAMLET   They are sheep and calves which seek out assurance in that. I will speak to this fellow. Whose
grave's this, sirrah?

CLOWN   Mine, sir.
   [Sings.]

         O, a pit of clay for to be made –

HAMLET   I think it be thine indeed, for thou liest in't.

CLOWN   You lie out on't, sir, and therefore 'tis not yours.
For my part, I do not lie in't, yet it is mine.

HAMLET   Thou dost lie in't, to be in't and say it is thine.
119   'Tis for the dead, not for the quick; therefore thou liest.
120   CLOWN   'Tis a quick lie, sir; 'twill away again from me to
you.

HAMLET   What man dost thou dig it for?

CLOWN   For no man, sir.

---

94 *tenures* holdings of property   95 *sconce* head (another slang term)   98
statutes, recognizances (two forms of legal acknowledgments of debt)   99 *fines,*
recoveries (legal ways of converting from a limited to a more absolute form of
property ownership); *vouchers* persons called on ("vouched") to warrant a
legal title   100 *fine* conclusion, end (the word introduces wordplay punning
on four meanings of *fine*)   103–4 *pair of indentures* deed or legal agreement
in duplicate   104 *conveyances* deeds   119 *quick* living

HAMLET What woman then?

CLOWN For none neither.

HAMLET Who is to be buried in't?

CLOWN One that was a woman, sir; but, rest her soul, she's dead.

HAMLET How absolute the knave is! We must speak by 129
the card, or equivocation will undo us. By the Lord, 130
Horatio, this three years I have took note of it, the age
is grown so picked that the toe of the peasant comes so 132
near the heel of the courtier he galls his kibe. – How 133
long hast thou been gravemaker?

CLOWN Of all the days i' th' year, I came to't that day
that our last king Hamlet overcame Fortinbras.

HAMLET How long is that since?

CLOWN Cannot you tell that? Every fool can tell that. It
was that very day that young Hamlet was born – he
that is mad, and sent into England. 140

HAMLET Ay, marry, why was he sent into England?

CLOWN Why, because a was mad. A shall recover his
wits there; or, if a do not, 'tis no great matter there.

HAMLET Why?

CLOWN 'Twill not be seen in him there. There the men
are as mad as he.

HAMLET How came he mad?

CLOWN Very strangely, they say.

HAMLET How strangely?

CLOWN Faith, e'en with losing his wits. 150

HAMLET Upon what ground?

CLOWN Why, here in Denmark. I have been sexton
here, man and boy, thirty years.

HAMLET How long will a man lie i' th' earth ere he rot?

CLOWN Faith, if a be not rotten before a die (as we have
many pocky corpses nowadays that will scarce hold the 156

---

129 *How absolute* how strict, what a stickler for accuracy 129–30 *by the card* accurately (*card* = mariner's chart?), to the point 130 *equivocation* ambiguity 132 *picked* refined, spruce 133 *galls* chafes; *kibe* chilblain (the analogy means the peasant affects a courtier's garb and hence diminishes the latter's status) 156 *pocky* rotten by pox (syphilis)

157   laying in), a will last you some eight year or nine year. A
tanner will last you nine year.

HAMLET   Why he more than another?

160 CLOWN   Why, sir, his hide is so tanned with his trade
that a will keep out water a great while, and your water
162 is a sore decayer of your whoreson dead body. Here's a
skull now hath lien you i' th' earth three and twenty
years.

HAMLET   Whose was it?

CLOWN   A whoreson mad fellow's it was. Whose do you
think it was?

HAMLET   Nay, I know not.

CLOWN   A pestilence on him for a mad rogue! A poured
170 a flagon of Rhenish on my head once. This same skull,
171 sir, was Sir Yorick's skull, the king's jester.

HAMLET   This? *[Takes the skull.]*

CLOWN   E'en that.

HAMLET   Alas, poor Yorick! I knew him, Horatio, a fellow of infinite jest, of most excellent fancy. He hath
bore me on his back a thousand times. And now how
abhorred in my imagination it is! My gorge rises at it.
Here hung those lips that I have kissed I know not how
oft. Where be your gibes now? Your gambols, your
180 songs, your flashes of merriment that were wont to set
the table on a roar? Not one now to mock your own
182 grinning? Quite chopfallen? Now get you to my lady's
183 table, and tell her, let her paint an inch thick, to this
184 favor she must come. Make her laugh at that. Prithee,
Horatio, tell me one thing.

HORATIO   What's that, my lord?

HAMLET   Dost thou think Alexander looked o' this fashion i' th' earth?

---

157 *laying in* i.e., in the ground   162 *whoreson* (coarse, here jocular, term of familiarity, perhaps of contempt)   170 *Rhenish* Rhine wine   171 *Sir* (the title is ironic, affectionate, and a common Shakespearean quip; cf. "Lady Worm," l. 83)   182 *chopfallen* lacking the lower chop, or jaw (also "down in the mouth," "dejected")   183 *table* (1) piece of furniture, (2) painted portrait   184 *favor* countenance, aspect

HORATIO   E'en so.

HAMLET   And smelt so? Pah!   *190*
   [Puts down the skull.]

HORATIO   E'en so, my lord.

HAMLET   To what base uses we may return, Horatio!
  Why may not imagination trace the noble dust of
  Alexander till a find it stopping a bunghole?   *194*

HORATIO   'Twere to consider too curiously, to consider   *195*
  so.

HAMLET   No, faith, not a jot, but to follow him thither
  with modesty enough, and likelihood to lead it. Alexan-   *198*
  der died, Alexander was buried, Alexander returneth to
  dust; the dust is earth; of earth we make loam; and why   *200*
  of that loam whereto he was converted might they not   *201*
  stop a beer barrel?

  Imperious Caesar, dead and turned to clay,   *203*
  Might stop a hole to keep the wind away.
  O, that that earth which kept the world in awe
  Should patch a wall t' expel the winter's flaw!   *206*
  But soft, but soft awhile! Here comes the king –
    Enter King, Queen, Laertes, and the Corpse [with
    Lords attendant and a Doctor of Divinity as Priest].
  The queen, the courtiers. Who is this they follow?
  And with such maimed rites? This doth betoken
  The corpse they follow did with desp'rate hand   *210*
  Fordo it own life. 'Twas of some estate.   *211*
  Couch we awhile, and mark.   *212*

LAERTES
  What ceremony else?

HAMLET   That is Laertes,
  A very noble youth. Mark.

---

194 *a bunghole* an opening in a barrel (e.g., of wine or beer)   195 *curiously*
(1) minutely, (2) ingeniously   198 *modesty* moderation   201 *loam* clay or
cement (called "lute" in archaic English) used to seal an opening (in a barrel,
l. 194, or a *wall*, l. 206)   203 *Imperious* imperial   206 *flaw* gust of wind   211
Fordo destroy; *it* its; *estate* rank   212 *Couch* hide (Hamlet and Horatio are
not seen or heard by the other characters until l. 244)

LAERTES
    What ceremony else?
DOCTOR
    Her obsequies have been as far enlarged
    As we have warranty. Her death was doubtful,
    And, but that great command o'ersways the order,
    She should in ground unsanctified have lodged
220 Till the last trumpet. For charitable prayers,
    Flints and pebbles should be thrown on her.
222 Yet here she is allowed her virgin crants,
223 Her maiden strewments, and the bringing home
    Of bell and burial.
LAERTES
    Must there no more be done?
DOCTOR   No more be done.
    We should profane the service of the dead
    To sing a requiem and such rest to her
    As to peace-parted souls.
LAERTES   Lay her i' th' earth,
    And from her fair and unpolluted flesh
230 May violets spring! I tell thee, churlish priest,
    A minist'ring angel shall my sister be
232 When thou liest howling.
HAMLET   What, the fair Ophelia?
QUEEN
    Sweets to the sweet! Farewell.
        [Scatters flowers.]
    I hoped thou shouldst have been my Hamlet's wife.
    I thought thy bridebed to have decked, sweet maid,
    And not have strewed thy grave.
LAERTES   O, treble woe
    Fall ten times double on that cursèd head
238 Whose wicked deed thy most ingenious sense
    Deprived thee of! Hold off the earth awhile,

---

222 *crants* garlands, chaplets   223 *strewments* strewings of the grave with flowers; *bringing home* laying to rest   232 *howling* i.e., in hell (see Matthew 13:42)   238 *most ingenious* of quickest apprehension

Till I have caught her once more in mine arms.   240
   [Leaps in the grave.]
Now pile your dust upon the quick and dead
Till of this flat a mountain you have made
T' o'ertop old Pelion or the skyish head   243
Of blue Olympus.
HAMLET   What is he whose grief
   Bears such an emphasis? whose phrase of sorrow   245
   Conjures the wand'ring stars, and makes them stand   246
   Like wonder-wounded hearers? This is I,
   Hamlet the Dane.   248
LAERTES   The devil take thy soul!
   [Grapples with him.]
HAMLET
   Thou pray'st not well.
   I prithee take thy fingers from my throat,   250
   For, though I am not splenitive and rash,   251
   Yet have I in me something dangerous,
   Which let thy wisdom fear. Hold off thy hand.
KING
   Pluck them asunder.
QUEEN   Hamlet, Hamlet!
ALL
   Gentlemen!
HORATIO   Good my lord, be quiet.
HAMLET
   Why, I will fight with him upon this theme
   Until my eyelids will no longer wag.

---

243 *Pelion* (a mountain in Thessaly, as are *Olympus,* l. 244, and *Ossa,* l. 273; when the Titans fought the gods [cf. IV.5.121 n.], the Titans attempted to heap Ossa and Olympus on Pelion, or Pelion and Ossa on Olympus, in order to scale heaven)   **245** *an emphasis* violent, exaggerated language   **246** *Conjures* charms, puts a spell upon; *wand'ring stars* planets   **248** *Hamlet . . . Dane* (Q1 directs Hamlet to join Laertes in the "grave" following this line, and near-contemporary comment supports a struggle there – perhaps an open trapdoor – but many different stagings have been tried, and precisely what happened in early performances is unknown)   **251** *splenitive* hot-tempered (the spleen was considered the seat of anger)

QUEEN
  O my son, what theme?

HAMLET
  I loved Ophelia. Forty thousand brothers
260 Could not with all their quantity of love
  Make up my sum. What wilt thou do for her?

KING
  O, he is mad, Laertes.

QUEEN
263 For love of God, forbear him.

HAMLET
  'Swounds, show me what thou't do.
265 Woo't weep? woo't fight? woo't fast? woo't tear thyself?
266 Woo't drink up eisel? eat a crocodile?
  I'll do't. Dost come here to whine?
  To outface me with leaping in her grave?
  Be buried quick with her, and so will I.
270 And if thou prate of mountains, let them throw
  Millions of acres on us, till our ground,
272 Singeing his pate against the burning zone,
  Make Ossa like a wart! Nay, an thou't mouth,
274 I'll rant as well as thou.

QUEEN   This is mere madness;
  And thus a while the fit will work on him.
  Anon, as patient as the female dove
277 When that her golden couplets are disclosed,
  His silence will sit drooping.

HAMLET   Hear you, sir.
  What is the reason that you use me thus?
280 I loved you ever. But it is no matter.
281 Let Hercules himself do what he may,

---

260 *quantity* (used here as a contemptuous term: "a small amount") **263**
forbear him leave him alone   **265** *Woo't* wilt (thou)   **266** *eisel* vinegar **272**
burning zone i.e., where the sun is   **274** *mere* absolute   **277** *couplets* pair of
fledgling birds; *disclosed* hatched   **281** *Hercules* (1) a legendary and mighty
demigod, (2) literally famous as a boastful ranter (Hamlet casts Laertes as
Hercules)

The cat will mew, and dog will have his day.   *Exit.*   282
KING
  I pray thee, good Horatio, wait upon him.

                                          Exit Horatio.

  [To Laertes]
  Strengthen your patience in our last night's speech.   284
  We'll put the matter to the present push. –   285
  Good Gertrude, set some watch over your son. –
  This grave shall have a living monument.
  An hour of quiet shortly shall we see;
  Till then in patience our proceeding be.   *Exeunt.*

                              ✻

ॐ **V.2**   *Enter Hamlet and Horatio.*

HAMLET
  So much for this, sir; now shall you see the other.
  You do remember all the circumstance?
HORATIO
  Remember it, my lord!
HAMLET
  Sir, in my heart there was a kind of fighting
  That would not let me sleep. Methought I lay
  Worse than the mutines in the bilboes. Rashly,   6
  And praised be rashness for it – let us know,
  Our indiscretion sometime serves us well
  When our deep plots do pall, and that should learn us   9
  There's a divinity that shapes our ends,   10
  Rough-hew them how we will –   11
HORATIO   That is most certain.

---

282 *dog . . . day* (proverbially, even the least creature will have a turn at success and happiness: Hamlet views himself as *cat* and *dog*); **s.d.** *Exit* (Q2's exit
s.d. is on two lines in the margin and seems to demand the separate exits indicated here)   284 *in* in the thought of, by calling to mind   285 *the present
push* immediate action

  V.2 Elsinore   **6** *mutines* mutineers; *bilboes* fetters   **9** *pall* fail   **10** *ends* (1)
purposes, (2) outcomes   **11** *Rough-hew* shape roughly in trial form

HAMLET
    Up from my cabin,
    My sea gown scarfed about me, in the dark
    Groped I to find out them, had my desire,
15   Fingered their packet, and in fine withdrew
    To mine own room again, making so bold,
    My fears forgetting manners, to unseal
    Their grand commission; where I found, Horatio –
    Ah, royal knavery! – an exact command,
20   Larded with many several sorts of reasons,
21   Importing Denmark's health, and England's too,
22   With, ho! such bugs and goblins in my life,
23   That on the supervise, no leisure bated,
    No, not to stay the grinding of the ax,
    My head should be struck off.
HORATIO   Is't possible?
HAMLET
    Here's the commission; read it at more leisure.
    But wilt thou hear now how I did proceed?
HORATIO   I beseech you.
HAMLET
    Being thus benetted round with villainies,
30   Or I could make a prologue to my brains,
    They had begun the play. I sat me down,
32   Devised a new commission, wrote it fair.
33   I once did hold it, as our statists do,
    A baseness to write fair, and labored much
    How to forget that learning, but, sir, now
36   It did me yeoman's service. Wilt thou know
37   Th' effect of what I wrote?
HORATIO   Ay, good my lord.

---

15 *Fingered* filched; *in fine* finally   20 *Larded* garnished (a metaphor from cooking)   21 *Importing* relating to   22 *bugs* bugbears, bogeymen; *in my life* i.e., in my (Hamlet's) being allowed to live   23 *supervise* perusal; *no leisure bated* no time allowed   30 *Or* ere, before   32 *fair* with professional clarity (like a scrivener, not like a gentleman: see l. 34)   33 *statists* statesmen, politicians   36 *yeoman's service* brave service such as yeomen foot soldiers gave as archers   37 *effect* purport

HAMLET
> An earnest conjuration from the king,
> As England was his faithful tributary,   39
> As love between them like the palm might flourish,   40
> As peace should still her wheaten garland wear   41
> And stand a comma 'tween their amities,   42
> And many suchlike as's of great charge,   43
> That on the view and knowing of these contents,
> Without debatement further, more or less,
> He should those bearers put to sudden death,
> Not shriving time allowed.   47

HORATIO   How was this sealed?

HAMLET
> Why, even in that was heaven ordinant.   48
> I had my father's signet in my purse,
> Which was the model of that Danish seal,   50
> Folded the writ up in the form of th' other,   51
> Subscribed it, gave't th' impression, placed it safely,   52
> The changeling never known. Now, the next day
> Was our sea fight, and what to this was sequent   54
> Thou knowest already.

HORATIO
> So Guildenstern and Rosencrantz go to't.

HAMLET
> They are not near my conscience; their defeat
> Does by their own insinuation grow.   58
> 'Tis dangerous when the baser nature comes
> Between the pass and fell incensèd points   60
> Of mighty opposites.

HORATIO   Why, what a king is this!

---

39 *tributary* one who pays tribute   **40** *palm . . . flourish* (see Psalm 92:12, "The righteous shall flourish like the palm tree")   **41** *wheaten garland* (traditional symbol of peace)   **42** *comma* i.e., something small   **43** *charge* burden (with a double meaning to fit wordplay that makes *as's* into "asses")   **47** *shriving time* time for confession and absolution   **48** *ordinant* ordaining   **50** *model* likeness   **51** *writ* writing   **52** *impression* i.e., of the signet (a seal)   **54** *sequent* subsequent, following   **58** *insinuation* slipping in   **60** *pass* sword thrust; *fell* fierce

HAMLET

62   Does it not, think thee, stand me now upon –
      He that hath killed my king and whored my mother,
64   Popped in between th' election and my hopes,
65   Thrown out his angle for my proper life,
66   And with such coz'nage – is't not perfect conscience?
          Enter [Osric,] a courtier.
      OSRIC   Your lordship is right welcome back to Denmark.
      HAMLET   I humbly thank you, sir. *[Aside to Horatio]*
69   Dost know this waterfly?
70   HORATIO   *[Aside to Hamlet]* No, my good lord.
      HAMLET   *[Aside to Horatio]* Thy state is the more gra-
      cious, for 'tis a vice to know him. He hath much land,
      and fertile. Let a beast be lord of beasts, and his crib
74   shall stand at the king's mess. 'Tis a chough, but, as I
75   say, spacious in the possession of dirt.
      OSRIC   Sweet lord, if your lordship were at leisure, I
      should impart a thing to you from his majesty.
      HAMLET   I will receive it, sir, with all diligence of spirit.
      Your bonnet to his right use. 'Tis for the head.
80   OSRIC   I thank your lordship, it is very hot.
      HAMLET   No, believe me, 'tis very cold; the wind is
      northerly.
83   OSRIC   It is indifferent cold, my lord, indeed.
      HAMLET   But yet methinks it is very sultry and hot for
85   my complexion.
      OSRIC   Exceedingly, my lord; it is very sultry, as 'twere – I
      cannot tell how. My lord, his majesty bade me signify

---

62 *stand me now upon* am I now obliged (i.e., to do something about these facts: see Folio-only Passages in Note on the Text for F's elaboration of Hamlet's question here)   **64** *election* i.e., to the kingship (the Danish kingship was elective, not inherited, as the English and Scottish crowns were in Shakespeare's day)   **65** *angle* fishhook; *proper* own   **66** *coz'nage* cozenage, trickery **66 s.d.** *Osric* (here, this character's name is from F; in Q1, "a Bragart Gentleman"; in Q2, "a Courtier"; Q2 later uses "Ostricke" at l. 176)   **69** *waterfly* dragonfly (?) – some gaudy insect   **74** *mess* table; *chough* jackdaw (a screeching bird), chatterer   **74–75** *as I say* I'd guess   **75** *spacious in . . . dirt* (he) owns a lot of land   **83** *indifferent* somewhat   **85** *complexion* temperament

to you that a has laid a great wager on your head. Sir,   88
this is the matter –

HAMLET   I beseech you remember.   90

OSRIC   Nay, good my lord; for my ease, in good faith. Sir,   91
here is newly come to court Laertes – believe me, an   92
absolute gentleman, full of most excellent differences,   93
of very soft society and great showing. Indeed, to speak   94
feelingly of him, he is the card or calendar of gentry; for   95
you shall find in him the continent of what part a gen-   96
tleman would see.

HAMLET   Sir, his definement suffers no perdition in you,   98
though, I know, to divide him inventorially would
dozy th' arithmetic of memory, and yet but yaw neither   100
in respect of his quick sail. But, in the verity of extol-   101
ment, I take him to be a soul of great article, and his in-   102
fusion of such dearth and rareness as, to make true   103
diction of him, his semblable is his mirror, and who   104
else would trace him, his umbrage, nothing more.   105

OSRIC   Your lordship speaks most infallibly of him.

HAMLET   The concernancy, sir? Why do we wrap the   107
gentleman in our more rawer breath?   108

OSRIC   Sir?

HORATIO   Is't not possible to understand in another   *110*
tongue? You will to't, sir, really.   111

HAMLET   What imports the nomination of this gentle-   112
man?

OSRIC   Of Laertes?

---

88 *a* he   **90** *remember* i.e., to put on your hat (see l. 79)   **91** *for my ease* i.e.,
I keep my hat off just for comfort (a conventional polite phrase)   **92–93** *an
absolute* a complete, flawless   **93** *differences* differentiating qualities   **94** *soft
society* refined manners; *great showing* noble appearance   **95** *feelingly* appropriately; *card* map; *calendar* guide; *gentry* gentlemanliness   **96** *continent*
containment (but with wordplay on *card*)   **98** *definement* definition; *perdition* loss   **100** *dozy* dizzy; *yaw* veer like a ship that steers wild; *neither* for all
that   **101** *in respect of* in comparison with   **102** *article* scope, importance
102–3 *infusion* essence   **103** *dearth* scarcity   **104** *semblable* likeness   **105**
trace follow (from hunting terminology); *umbrage* shadow   **107** *concernancy*
relevance   **108** *rawer breath* cruder speech   **111** *to't* i.e., get to an understanding   **112** *nomination* mention

HORATIO   *[Aside to Hamlet]* His purse is empty already.
  All's golden words are spent.

HAMLET   Of him, sir.

OSRIC   I know you are not ignorant —

HAMLET   I would you did, sir; yet, in faith, if you did, it
120 would not much approve me. Well, sir?

OSRIC   You are not ignorant of what excellence Laertes
  is —

123 HAMLET   I dare not confess that, lest I should compare
  with him in excellence; but to know a man well were to
  know himself.

OSRIC   I mean, sir, for his weapon; but in the imputation
127 laid on him by them, in his meed he's unfellowed.

HAMLET   What's his weapon?

OSRIC   Rapier and dagger.

130 HAMLET   That's two of his weapons — but well.

OSRIC   The king, sir, hath wagered with him six Barbary
132 horses, against the which he has impawned, as I take it,
133 six French rapiers and poniards, with their assigns, as
134 girdle, hanger, and so. Three of the carriages, in faith,
135 are very dear to fancy, very responsive to the hilts, most
136 delicate carriages, and of very liberal conceit.

HAMLET   What call you the carriages?

HORATIO   *[Aside to Hamlet]* I knew you must be edified
139 by the margent ere you had done.

140 OSRIC   The carriage, sir, are the hangers.

HAMLET   The phrase would be more germane to the
  matter if we could carry a cannon by our sides. I would it
  might be hangers till then. But on! Six Barbary horses
  against six French swords, their assigns, and three liberal-

---

120 *approve* commend   123 *compare* compete   127 *meed* reward   132 *impawned* staked   133 *assigns* appurtenances   134 *hanger* straps by which the sword hangs from the belt   135 *dear to fancy* finely designed; *responsive* corresponding closely   136 *liberal conceit* tasteful design, refined conception   139 *margent* margin (i.e., explanatory notes printed in the margin of a page)

conceited carriages – that's the French bet against the
Danish. Why is this all impawned, as you call it?   146

OSRIC   The king, sir, hath laid, sir, that in a dozen passes
between yourself and him he shall not exceed you three
hits; he hath laid on twelve for nine, and it would come
to immediate trial if your lordship would vouchsafe the   *150*
answer.

HAMLET   How if I answer no?

OSRIC   I mean, my lord, the opposition of your person in
trial.

HAMLET   Sir, I will walk here in the hall. If it please his
majesty, it is the breathing time of day with me. Let the   156
foils be brought, the gentleman willing, and the king
hold his purpose, I will win for him and I can; if not, I   158
will gain nothing but my shame and the odd hits.

OSRIC   Shall I deliver you so?   *160*

HAMLET   To this effect, sir, after what flourish your nature will.

OSRIC   I commend my duty to your lordship.

HAMLET   Yours. *[Exit Osric.]* He does well to commend
it himself; there are no tongues else for's turn.

HORATIO   This lapwing runs away with the shell on his   166
head.

HAMLET   A did comply with his dug before a sucked it.   168
Thus has he, and many more of the same breed that I
know the drossy age dotes on, only got the tune of the   *170*
time and, out of an habit of encounter, a kind of yeasty
collection, which carries them through and through the
most [fanned] and [winnowed] opinions; and do but   173
blow them to their trial, the bubbles are out.

    Enter a Lord.

---

146 *impawned . . . it* (in F, Hamlet seems to mock Osric's *impawned,* but in
Q2 the compositor apparently misunderstood the word here, but not at
l. 132; see Emendations in Note on the Text)   156 *breathing time* exercise
hour   158 *and* if   166 *lapwing* (a bird reputed to be so precocious as to run
as soon as hatched)   168 *comply* observe formalities of courtesy; *dug* nipple
170 *drossy* frivolous   173 *fanned and winnowed* select and refined (see
Emendations in Note on the Text)

LORD   My lord, his majesty commended him to you by young Osric, who brings back to him that you attend him in the hall. He sends to know if your pleasure hold to play with Laertes, or that you will take longer time.

HAMLET   I am constant to my purposes; they follow the
180   king's pleasure. If his fitness speaks, mine is ready; now or whensoever, provided I be so able as now.

LORD   The king and queen and all are coming down.

183 HAMLET   In happy time.

184 LORD   The queen desires you to use some gentle entertainment to Laertes before you fall to play.

HAMLET   She well instructs me.   *[Exit Lord.]*

HORATIO   You will lose, my lord.

HAMLET   I do not think so. Since he went into France I have been in continual practice. I shall win at the odds.
190   Thou wouldst not think how ill all's here about my heart, but it is no matter.

HORATIO   Nay, good my lord –

193 HAMLET   It is but foolery, but it is such a kind of gain-giving as would perhaps trouble a woman.

HORATIO   If your mind dislike anything, obey it. I will forestall their repair hither and say you are not fit.

HAMLET   Not a whit, we defy augury. There is special providence in the fall of a sparrow. If it be now, 'tis not to come; if it be not to come, it will be now; if it be not
200   now, yet it will come. The readiness is all. Since no man of aught he leaves knows, what is't to leave betimes? Let
202   be.

> *A table prepared. [Enter] Trumpets, Drums, and Officers with cushions; King, Queen, [Osric,] and all the State, [with] foils, daggers, and Laertes.*

KING
203   Come, Hamlet, come, and take this hand from me.

---

183 *In happy time* I am happy (a polite response)   **184–85** *entertainment* courtesy   **193–94** *gaingiving* misgiving   **200** *all* all that matters   **202 s.d.** *State* court and courtiers (there must also be props for serving wine)   **203** *this hand* i.e., Laertes' hand

HAMLET
> Give me your pardon, sir. I have done you wrong,
> But pardon't, as you are a gentleman.
> This presence knows, and you must needs have heard,　206
> How I am punished with a sore distraction.
> What I have done
> That might your nature, honor, and exception　209
> Roughly awake, I here proclaim was madness.　*210*
> Was't Hamlet wronged Laertes? Never Hamlet.
> If Hamlet from himself be ta'en away,
> And when he's not himself does wrong Laertes,
> Then Hamlet does it not, Hamlet denies it.
> Who does it then? His madness. If't be so,
> Hamlet is of the faction that is wronged;　216
> His madness is poor Hamlet's enemy.
> [Sir, in this audience,]
> Let my disclaiming from a purposed evil
> Free me so far in your most generous thoughts　*220*
> That I have shot my arrow o'er the house
> And hurt my brother.　222

LAERTES　　　　　　　　I am satisfied in nature,
> Whose motive in this case should stir me most
> To my revenge. But in my terms of honor　224
> I stand aloof, and will no reconcilement
> Till by some elder masters of known honor
> I have a voice and precedent of peace　227
> To keep my name ungored. But till that time　228
> I do receive your offered love like love,
> And will not wrong it.　*230*

HAMLET　　　　　　　　I embrace it freely,
> And will this brother's wager frankly play.
> Give us the foils.

LAERTES　　　　　　Come, one for me.

---

206 *presence* assembly **209** *exception* disapproval **216** *faction* political group in opposition to another group **222** *nature* natural feeling **224** *terms of honor* position as a man of honor **227** *a voice* an authoritative statement **228** *ungored* uninjured

HAMLET

233   I'll be your foil, Laertes. In mine ignorance
Your skill shall, like a star i' th' darkest night,
235   Stick fiery off indeed.

LAERTES   You mock me, sir.

HAMLET

No, by this hand.

KING

Give them the foils, young Osric. Cousin Hamlet,
You know the wager?

HAMLET   Very well, my lord.
Your grace has laid the odds o' th' weaker side.

KING

240   I do not fear it, I have seen you both;
241   But since he is bettered, we have therefore odds.

LAERTES

This is too heavy; let me see another.

HAMLET

This likes me well. These foils have all a length?
[Prepare to play.]

OSRIC

Ay, my good lord.

KING

Set me the stoups of wine upon that table.
If Hamlet give the first or second hit,
247   Or quit in answer of the third exchange,
Let all the battlements their ordnance fire.
The king shall drink to Hamlet's better breath,
250   And in the cup an union shall he throw
Richer than that which four successive kings
In Denmark's crown have worn. Give me the cups,
253   And let the kettle to the trumpet speak,
The trumpet to the cannoneer without,

---

233 *foil* setting that displays a jewel advantageously (punning on *foil* as a weapon) 235 *Stick fiery off* show off in brilliant relief 241 *bettered* said to be better by public opinion (?) 247 *quit* repay by a hit 250 *an union* a pearl 253 *kettle* kettledrum

The cannons to the heavens, the heaven to earth,
"Now the king drinks to Hamlet." Come, begin.
 Trumpets the while.
And you, the judges, bear a wary eye.
HAMLET Come on, sir.
LAERTES Come, my lord.
 [They play.]
HAMLET One.   *260*
LAERTES No.
HAMLET Judgment?
OSRIC A hit, a very palpable hit.   *263*
 Drum, trumpets, and shot. Flourish; a piece goes off.
LAERTES Well, again.
KING
Stay, give me drink. Hamlet, this pearl is thine.
Here's to thy health. Give him the cup.
HAMLET
I'll play this bout first; set it by awhile.
Come. *[They play.]* Another hit. What say you?
LAERTES I do confess't.
KING
Our son shall win.   *270*
QUEEN   He's fat, and scant of breath.
Here, Hamlet, take my napkin, rub thy brows. *271*
The queen carouses to thy fortune, Hamlet. *272*
HAMLET
Good madam!
KING   Gertrude, do not drink.
QUEEN
I will, my lord; I pray you pardon me.
 [Drinks.]
KING *[Aside]*
It is the poisoned cup; it is too late.
HAMLET
I dare not drink yet, madam – by and by.

---

263 s.d. *piece* cannon **270** *fat* (1) not physically fit (?), (2) sweaty (?) **271**
napkin handkerchief **272** *carouses* drinks a toast

QUEEN
    Come, let me wipe thy face.
LAERTES
    My lord, I'll hit him now.
KING   I do not think't.
LAERTES   *[Aside]*
    And yet it is almost against my conscience.
HAMLET
280   Come for the third, Laertes. You do but dally.
281   I pray you pass with your best violence;
282   I am sure you make a wanton of me.
LAERTES
    Say you so? Come on.
        [They play.]
OSRIC
    Nothing neither way.
LAERTES
    Have at you now!
        [In scuffling they change rapiers.]
KING   Part them. They are incensed.
HAMLET
    Nay, come – again!
        [The Queen falls.]
OSRIC   Look to the queen there, ho!
HORATIO
    They bleed on both sides. How is it, my lord?
OSRIC
    How is't, Laertes?
LAERTES
289   Why, as a woodcock to mine own springe, Osric.
290   I am justly killed with mine own treachery.
HAMLET
    How does the queen?
KING   She swoons to see them bleed.

---

281 *pass* thrust (with a sword)   **282** *wanton* spoiled child   **289** *woodcock* (a
bird reputed to be stupid and easily trapped); *springe* trap

QUEEN

No, no, the drink, the drink! O my dear Hamlet!
The drink, the drink! I am poisoned.
    [Dies.]

HAMLET

O villainy! Ho! let the door be locked.
Treachery! Seek it out.   *[Exit Osric.]*

LAERTES

It is here, Hamlet. Hamlet, thou art slain;
No med'cine in the world can do thee good.
In thee there is not half an hour's life.
The treacherous instrument is in thy hand,
Unbated and envenomed. The foul practice   300
Hath turned itself on me. Lo, here I lie,
Never to rise again. Thy mother's poisoned.
I can no more. The king, the king's to blame.

HAMLET

The point envenomed too?
Then venom, to thy work.
    [Wounds the King.]

ALL   Treason! treason!

KING

O, yet defend me, friends. I am but hurt.

HAMLET

Here, thou incestuous, murd'rous, damnèd Dane,
Drink off this potion. Is thy union here?   309
Follow my mother.   310
    [King dies.]

LAERTES   He is justly served.
It is a poison tempered by himself.   311
Exchange forgiveness with me, noble Hamlet.
Mine and my father's death come not upon thee,
Nor thine on me!
    [Dies.]

---

300 *Unbated* unblunted; *practice* trick   309 *union* (1) pearl (cf. l. 250 n.),
(2) marriage to Gertrude   311 *tempered* mixed

HAMLET
    Heaven make thee free of it! I follow thee.
    I am dead, Horatio. Wretched queen, adieu!
    You that look pale and tremble at this chance,
318   That are but mutes or audience to this act,
319   Had I but time – as this fell sergeant, Death,
320   Is strict in his arrest – O, I could tell you –
    But let it be. Horatio, I am dead;
    Thou livest; report me and my cause aright
    To the unsatisfied.

HORATIO   Never believe it.
324   I am more an antique Roman than a Dane.
    Here's yet some liquor left.

HAMLET   As th' art a man,
    Give me the cup. Let go. By heaven, I'll ha't!
    O God, Horatio, what a wounded name,
    Things standing thus unknown, shall I leave behind
      me!
    If thou didst ever hold me in thy heart,
330   Absent thee from felicity awhile,
    And in this harsh world draw thy breath in pain,
    To tell my story.
       A march afar off.
                What warlike noise is this?
      Enter Osric.

OSRIC
    Young Fortinbras, with conquest come from Poland,
    To the ambassadors of England gives
    This warlike volley.

HAMLET   O, I die, Horatio!
336   The potent poison quite o'ercrows my spirit.
    I cannot live to hear the news from England,
338   But I do prophesy th' election lights

---

318 *mutes* actors without speaking parts **319** *sergeant* court officer with power of arrest **320** *strict* (1) just, (2) inescapable **324** *antique Roman* i.e., someone who prefers suicide to a dishonored life **336** *o'ercrows* triumphs over (as a crow does over its meal? as a cock does in a cockfight?) **338** *election* i.e., for the throne of Denmark (cf. l. 64)

On Fortinbras. He has my dying voice.   339
So tell him, with th' occurrents, more and less,   340
Which have solicited – the rest is silence.   341
    [Dies.]

HORATIO
Now cracks a noble heart. Good night, sweet prince,
And flights of angels sing thee to thy rest!
    [March within.]
Why does the drum come hither?
    Enter Fortinbras, with the Ambassadors [and Drum,
    Colors, and Attendants].

FORTINBRAS
Where is this sight?

HORATIO   What is it you would see?
If aught of woe or wonder, cease your search.   346

FORTINBRAS
This quarry cries on havoc. O proud Death,   347
What feast is toward in thine eternal cell   348
That thou so many princes at a shot
So bloodily hast struck?   350

AMBASSADOR   The sight is dismal;
And our affairs from England come too late.
The ears are senseless that should give us hearing
To tell him his commandment is fulfilled,
That Rosencrantz and Guildenstern are dead.
Where should we have our thanks?

HORATIO   Not from his mouth,
Had it th' ability of life to thank you.
He never gave commandment for their death.
But since, so jump upon this bloody question,   358
You from the Polack wars, and you from England,
Are here arrived, give order that these bodies   360

---

339 *voice* vote   340 *occurrents* occurrences   341 *solicited* incited, provoked
346 *wonder* disaster (an archaic meaning in Shakespeare's day?)   347 *quarry*
pile of dead (literally, killed deer gathered after the hunt); *cries on* proclaims
loudly; *havoc* indiscriminate killing and destruction   348 *toward* forthcoming, about to occur (i.e., *Death* will feast on *so many princes*)   358 *jump* precisely

361   High on a stage be placèd to the view,
       And let me speak to th' yet unknowing world
       How these things came about. So shall you hear
       Of carnal, bloody, and unnatural acts,
365   Of accidental judgments, casual slaughters,
366   Of deaths put on by cunning and forced cause,
       And, in this upshot, purposes mistook
       Fall'n on th' inventors' heads. All this can I
       Truly deliver.

     FORTINBRAS   Let us haste to hear it,
370   And call the noblest to the audience.
       For me, with sorrow I embrace my fortune.
372   I have some rights of memory in this kingdom,
373   Which now to claim my vantage doth invite me.

     HORATIO
       Of that I shall have also cause to speak,
375   And from his mouth whose voice will draw on more.
376   But let this same be presently performed,
       Even while men's minds are wild, lest more mischance
378   On plots and errors happen.

     FORTINBRAS   Let four captains
       Bear Hamlet like a soldier to the stage,
380   For he was likely, had he been put on,
381   To have proved most royal; and for his passage
       The soldiers' music and the rite of war
       Speak loudly for him.
       Take up the bodies. Such a sight as this
       Becomes the field, but here shows much amiss.
       Go, bid the soldiers shoot.

                          Exeunt [marching; after the which
                          a peal of ordnance is shot off].

---

361 *stage* platform (the meaning for performance or the early modern audience is uncertain)   **365** *accidental* i.e., inscrutable to human eyes; *judgments* retributions; *casual* not humanly planned (the word reinforces *accidental*)   **366** *put on* instigated; *forced* contrived   **372** *of memory* unforgotten   **373** *vantage* advantageous opportunity   **375** *more* i.e., more voices, or votes, for the kingship   **376** *presently* immediately   **378** *On* on the basis of   **380** *put on* set to perform in office   **381** *passage* death

FOR THE BEST IN PAPERBACKS, LOOK FOR THE 🐧

In every corner of the world, on every subject under the sun, Penguin represents quality and variety—the very best in publishing today.

For complete information about books available from Penguin—including Puffins, Penguin Classics, and Compass—and how to order them, write to us at the appropriate address below. Please note that for copyright reasons the selection of books var___

In the Uni___ ___ ___ write to Dept. ___ ___ ___ ___, *Bath Road, Harmondsworth, West Drayton, Middlesex UB7 0DA.*

In the United States: Please write to *Penguin Putnam Inc., P.O. Box 12289 Dept. B, Newark, New Jersey 07101-5289* or call 1-800-788-6262.

In Canada: Please write to *Penguin Books Canada Ltd, 10 Alcorn Avenue, Suite 300, Toronto, Ontario M4V 3B2.*

In Australia: Please write to *Penguin Books Australia Ltd, P.O. Box 257, Ringwood, Victoria 3134.*

In New Zealand: Please write to *Penguin Books (NZ) Ltd, Private Bag 102902, North Shore Mail Centre, Auckland 10.*

In India: Please write to *Penguin Books India Pvt Ltd, 11 Panchsheel Shopping Centre, Panchsheel Park, New Delhi 110 017.*

In the Netherlands: Please write to *Penguin Books Netherlands bv, Postbus 3507, NL-1001 AH Amsterdam.*

In Germany: Please write to *Penguin Books Deutschland GmbH, Metzlerstrasse 26, 60594 Frankfurt am Main.*

In Spain: Please write to *Penguin Books S. A., Bravo Murillo 19, 1° B, 28015 Madrid.*

In Italy: Please write to *Penguin Italia s.r.l., Via Benedetto Croce 2, 20094 Corsico, Milano.*

In France: Please write to *Penguin France, Le Carré Wilson, 62 rue Benjamin Baillaud, 31500 Toulouse.*

In Japan: Please write to *Penguin Books Japan Ltd, Kaneko Building, 2-3-25 Koraku, Bunkyo-Ku, Tokyo 112.*

In South Africa: Please write to *Penguin Books South Africa (Pty) Ltd, Private Bag X14, Parkview, 2122 Johannesburg.*